PENGUIN CLASSICS

THE EUROPEANS

HENRY JAMES was born in 1843 in Washington Place, New York, of Scottish and Irish ancestry. His father was a prominent theologian and philosopher and his elder brother, William, was also famous as a philosopher. He attended schools in New York and later in London, Paris and Geneva, entering the Law School at Harvard in 1862. In 1865 he began to contribute reviews and short stories to American journals. In 1875, after two prior visits to Europe, he settled for a year in Paris, where he met Flaubert, Turgenev, and other literary figures. However, the next year he moved to London, where he became such an inveterate diner-out that in the winter of 1878–9 he confessed to accepting 140 invitations. In 1898 he left London and went to live at Lamb House, Rye, Sussex, Henry James became naturalized in 1915, was awarded the O.M., and died in 1916.

In addition to many short stories, plays, books of criticism, autobiography, and travel he wrote some twenty novels, the first published being *Roderick Hudson* (1875). They include *Washington Square, The Portrait of a Lady, The Bostonians, The Princess Casamassima, The Tragic Muse, The Spoils of Poynton, The Awkward Age, The Wings of the Dove, The Ambassadors* and *The Golden Bowl*.

TONY TANNER, who has also edited *Pride and Prejudice, Mansfield Park* and *Sense and Sensibility* by Jane Austen and *Villette* by Charlotte Brontë for the Penguin Classics, is a Fellow of King's College, Cambridge, and a Professor. He has taught and travelled extensively in America and Europe. Besides books on Conrad and Saul Bellow, he has published *The Reign of Wonder* (1965), a study of American literature, *City of Words* (1970), *Contract and Transgression: Adultery and the Novel* (1980) and *Jane Austen* (1986).

PATRICIA CRICK, one-time Scholar of Girton College, Cambridge, is currently Head of Modern Languages at Long Road Sixth Form College, Cambridge.

General Editor for the works of Henry James in Penguins is Geoffrey Moore.

HENRY JAMES

THE EUROPEANS

A SKETCH

WITH AN INTRODUCTION BY TONY TANNER
AND NOTES BY P. CRICK

PENGUIN BOOKS

PENGUIN BOOKS

Published by the Penguin Group
27 Wrights Lane, London W8 5TZ, England
Viking Penguin Inc., 40 West 23rd Street, New York, New York 10010, USA
Penguin Books Australia Ltd, Ringwood, Victoria, Australia
Penguin Books Canada Ltd, 2801 John Street, Markham, Ontario, Canada L3R 1B4
Penguin Books (NZ) Ltd, 182–190 Wairau Road, Auckland 10, New Zealand

Penguin Books Ltd, Registered Offices: Harmondsworth, Middlesex, England

First published 1878
Published in Penguin Books 1964
Reprinted in the Penguin English Library 1984
Reprinted in Penguin Classics 1985
5 7 9 10 8 6

Introduction copyright © Tony Tanner, 1984
Notes copyright © P. Crick, 1984
All rights reserved

Made and printed in Great Britain by
Richard Clay Ltd, Bungay, Suffolk
Filmset in 9/11 Monophoto Times

CONTENTS

INTRODUCTION

On 30 March 1877 Henry James wrote a letter to William Dean Howells in which he effectively outlined his plan for *The Europeans*. Howells was to publish this letter in the *Atlantic* (July–October 1878), and is worth quoting at length:

I suspect it is the tragedies in life that arrest my attention more than the other things and say more to my imagination; but on the other hand, if I fix my eyes on a sun-spot I think I am able to see the prismatic colours in it. You shall have the brightest possible sun-spot for the four-number tale of 1878. It shall fairly put your readers' eyes out. The idea of doing what you propose much pleases me; and I agree to squeeze my buxom muse, as you happily call her, into a hundred of your pages. I will lace her so tight that she shall have the neatest little figure in the world. It shall be a very joyous little romance. I'm afraid I can't tell you at this moment what it will be; for my dusky fancy contains nothing joyous enough: but I will invoke the jocund muse and come up to time. I shall probably develop an idea that I have, about a genial, charming youth of a Bohemian pattern, who comes back from foreign parts into the midst of a mouldering and ascetic old Puritan family of his kindred (some imaginary locality in New England 1830), and by his gayety and sweet audacity smooths out their rugosities, heals their dyspepsia and dissipates their troubles. *All* the women fall in love with him (and he with them – his amatory powers are boundless;) but even for a happy ending he can't marry them all. But he marries the prettiest, and from a romantic quality of Christian charity, produces a picturesque imbroglio (for the sake of the picturesque I shall play havoc with the New England background of 1830:) under cover of which the other maidens pair off with the swains who have hitherto been starved out: after which the beneficent cousin departs for Bohemia (*with his bride, oh yes!*) in a vaporous rosy cloud, to scatter new benefactions over man – and especially, woman-kind! – (Pray don't mention this stuff to anyone. It would be meant, roughly speaking, as the picture of the conversion of a dusky, dreary domestic circle to epicureanism. But I may be able to make nothing of it. The merit would be the amount of color I should be able to infuse into it.)

In the event, of course, he made a good deal of it. The novel not only has the brightness, that 'colour' – often a dazzling play of iridescent surfaces – which fairly puts the readers' eyes out; it has all the neatness and formal perfection that James promised. It is indeed one of his brightest sun-spots! Which makes it, perhaps, odd that he should, in a letter of 1878 to William James, promptly agree to his brother's criticism that the work was 'thin and empty'; and that within a year of its publication, he should, in another letter to his mother, repudiate it as a work 'which I never thought good', astonishingly preferring the interesting but distinctly slight *Confidence*. Nor did he include *The Europeans* in the collected edition of his works, though its reputation has only increased over the years.

One criticism in particular might have contributed to James's desire to distance himself from the work. To contemporary readers he does not exactly 'play havoc' with the New England background of 1830;* or, rather, we are unconcerned if he does. In enjoying the playing off of effects in a slightly unreal atmosphere (it is clear and bright enough but occasionally there is a timeless, almost fairy-tale quality about it) we neither notice nor cavil at possible inadequacies of historical detail. But one critic did. Thomas Wentworth Higginson, a constant disparager of James's work, wrote in *Literary World* (22 November 1879) a bitter denunciation of the radical anachronisticity of the novel.

He opens his *The Europeans* by exhibiting horsecars in the streets nearly ten years before their introduction ... The family portrayed has access to 'the best society in Boston'; yet the daughter, twenty-three years old, has 'never seen an artist', though the picturesque figure of Allson had just disappeared from the streets, when Cheney, Staigg, and Eastman Johnson might be seen any day, with plenty of others less known. The household is perfectly amazed and overwhelmed by the sight of two foreigners, although there were more cultivated Europeans in Boston thirty years ago than now ... Mr James's cosmopolitanism is after all limited; to be really cosmopolitan a man must be at home even in his own country.

---

*From internal evidence, it would seem that in the course of writing the novel James decided to set it in the 1840s instead of the 1830s.

This criticism was first reprinted by the late F. W. Dupee and then by Oscar Cargill. Today these reproaches seem petty and basically irrelevant. James was not trying to reduplicate in mimetic detail the actual New England of the time. Nor was he merely creating some never-never land, a fantasy of Puritan New England. He did, indeed, play a certain amount of 'havoc' and he gaily admitted as much to Howells but, as can happen in art, there may be more 'truth' in the havoc than in purely, exemplary historical documentation. But, though he may be playing, his is a game with a purpose. He evoked an essentially – a quintessentially – New England Puritan atmosphere, and if, to do this, he put a few horses in and took a few minor artists out we cannot take it so amiss as did the stern literalist, Higginson. But it is conceivable that James was hurt by the accusation of wanton anachronism. Certainly, his precipitous down-grading of the work – after his ebullient letter to Howells – is unusual, and hard to comprehend. And, as Oscar Cargill noted, James never again attempted a 'historical' work until the end of his life in *The Sense of the Past*. But to understand fully the New England which James was evoking it is best to consider two other works of the same period: namely, James's important essay on Emerson (published the previous year, in December 1877) and his study of Hawthorne (published a year after *The Europeans*, in December 1879). It is here that we can find that earlier New England in the days before horsecars first appeared in the Boston streets.

Before having a glance at these works, one other aspect of James's letter to Howells should be noted. Though it would be absurd to criticize a hypothetical outline – to point out, for instance, that Felix does not fall in love with 'all the women' and that his 'amatory powers' are not boundless but, if anything, unusually single-minded and sharp-focused – what *is* strange is that James does not mention in his outline the crucial figure of Eugenia. Given how relatively uncomplicated – if 'happy' – Felix is, without the distinctly complex figure of Eugenia the novel might have been little more than a trifle; indeed, the opposition between Bohemian epicureanism and dyspeptic Puritanism might have become embarrassingly obvious and banal. But Eugenia changes all that, and not only complicates many of the issues of the book, but in her own way casts something of a shadow over the end of this 'sun-spot' of a tale. It would seem that James could not repress or extrude his 'dusky fancy' after all. In a sense, she is too rich, too ambiguous, too large a character for the book. There is a real danger that she will make Felix seem merely trivial, vacuously good-natured and shallow. In the same way, there is also a danger that she will make us see the American Puritans as hopelessly rigid, monocular, self-stereotyping and unnuanced. (An exception would be Gertrude who, in her sometimes abrasive and abrupt way, struggles against the dominant Puritan ethos. Yet here we have another surprise, for in a letter to Elizabeth Boott (1878) James writes: 'You are quite right to hate Gertrude, whom I personally dislike!' It would seem that James's sympathies – and his oppositions – were not so obvious as we might think on first reading.) And if Eugenia manages to fend off the 'tragic' she is certainly not included in the 'swains' and 'maidens' who 'pair off' in deference to James's promised happy ending. The book is an idyll, right enough, but there *is* a darkness in it and there are some ambiguous, potentially unsettling moments in it – as one might discern, perhaps, in a painting by Watteau.

Before moving on to the novel we might remind ourselves that it was subtitled – not obviously provocatively – 'A Sketch'. But James has left us a fairly extended record of a disagreement he had with a fellow-compatriot about 'sketching' which is included in 'The Picture Season in London' of 1877 (reprinted in *The Painter's Eye*).

English culture, then, in so far as it is a luxury, is a child of leisure, whereas leisure, in America, has not yet reached that interesting period at which the parental function begins to operate. We have, it is true, a great many young ladies who 'play', but we have, as compared with the English, a very small number who sketch, either in oils or water colours, who write three-volume novels, or produce historical monographs. For my own part, I regret it; for I subscribe to the axiom that culture lends a charm to life. But I have a friend, a compatriot, with whom I often discuss these matters, who takes a very different view, and who pretends that (speaking particularly of sketching) it is better not to sketch at all than to sketch badly. He here makes, as you see, two questionable assumptions: one is that we Americans do not sketch at all, the other is that the English sketch badly. In fact I should say that we do sketch a little, and that the English often sketch very well ... if, as a society, we don't sketch, it is not because we won't, but because we can't; and if we don't hang indifferent water colours on our parlour walls, it is because we have not got them to hang. If we had them, I say, we should be only too happy. It is mere want of culture, I say, and not our native delicacy. Delicacy is shown, not in barren abstinence, but in beautiful performance.

Here, then, we have a pair of terms which may perhaps guide us in our understanding of the novel or 'sketch'. James was aiming at a 'beautiful performance' to put against the 'barren abstinence' or lack of 'delicacy' of his native culture. As we shall see, 'performance' becomes a key-word in appreciating some of the differences between the 'Europeans' and the Puritans, though here again it should not be assumed that 'performance' is the prerogative of the Europeans – or that all 'Puritans' are barren abstainers.

What of this slightly ahistorical Puritan New England which James evoked in the novel? It was first of all the New England of familial memories, but above all it was the world of Emerson and Hawthorne. Writing about a memoir of Emerson by James Elliot Cabot, James has a number of observations to make which are very germane to our reading of *The Europeans*. He notes in general, as he surveys Emerson's life, a lack of 'colour', 'a singular impression of paleness': 'The life seems curiously devoid of complexity' – 'passions, alternations, affairs, adventures had absolutely no part in it.' James sees Emerson as living 'in a kind of high, vertical moral light, the brightness of a society at once very simple and very responsible . . . he was *all* the warning moral voice, without distraction or counter-solicitation'. He speaks of a 'terrible paucity of alternatives' – 'in the world in which he grew up and lived, the bribes and lures, the beguilements and bribes were few'. James hints that 'the will, in the old New England, was a clue without a labyrinth', and speaks of the impression 'of a conscience gasping in the void, panting for sensations, with something of the movement of the gills of a landed fish'. What, in particular, he notes as missing from the work (and life) of Emerson is a 'sense of wrong' – 'no sense of the dark, the foul, the base'. The reader may decide for himself how much this sheds light on the deportment and outlook of the various Wentworths and their friends, and on the atmosphere in which they live, though with obvious reservations. James writing a long review essay is one writer: James attempting a certain kind of fictional 'sketch' writes in a different way – with more sense of latent ambiguities and contradictions. Nevertheless, there are undoubtedly strong similarities between James's evocation of Emerson and his society and the Wentworths and theirs. (No reader will miss the clue recumbent in the description of the ailing and bed-bound Mrs Acton: 'On a chair, beside her, lay a volume of Emerson's Essays.')

But if it was Emerson's New England James was recalling it was also Hawthorne's. There were, in any case, similarities: they both had the same America to write about. And James finds in Hawthorne's American diaries a quality as pallid and empty as he had found in Emerson's: 'It is characterised by an extraordinary blankness – a curious paleness of colour and paucity of detail.' And James's indictment of the American's lack of sense of history could have been prompted by either work:

History, as yet, has left in the United States but so thin and impalpable a deposit that we very soon touch the hard substratum of nature; and nature herself, in the Western World, has the peculiarity of seeming rather crude and immature. The very air looks new and young; the light of the sun seems fresh and innocent, as if it knew as yet but few of the secrets of the world and none of the weariness of shining; the vegetation has the appearance of not having reached its majority. A large juvenility is stamped upon the face of things, and in the vividness of the present, the past, which dies so young and had time to produce so little, attracts but scant attention.

One point which James makes is of central relevance to *The Europeans*: 'American life had begun to constitute itself from the foundations; it had begun to *be* simply; it was at an immeasurable distance from having begun to enjoy.' This is why James has no hesitation about regarding the 'tone of the American world' as 'in some respects provincial'. It is why, as he surveys Hawthorne's life, he seems to see 'the image of the crude and simple society in which he lived'. It was why he would compose that famous – or infamous – list of all that was lacking in American life which starts: 'No sovereign, no court, no personal loyalty, no aristocracy' and runs on until it concludes: 'no Epsom nor Ascot!' at which point one cannot help but wonder whether James isn't having his own kind of fun. The passage attracted a decent, patriotic answer from Howells, but still, in varying ways, James is pointing to some general *lack* in Hawthorne's New England, a lack which not only hampered the artist (as Hawthorne lamented), but which severely limited the average American's sense of life's possibilities.

James could, of course, see a radical difference between Emerson and Hawthorne ('Emerson as a sort of spiritual sun-worshipper, could have attached but a moderate value to Hawthorne's cat-like faculty of seeing in the dark' is one memorable formulation); and he approves of Hawthorne's 'duskily-sportive imagination' – an epithet which, we recall, he applied to his own imagination. He saw that Hawthorne had 'a haunting care for moral problems', and applauded his imagination: 'always entertaining itself, always engaged in a game of hide-and-seek in the region in which it seemed to him that the game could best be played – among the shadows and substructions, the dark-based pillars and supports of our moral nature'. He admires Hawthorne because 'he cared for the deeper psychology'. At the same time – and here James (with his eyes fixed on European models) is clearly attempting to make a distinction between the first major American novelist and himself – he is somewhat deprecating, and at times patronizing, in his account of Hawthorne. He is 'charming' but something is missing or, for Hawthorne, simply not there to be had. Hawthorne concedes as much when he complains of his 'great difficulty in the lack of materials'. James quotes him to this effect:

No author, without a trial, can conceive of the difficulty of writing a romance about a country where there is no shadow, no antiquity, no mystery, no picturesque and gloomy wrong, nor anything but a commonplace prosperity, in broad and simple daylight as is happily the case with my dear native land.

James was determined to avoid that 'lack'. He had, after all, only recently decided to settle in London when he wrote *Hawthorne* and, indeed, *The Europeans*. To reinforce his point he makes much of his image of the pre-Civil War type of Americans. This was an important – even crucial – 'divide' in the life of Americans, and it is worth quoting his statement at some length, particularly as he decided to cast *The Europeans* in the pre-Civil War period:

Our hero was an American of the earlier and simpler type – the type of which it is doubtless premature to say that it has wholly passed away, but of which it may at least be said that the circumstances that produced it have been greatly modified. The generation to which he belonged, that generation which grew up with the century, witnessed during a period of fifty years the immense, uninterrupted material development of the young Republic; and when one thinks of the scale on which it took place, of the prosperity that walked in its train and waited on its course, of the hopes it fostered and the blessings it conferred – of the broad morning sunshine, in a word, in which it all went forward – there seems to be little room for surprise that it should have implanted a kind of superstitious faith in the grandeur of the country, its duration, its immunity from the usual troubles of earthly empires. This faith was a simple and uncritical one, enlivened with an element of genial optimism ... From this conception of the American future the sense of its having problems to solve was blissfully absent; there were no difficulties in the programme, no looming complications, no rocks ahead.

Then came the Civil War.

Hawthorne had no idea that the respectable institution which he contemplated in impressive contrast to humanitarian 'mistiness', was presently to cost the nation four long years of bloodshed and misery, and a social revolution as complete as any the world has seen ... The subsidence of that great convulsion has left a different tone from the tone it found, and one may say that the Civil War marks an era in the history of the human mind. It introduced into the national consciousness a certain sense of proportion and relation, of the world being a more complicated place than it had hitherto seemed, the future more treacherous, success more difficult. At the rate at which things are going, it is obvious that good Americans will be more numerous than ever; but the good American, in days to come, will be a more critical person than his complacent and confident grandfather. He has eaten of the tree of knowledge. He will not, I think, be a sceptic, and still less, of course, a cynic; but he will be, without discredit to his well-known capacity for action, an observer.

James could almost be writing out a prescription – and justification – for the many 'observers' who were to appear in his subsequent works. Of course, Hawthorne himself produced at least one notable 'observer' – Miles Coverdale in *The Blithedale Romance* (1852), of whom James himself wrote 'Coverdale is a picture of the contemplative, observant, analytic nature ...' But his main point, though not necessarily historically justified, is that there prevailed a certain kind of complacent optimism – blessed or fatuous – before the Civil War and that such a particular kind of optimism was no longer possible. So in writing *The Europeans* he was looking back across a certain 'shadow line' at his notion of an almost mythical pre-Civil War New England. It is this that we should bear in mind in reading the novel, and not whether he got the date of the introduction of horsecars sadly wrong.

The novel is divided into twelve chapters – 'sketches' or scenes. It probably owes much in structure and tone to the work of Octave Feuillet and V. Cherbuliez, as well as to the French playwrights Dumas *fils*, Augier and Sardou, whom James in a letter of 1878 to his brother claimed to have 'thoroughly mastered'. (For examples of his admiration of the contemporary French theatre see the essays in *The Scenic Art*; for a discussion of all these influences see *The Novels of Henry James* (1961) by Oscar Cargill, and Leon Edel's introduction to *The Complete Plays of Henry James*.

In the very first chapter we are given a vivid sense both of the opening situation and of the differences between Eugenia and her brother Felix. Eugenia is preoccupied with the 'scene' – from the window and in the room – and with her own image as reflected in the mirror. The scene is bleak enough. Indeed, the chapter starts with a description of a graveyard in snow and drizzle and, although the climate changes to a sunlit atmosphere more appropriate to comedy, we may say in retrospect that Eugenia will stay long enough to see the 'grave-yard' of the hopes and ambitions she brought with her to America. Two things about her appear immediately. She is constantly concerned with her 'performance' – and with her appearance or style. From the start, even in this depressing hotel room with her brother, she is never really 'off stage'. When she looks in the mirror she becomes in effect a narcissistic would-be seductress:

Here she paused a moment, gave a pinch to her waist with her two hands, or raised these members – they were very plump and pretty – to the multifold braids of her hair, with a movement half-caressing, half-corrective. An attentive observer might have fancied that during these periods of desultory self-inspection her face forgot its melancholy ...

But once she turns to the window and the room again she becomes the melancholy, discontented actress. And she is 'restless' – a key-word which recurs in the book. The notable features about her are not her beauty – which is denied – but the potency and brilliance of her presence and style. She is exotic and she is richly dressed:

> Her forehead was very low – it was her only handsome feature; and she had a great abundance of crisp dark hair, finely frizzled, which was always braided in a manner that suggested some Southern or Eastern, some remotely foreign, woman. She had a large collection of earrings, and wore them in alternation; and they seemed to give a point to her Oriental or exotic aspect.

Since clothes and dress and adornments are to loom large in the novel I might quote here from one of James's essays on paintings which, after a discussion of more modern works, he concludes by referring to portraits and group studies of Tudors and Stuarts.

> On this odd phenomenon there would be more to say, were it not that every lesson fades, in the halls in question, in the light of the great moral phrased for us by the Tudor and Stuart groups. This moral, startling perhaps in its levity, is simply the glory of costume, the gospel of clothes. From the ages of costume to the ages of none the drop is more than pitiful, and distinction is shattered by the fall. If you are to be represented, if you are to be perpetuated, in short, it is nothing that you be great or good – it is everything that you be dressed. (From 'The Grafton Galleries' in *The Painter's Eye*.)

It remains uncertain whether Eugenia is 'great or good' – but she is certainly 'dressed'. What happens when she drops from the *place* of costume to the place of – apparently – none, is one of the comic/serious issues in the book and a deft meditation on 'the gospel of clothes'.

In this opening scene, as an actress, she is very much the *malcontente*. Her comments of disgust at everything she sees around her – and outside her – are almost theatrically exaggerated, as are her gestures and mannerisms. ' "It's too horrible!" she exclaimed. "I shall go back – I shall go back!" And she flung herself into a chair before the fire.' Among other things, she seems to suffer from the lack of an appreciative audience. For while she is performing – to and for herself – her brother Felix is 'sketching' – to and for himself. He seems imperturbably good-natured and totally at his ease – a *biencontent*, and too much so for his sister's patience. ' "Remember ... that you are nothing but an obscure Bohemian – a penniless correspondent of an illustrated paper." ' But nothing can put him out or dismay him, be it graveyard or hotel room. Or America. ' "This comical country, this delightful country! The women are very pretty ... and the whole affair is very amusing. I must make a sketch of it." ' And so he sketches and smiles while his sister performs and rants. Both are slightly parodic versions of 'European' artists in this opening scene, both equally ignorant of what America is or may be. They have American relations whose portraits Felix means to sketch and whose money, in some way, Eugenia hopes to benefit from. She is deadly serious; though he says, ' "I hoped we had left seriousness in Europe." ' Both are right: America does offer opportunities which Felix, with his endless, adaptable good nature and lightness of touch, will avail himself of. But as to 'seriousness', Eugenia says tersely, ' "I fancy you will find it here." ' In the event, it might be said that it is she who finds 'seriousness'. But in this first chapter James comically and economically depicts his two Europeans in characteristic modes: one turning all to jest and sketch; the other concerned, above all, with preening and performance. Two 'artists' then, and taken together reflecting something of what James – sketching and performing – was doing himself.

The contrast with the habitation of the Wentworths which provides the next scene, is not such a total contrast as the apparent European/Puritan opposition might suggest or promise. The house is 'large' and 'square' and the plants are 'neatly-disposed'. There is a sound of 'a distant church-bell' but we are introduced to a girl 'not dressed for church'. She is an 'innocent Sabbath-breaker', not 'especially pretty', but she is, like Eugenia, 'restless'. The house is 'wide open' but here again there is a suggestion of a connection with the East; not in terms of style but trade: 'small cylindrical stools in green and blue porcelain, which suggest an affiliation between the residents and the Eastern trade'. Eastern objects will recur later in a rather more sombre context.

We also may notice that Gertrude, the 'innocent Sabbath-breaker', is first seen as having an interest in clothes and appearance. She cannot exactly say what is wrong with the way her sister wears her scarf but she would know by instinct how to wear it correctly. There follows a crucial exchange. The grave sister Charlotte dismisses the scarf problem by saying, ' "I don't think it matters how one looks behind." ' To which Gertrude has a quick, pert answer:

'I should say it mattered more,' said Gertrude. 'Then you don't know who may be observing you. You are not on your guard. You can't try to look pretty.'

Charlotte received this declaration with extreme gravity. 'I don't think one should ever try to look pretty,' she rejoined earnestly.

Her companion was silent. Then she said, 'Well, perhaps it's not of much use.'

Presentation of the self, 'performance' of the self through 'style', or a grave indifference to personal appearance in face of the world: these are some of the underlying controversies of the book. The would-be suitor of Gertrude, Mr Brand – 'handsome, but rather too stout' (not quite a heroic figure) – says all the orthodox things, but Gertrude is quite consciously perverse and contrary in her replies to all his lumbering, decent questions ('he looked, as the phrase is, as good as gold'). Gertrude styles herself as 'wicked' but it is a wickedness of a spirit of contrariness and play. She likes to say apparently frivolous things which baffle her serious and literal-minded family and friends, as she confesses about her conversation with her sister, ' "I said things that puzzled her – on purpose." ' When Brand asks why, she simply says, ' "Because the sky is so blue!" ' As he says, ' "I don't know whether you are wicked ... but you are certainly puzzling." ' So quite before the Europeans arrive we are shown that the apparently serene Puritan household contains an uncontrollable puzzle – in the figure of Gertrude. She continues the Eastern theme when she takes down the *Arabian Nights* to read instead of going to church. And, of course, when Felix arrives he seems to come straight from the book. 'There, for a quarter of an hour, she read the history of the loves of the Prince Camaralzaman and the Princess Badoura.

At last looking up, she beheld as it seemed to her, the Prince Camaralzaman standing before her.' So, while the others are at church, Felix comes to her from an exotic fairy-tale. It is another tension of the book that what (or who) goes to church cannot come from fairy stories; and the reverse is true. In trying to explain their origin and life, Felix says of himself and his sister, ' "I am afraid you will think we are little better than vagabonds. I have lived anywhere – everywhere." ' Everywhere is really nowhere and truly he seems to be without origin: his rootlessness is total. But such vagueness of origin, such deracination, is obviously attractive to the clearly descended and very firmly rooted Gertrude.

Felix is always said to be laughing and smiling (though once his smile is oddly described as a 'grimace'). 'You would have said that American civilisation expressed itself to his sense in a tissue of capital jokes.' His description of the Wentworth household and its inhabitants is that they have a 'style' but it is a style of their own: ' "How shall I describe it? It's primitive; it's patriarchal; it's the *ton* of the golden age." ' Eugenia, who after all came to make her fortune, asks directly, ' "And have they nothing golden but their *ton*? Are there no symptoms of wealth?" ' To which Felix astutely replies, ' "I should say there was wealth without symptoms." ' Perhaps more to the point Felix admits that the Wentworths are not 'gay'. ' "They are sober; they are even severe. They are of a pensive cast; they take things hard. I think there is something the matter with them; they have some melancholy memory or some depressing expectation. It's not the epicurean temperament ... But we shall cheer them up." ' Whether the Europeans really do cheer the Puritans up is open to question (though Felix must to some extent succeed with Gertrude whom he marries and takes away to some never-never land where, no doubt, all will be smiles and everything 'gay').

But, apart from Gertrude, there are at least two others who do not quite fit into the Puritan mould. The Wentworth son is inclined to drinking, and we learn of a relative, Robert Acton, who has been to China and returned with a fortune. (I have mentioned the subtly consistent ways in which the theme of the East pervades the book, and there is some truth in Felix's remark that ' "Instead of coming to the West we seem to have gone to the

East."' The cultural codes are more confusing than a simple Europe/Puritan opposition might suggest.) Eugenia will show an interest in both of these slightly deviant or atypical figures, as though her hopes lay with them rather than with any orthodox Puritan. When Eugenia arrives at the Wentworth house she obviously causes a stir of surprise with her foreign airs and graces. But in a way she is regarded as some kind of brilliant performer. She is watched and listened to almost as some foreign object. 'Their attitude seemed to imply that she was a kind of conversational mountebank, attired, intellectually, in gauze and spangles.' She is welcomed gravely and cautiously yet she seems genuinely touched by the novel atmosphere, as she indicates in a moving speech.

'I came to look – to try – to ask,' she said. 'It seems to me I have done well. I am very tired; I want to rest.' There were tears in her eyes. The luminous interior, the gentle, tranquil people, the simple, serious life – the sense of these things pressed upon her with an overmastering force, and she felt herself yielding to one of the most genuine emotions she had ever known. 'I should like to stay here,' she said. 'Pray take me in.'

As she speaks, Robert Acton turns away – 'with his hands stealing into his pockets'. The pathos of the book is that finally they will not 'take her in' and her most genuine hope of acceptance and assimilation – in the eligible figure of Robert Acton – does indeed 'turn away'. That moment of 'genuine emotion' indicates that she is no mere fortune-hunter – though she is 'ambitious'. And in not taking her in the community really reveals its inability, too, to take in the style and graces of social performance which she incarnates. The loss is hers, certainly. But it is also theirs.

Eugenia's advent is felt as a possible threat: 'The sudden irruption into the well-ordered consciousness of the Wentworths of an element not allowed for in its scheme of usual obligations, required a readjustment of that sense of responsibility which constituted its principal furniture.' Mr Wentworth cannot quite see Eugenia as part of his house; nor, indeed, can Eugenia herself. The decision to lodge her in a separate house 'over the way' represents a compromise: hospitality without assimilation. It also keeps the threat of foreignness somewhat at bay. The young Gertrude is excited by the idea and welcomes it. ' "It will be a foreign house."' To which Mr Wentworth gravely replies, '"Are we very sure that we need a foreign house ... Do you think it desirable to establish a foreign house – in this quiet place?"' He feels that they must be perpetually on their guard against 'Europeanism' – '"we must all be careful. This is a great change; we are to be exposed to peculiar influences. I don't say they are bad; I don't judge them in advance. But they may perhaps make it necessary that we should exercise a great deal of wisdom and self-control. It will be a different tone."' Mr Wentworth lives by a Puritan monotone and is deeply suspicious of anything and anyone who exhibits a multiplicity – or even just a difference – of tone. His reactions offer a clear statement of a deep-rooted idea that America might retain her moral purity more readily by excluding European influences and habits. (In his study Mr Wentworth's only accessories are law books and a map of America. Together, these are sufficient to tell him where he is and what to do.) '"I shall keep them in the other house,"' resolves Mr Wentworth firmly. This, in effect, is the Puritan rejection of the expressive delights of style in favour of a few rigidly simplistic concepts of obligation and responsibility. (When Felix asks for the hand of Gertrude, he says that she needs a place in the world that '"would bring her out"'. '"A place to do her duty!"' counters Mr Wentworth, thus implicitly revealing the opposition between self-exfoliation and self-contraction which runs through the book.)

But while Eugenia is an ambiguous figure and not without a streak of what might be called duplicity ('nothing that the Baroness said was wholly untrue. It is but fair to add, perhaps, that nothing that she said was wholly true'), she is not a simple deceiver. Her strange 'morganatic' marriage and her many names are indeed 'new names and new words' to her American relations. The multiplicity of her names – Eugenia, Camilla, Dolores, the Baroness Münster, wife, through 'morganatic' marriage, to the Prince of Silberstadt-Schreckenstein – variously suggest, as Richard Poirier notes in a brilliant essay (in *The Comic Sense of Henry James* (1960)), a recently deposed queen, a courtesan made mythic by Dumas *fils*, and a traditional lady of the sorrows. Her German name contains both wealth and fear. She is not simple and her many-sidedness raises suspicions among those Puritans who prefer things to be as open and clear as the totally illuminated house of the Wentworths, prefer character to be reduced to a single clear facet. But Gertrude – 'restless' in her simple surroundings – responds to the intriguing multiplicity and ambiguity of Eugenia's presence. When Eugenia imports all her ornaments, shawls and draperies into the little cottage (she had brought with her to the New World 'a copious provision of the element of costume'), Gertrude responds to the varied and nuanced richness of the place, feeling that she has 'been leading hitherto an existence singularly garish and totally devoid of festoons'. '"What is life, indeed, without curtains?"' she sighs secretly to herself, thus perhaps adumbrating her final departure from Mr Wentworth's excessively well-lighted abode.

It is Gertrude, too, who asks Felix to paint her, after Mr Wentworth has revealed that deep Puritan suspicion of art by refusing to have his head 'made over again' for aesthetic purposes (Felix finds it '"delightfully wasted and emaciated. The complexion is wonderfully bleached."'). And it is Gertrude who brings into the open one of the book's crucial issues, when she cries out to the importunate clergyman Mr Brand in defence of her relationship with Felix: '"I am trying for once to be natural! ... I have been pretending, all my life; I have been dishonest; it is you that have made me so!"' The Puritans' self-conceit was that their way of life represented something absolutely simple and natural, whereas the amoral Europeans were given over to concealment and pretence. But here is a spirited girl revealing that it is those honest, simple Puritans who have imposed a life of concealment and pretence on her, while it is with the adorned and eloquent Europeans that she feels most 'natural'. The paradox is potentially a deep one. Perhaps it is with the aid of art and style that we may most readily discover   and be   our most natural selves; while the attempt to deny and exclude art (keep it in 'the other house') in the interests of purity and radical integrity and godliness may involve a falsification of the self more destructive than the artifice in the flexible performances of the Baroness, for instance. Felix may be the most 'natural' figure in the book. Art might make for 'nature'. In rejecting European civilizing influences the Puritans may make themselves 'unnatural'. As Gertrude complains, ' "There must be a thousand different ways of being dreary ... and sometimes I think we make use of them all." ' Is it 'dreary' to be natural? Is it natural to be dreary? The Baroness says to Robert Acton: ' "I had a sort of longing to come into those natural relations which I knew I should find here. Over there I had only, as I may say, artificial relations. Don't you see the difference?" ' But the difference is not so clearly marked out. Acton immediately reacts with an almost crude suggestion. We may say that the supposedly 'artificial' Eugenia gets the better of the exchange, showing both more subtlety and dignity.

'Well, there is one way in which the relation of a lady and a gentleman may always become natural,' said Acton.
'You mean by their becoming lovers? That may be natural or not. At any rate,' rejoined Eugenia, *nous n'en sommes pas là!*'

If Eugenia is an 'artificial', complex European, then Robert Acton in his own way at least is just as 'artificial', complex – and arguably more devious than Eugenia.

We must look a little more closely at Robert Acton for if Eugenia complicates James's original simple scheme for his story in one way, Robert Acton does so in another. Robert Acton ('Action' without the 'I' – though he does 'act on' other people) is said to be a man who 'exercised great discretion in all things – beginning with his estimate of himself'. He knows his limitations but he is also aware of his 'natural shrewdness'. He takes 'the humorous view of things' and in all this we can discern a marked defensiveness. He is usually presented in some posture of 'lounging' though we are told 'he was not quite so relaxed as he pretended'. It is a cover for a habit of 'vigilant observation'. His cautious observation is certainly in excess of his feelings, over which he exercises a vigilant restraint. The Baroness interests him, certainly: ' "It's what I call a very clever woman" ' is his first somewhat ambiguous comment on her and her social performance and conversation. He has a 'handsome library' and collects paintings which are, however, described as 'abortive masterpieces'. His house is a 'much more modern dwelling than Mr Wentworth's, and [is] more redundantly upholstered and expensively ornamented'. He has a fine collection of 'the most delightful *chinoiseries*' (more evidence of that displaced East that runs through the book). He is indeed a 'collector' – and a calculator. For him the Baroness poses an interesting problem: 'He was constantly pondering her words and motions; they were as interesting as the factors in an algebraic problem. This is saying a good deal; for Acton was extremely fond of mathematics.' He is vaguely prepared to marry – but he has a negative feeling about 'love': 'Love was a poetic impulse, and his own state of feeling with regard to the Baroness was largely characterized by that eminently prosaic sentiment – curiosity.' He is one of those emotionally arid observers who, for good or bad (usually bad), often turn up in James's works. The 'prose' of curiosity is more self-defensive, self-retracting than the 'poetry' of love, the opening and giving of oneself to another. He is positively delighted when Clifford Wentworth (with whom Eugenia has been maintaining a slight secondary flirtation) says to him, ' "Eugenia doesn't care for anything!" ' As if that boy could pronounce with any finality on anything so subtle and complex as Eugenia's feelings. Acton, with his travelling, his collections and furniture and his wry detachment, appears to have transcended the limitations and suspicions of the Puritan mind. He seems tolerant and open and, perhaps, the only American in the book capable of appreciating Eugenia. Indeed, he is said to fall in love with her – but love is soon smothered in mistrust. Whereas Gertrude seeks true emancipation, Acton, in his languourousness and worldliness, is the reverse of emancipated. He is, for one thing, tied to his mother – that pale, ailing devotee of Emerson – as the last sentence of the book indicates. More notably, there is that vitiating inertia about him (as often as not hanging around with his hands in his pockets, leaning against things, even lying down). As has been intimated, this tendency to the supine state clearly indicates some more serious lack of emotional energy. His mother, 'wonderfully white and transparent', has a voice which, as Eugenia detects, 'had never expressed any human passions'. Acton is, moreover, incapable of any spontaneous feelings. Instead, he coldly experiments on Eugenia, proposing sex without marriage, trying to catch her out, force her into a lie, make her break down. Given Eugenia's particular plight, such detached experimentation is real cruelty. For James, as for Hawthorne, to use people in this way is the

epitome of immorality. Thus, early in his career James shows that
the Puritan preoccupation with rigid rules of conduct may testify
not to great passions manfully resisted, but simply to an absence
of passion, and that 'the great standard of morality' so often
invoked may only be a rationalization for a great emotional
anaesthesia.

In Chapter 10 the weather is again 'cold and dreary' as it was
at the start. Even a rose tree scattering rain drops appears to have
a 'menacing, warning intention'. Eugenia keeps up the pretence
that she has rejected Robert Acton but she realizes that it is in
fact he who has decided against her; and towards the conclusion
of this 'idyllic' story a serious passage, verging on pathos, sums
up Eugenia's thoughts and feelings:

If she could have done something at the moment, on the spot, she would
have stepped upon a European steamer and turned her back, with a kind
of rapture, upon that profoundly mortifying failure, her visit to her
American relations. It is not exactly apparent why she should have termed
this enterprise a failure, inasmuch as she had been treated with the highest
distinction for which allowance has been made in American institutions.
Her irritation came, at bottom, from the sense, which, always present,
had suddenly grown acute, that the social soil on this big, vague continent
was somehow not adapted for growing those plants whose fragrance she
especially inclined to inhale, and by which she liked to see herself surrounded
– a species of vegetation for which she carried a collection of seedlings,
as we may say, in her pocket. She found her chief happiness in the sense
of exerting a certain power and making a certain impression; and now
she felt the annoyance of a rather wearied swimmer who, on nearing shore,
to land, finds a smooth straight wall of rock when he had counted on
a clean firm beach. Her power, in the American air, seemed to have lost
its prehensile attributes; the smooth wall of rock was insurmountable.

The passage can be read as a criticism of Eugenia whose ambitions
have been disappointed and whose 'plots' have been foiled, or
have foiled themselves. Certainly she came to serve herself, even
to save herself, and has not been above intrigue and dissimulation.
But she does bring with her 'seedlings' of civilization to which
the American soil proves innutritive; and the wall of rock which
should have been an hospitable beach may indicate as much a
loss for America as it does a rebuff to Eugenia. Indeed, the

implicit comment on the Wentworths' America can be seen as fairly severe – admirable and decent enough though the Wentworths are themselves. Since Gertrude leaves this America in pursuit of 'naturalness' and Eugenia is effectively excluded from it because of her 'arts', it becomes something of a problem to define what exactly does flourish on that rich but profoundly inhospitable soil. ' *"Les beaux jours sont passés"* ' says the Baroness: ' "Never, never! They have only begun," ' replies Felix, but then he is 'a highly successful comedian' while there is something deeply serious about Eugenia. When she looks round Robert Acton's house and admires all its furnishings and arrangings – ' *"Comme c'est bien!"* ' she says to herself – and when we are told 'she had thought of just such a house as this when she decided to come to America' we may feel that her basic motives were cynically materialistic. Nevertheless, as she walks home alone and wonders, 'Was she to have gained nothing – was she to have gained nothing?' we sense the genuine sadness of her situation. She does, after all, have so much to give. (It should be noted that the 'aristocratic' court and castle from which Eugenia has come is described as 'meagre' and that the family she has left is, as 'royalty', something of a sham. There is something much more substantial about the Acton house than what she has left in Europe, which cannot but strike us as something of an empty shell, an impoverished 'aristocracy' with little reality to it.)

Having said this, it should perhaps be remembered that the 'Europeans' are not in fact pure Europeans. Eugenia and Felix are not true Europeans but Europeanized Americans. They are American cousins of the Wentworths who simply happen to have been born and brought up in various European countries. The point is not an idle one: James's work exhibits many Americans whose 'Europeanization' is not always to their advantage. Think of Osmond and Madame Merle in *Portrait of a Lady*, who turn out to be the most sinister, plotting figures. They are *not* 'Europeans' but perverted Americans. Similarly, although one can see that Felix and Eugenia bring to America the best of Europe, it behoves one to recognize that they are – in a metamorphosed form – 'Americans'. Which makes the idea of a simple confrontation between Europeans and Americans inapplicable to the book. They are *all* Americans, albeit that the places of upbringing have produced very marked and noticeable differences. And it should be recognized that, despite the light (or heavy) ironic criticisms of the Puritans, they not only have many admirable qualities which are not undermined by irony, but that with them both Felix and Eugenia feel 'a sacred satisfaction to have found a family'. The positive values associated with this Puritan family are criticized but not nullified by the unexpected irruption of the Europeanized cousins into their midst. The criticisms of the family are rather of the order: Why must they be so sad? Why must they be so dreary? Why can't they begin to learn to 'enjoy'? But there is misreading on both sides. It could be said that if the Wentworths do not appreciate the particular style and performance of Eugenia and Felix, the latter do not really appreciate the profound and unmasked simplicity of the Wentworths. A comment by Richard Poirier is relevant here: 'The comedy in the novel is the result of a dramatic confrontation not of Europe and America but of misconceptions about both of them.' Underestimation, mis-assessment, and mis-evaluations are ubiquitous, and if there is some implied criticism of Eugenia's somewhat histrionic role-playing, so there is also some quiet, if understated, appreciation of the more reticent Wentworth virtues. *The Europeans* may be light in tone and basically comic in texture – but it is not a simple book.

There were, of course, a number of authentic Europeans who visited and observed America during the nineteenth century. Alexis de Tocqueville has left us with perhaps the most probing account of nineteenth-century America from a European point of view – but there were also the Trollopes, Dickens, Oscar Wilde and others (for an account of their responses see Peter Conrad's *Imagining America* (1980)). To summarize the truly European response to America would be another story. But we might do well to conclude with the later responses of that most subtly 'Europeanized' American of them all – Henry James himself. He returned to America in 1905 and recorded his impressions in *The American Scene* (1907); the first chapter, aptly enough, is on New England.

He starts in New York but one of his first impressions sounds the keynote of what is to come. He senses 'the great adventure of a society reaching out into the apparent void for the amenities, the consummations, after having earnestly gathered in so many of the preparations and necessities'. 'Void' and 'vacancy' are to be words that recur in his ensuing account. New England he still finds 'Arcadian' and 'idyllic' – as it is in the novel – but he detects a cost, even as the novel does: 'One was in the presence, everywhere, of the refusal to consent to history, and of the consciousness, on the part of every site, that this precious compound is in no small degree being made, on the other side of the continent, at the expense of such sites.' If he is struck by 'the very high standard of propriety' he also notes what amounts to 'the complete abolition of *forms*'. He responds to the great rural beauty of the place but (he is talking of Cape Cod but the observation carries over into America as a whole): 'the life of the little community was practically locked up tight as if it had *all* been a question of painted Japanese silk. And that was doubtless, for the story-seeker, absolutely the little story: the constituted blankness was the whole business, and one's opportunity was all, thereby, for a study of exquisite emptiness.' There is also a radical lack of true variety – 'the scene is everywhere the same' – which applies to the inhabitants as well in an atmosphere 'that so often affects us as drained precisely, and well-nigh to our gasping, of any exception to the common'.

Another way of rendering this impression is to note the apparent absence of any inwardness and 'secrets': '*Were* there any secrets at all, or had the outward blankness, the quantity of absence, its inward equivalent as well?' Once again he comes back to that sense of a 'visible vacancy' – 'the thinness, the passivity ... that absence of the settled standard which contains, as I more and more felt, from day to day, the germ of the most final of all my generalizations'. The atmosphere is 'thin and clear and colourless, what would it ever say "no" to? or what would it ever paint thick, indeed, with sympathy and sanction?' (The same atmosphere finally said 'no' to Eugenia, a figure whom it distinctly did not 'paint thick with sympathy and sanction'.) James finds 'a perpetual repudiation of the past' all around him: instead there is 'the working of democratic institutions' – 'a revelation that has its full force and its lively interest only on the spot, where, once caught, it becomes the only clue worth mentioning in the labyrinth': 'The democratic consistency, consummately and immitigably complete, shines through with its hard light, whatever equivocal gloss may happen momentarily to prevail.' And, again and again, James comes back to the sense of 'extraordinary virtuous vacancy' as later, in his account of Boston, the words 'vacant' and 'void' echo once more; a consequence – or result – of his 'vain quest ... of the deeper depths'. There *are* no 'deeper depths', any more than the Wentworth house concealed depths (though it contained puzzles), and perhaps that totally illuminated house was also a kind of 'void' and 'vacancy' for all its foreground decency and propriety. Though whether the two American 'Europeans' – who, for all their brilliance, have a slight aura of meretriciousness about them – could have filled that 'void' is a question which the book does not seek to resolve.

TEXTUAL NOTE

The text of *The Europeans* is from the original edition published by Macmillan and Company in 1878 which James never revised.

THE EUROPEANS

A SKETCH

CHAPTER 1

A NARROW grave-yard in the heart of a bustling, indifferent city, seen from the windows of a gloomy-looking inn,[1] is at no time an object of enlivening suggestion; and the spectacle is not at its best when the mouldy tombstones and funereal umbrage have received the ineffectual refreshment of a dull, moist snow-fall. If, while the air is thickened by this frosty drizzle, the calendar should happen to indicate that the blessed vernal season is already six weeks old, it will be admitted that no depressing influence is absent from the scene. This fact was keenly felt on a certain 12th of May, upwards of thirty years since,[2] by a lady who stood looking out of one of the windows of the best hotel in the ancient city of Boston. She had stood there for half an hour – stood there, that is, at intervals; for from time to time she turned back into the room and measured its length with a restless step. In the chimney-place was a red-hot fire, which emitted a small blue flame; and in front of the fire, at a table, sat a young man who was busily plying a pencil. He had a number of sheets of paper cut into small equal squares, and he was apparently covering them with pictorial designs – strange-looking figures. He worked rapidly and attentively, sometimes threw back his head and held out his drawing at arm's length, and kept up a soft, gay-sounding humming and whistling. The lady brushed past him in her walk; her much-trimmed skirts were voluminous.[3] She never dropped her eyes upon his work; she only turned them, occasionally, as she passed, to a mirror suspended above a toilet-table on the other side of the room. Here she paused a moment, gave a pinch to her waist with her two hands, or raised these members – they were very plump and pretty – to the multifold braids of her hair, with a movement half-caressing, half-corrective. An attentive observer might have fancied that during these periods of desultory self-inspection her

33

face forgot its melancholy; but as soon as she neared the window again it began to proclaim that she was a very ill-pleased woman. And indeed in what met her eyes there was little to be pleased with. The window-panes were battered by the sleet; the head-stones in the grave-yard beneath seemed to be holding themselves askance to keep it out of their faces. A tall iron railing protected them from the street, and on the other side of the railing an assemblage of Bostonians were trampling about in the liquid snow. Many of them were looking up and down; they appeared to be waiting for something. From time to time a strange vehicle drew near to the place where they stood – such a vehicle as the lady at the window, in spite of a considerable acquaintance with human inventions, had never seen before: a huge, low omnibus,[4] painted in brilliant colours, and decorated apparently with jingling bells, attached to a species of groove in the pavement,[5] through which it was dragged, with a great deal of rumbling, bouncing, and scratching, by a couple of remarkably small horses. When it reached a certain point the people in front of the grave-yard, of whom much the greater number were women, carrying satchels and parcels, projected themselves upon it in a compact body – a movement suggesting the scramble for places in a life-boat at sea – and were engulfed in its large interior. Then the life-boat – or the life-car, as the lady at the window of the hotel vaguely designated it – went bumping and jingling away upon its invisible wheels, with the helmsman (the man at the wheel) guiding its course incongruously from the prow. This phenomenon was repeated every three minutes, and the supply of eagerly-moving women in cloaks, bearing reticules and bundles, renewed itself in the most liberal manner. On the other side of the grave-yard was a row of small red-brick houses, showing a series of homely, domestic-looking backs; at the end opposite the hotel a tall wooden church spire, painted white,[6] rose high into the vagueness of the snow-flakes. The lady at the window looked at it for some time; for reasons of her own she thought it the ugliest thing she had ever seen. She hated it, she despised it; it threw her into a state of irritation that was quite out of proportion to any sensible motive. She had never known herself to care so much about church spires.

She was not pretty; but even when it expressed perplexed irritation her face was most interesting and agreeable. Neither was she in her first youth; yet, though slender, with a great deal of extremely well-fashioned roundness of contour – a suggestion both of maturity and flexibility – she carried her three-and-thirty years as a light-wristed Hebe[7] might have carried a brimming wine-cup. Her complexion was fatigued, as the French say; her mouth was large, her lips too full, her teeth uneven, her chin rather commonly modelled; she had a thick nose, and when she smiled – she was constantly smiling – the lines beside it rose too high, toward her eyes. But these eyes were charming: grey in colour, brilliant, quickly glancing, gently resting, full of intelligence. Her forehead was very low – it was her only handsome feature; and she had a great abundance of crisp dark hair, finely frizzled, which was always braided in a manner that suggested some Southern or Eastern, some remotely foreign, woman. She had a large collection of earrings, and wore them in alternation; and they seemed to give a point to her Oriental or exotic aspect. A compliment had once been paid her which, being repeated to her, gave her greater pleasure than anything she had ever heard. 'A pretty woman?' someone had said. 'Why, her features are very bad.' 'I don't know about her features,' a very discerning observer had answered; 'but she carries her head like a pretty woman.' You may imagine whether, after this, she carried her head less becomingly.

She turned away from the window at last, pressing her hands to her eyes. 'It's too horrible!' she exclaimed. 'I shall go back – I shall go back!' And she flung herself into a chair before the fire.

'Wait a little, dear child,' said the young man softly, sketching away at his little scraps of paper.

The lady put out her foot; it was very small, and there was an immense rosette on her slipper. She fixed her eyes for a while on this ornament, and then she looked at the glowing bed of anthracite coal in the grate. 'Did you ever see anything so hideous as that fire?' she demanded. 'Did you ever see anything so – so *affreux*[8] as – as everything?' She spoke English with perfect purity; but she brought out this French epithet in a manner that indicated that she was accustomed to using French epithets.

'I think the fire is very pretty,' said the young man, glancing

35

at it a moment. 'Those little blue tongues, dancing on top of the crimson embers, are extremely picturesque. They are like a fire in an alchemist's laboratory.'[9]

'You are too good-natured, my dear,' his companion declared.

The young man held out one of his drawings, with his head on one side. His tongue was gently moving along his under-lip. 'Good-natured – yes. Too good-natured – no.'

'You are irritating,' said the lady, looking at her slipper.

He began to retouch his sketch. 'I think you mean simply that you are irritated.'

'Ah, for that, yes!' said his companion, with a little bitter laugh. 'It's the darkest day of my life – and you know what that means.'

'Wait till tomorrow,' rejoined the young man.

'Yes, we have made a great mistake. If there is any doubt about it today, there certainly will be none tomorrow. *Ce sera clair, au moins!*'[10]

The young man was silent a few moments, driving his pencil. Then at last, 'There are no such things as mistakes,' he affirmed.

'Very true – for those who are not clever enough to perceive them. Not to recognise one's mistakes – that would be happiness in life,' the lady went on, still looking at her pretty foot.

'My dearest sister,' said the young man, always intent upon his drawing, 'it's the first time you have told me I am not clever.'

'Well, by your own theory I can't call it a mistake,' answered his sister, pertinently enough.

The young man gave a clear, fresh laugh. 'You, at least, are clever enough, dearest sister,' he said.

'I was not so when I proposed this.'

'Was it you who proposed it?' asked her brother.

She turned her head and gave him a little stare. 'Do you desire the credit of it?'

'If you like, I will take the blame,' he said, looking up with a smile.

'Yes,' she rejoined in a moment, 'you make no difference in these things. You have no sense of property.'

The young man gave his joyous laugh again. 'If that means I have no property, you are right!'

'Don't joke about your proverty,' said his sister. 'That is quite as vulgar as to boast about it.'

'My poverty! I have just finished a drawing that will bring me fifty francs!'

'*Voyons*,'[11] said the lady, putting out her hand.

He added a touch or two, and then gave her his sketch. She looked at it, but she went on with her idea of a moment before. 'If a woman were to ask you to marry her you would say, "Certainly, my dear, with pleasure!" And you would marry her, and be ridiculously happy. Then at the end of three months you would say to her, "You know that blissful day when I begged you to be mine!"'

The young man had risen from the table, stretching his arms a little; he walked to the window. 'That is a description of a charming nature,' he said.

'Oh yes, you have a charming nature; I regard that as our capital. If I had not been convinced of that I should never have taken the risk of bringing you to this dreadful country.'

'This comical country, this delightful country!' exclaimed the young man; and he broke into the most animated laughter.

'Is it those women scrambling into the omnibus?' asked his companion. 'What do you suppose is the attraction?'

'I suppose there is a very good-looking man inside,' said the young man.

'In each of them? They come along in hundreds, and the men in this country don't seem at all handsome. As for the women – I have never seen so many at once since I left the convent.'

'The women are very pretty,' her brother declared, 'and the whole affair is very amusing. I must make a sketch of it.' And he came back to the table quickly, and picked up his utensils – a small sketching-board, a sheet of paper, and three or four crayons. He took his place at the window with these things, and stood there glancing out, plying his pencil with an air of easy skill. While he worked he wore a brilliant smile. Brilliant is indeed the word at this moment for his strongly-lighted face. He was eight-and-twenty years old; he had a short, slight, well-made figure. Though he bore a noticeable resemblance to his sister, he was a better-favoured person: fair-haired, clear-faced, witty-looking, with a delicate finish of feature and an expression at once urbane and not at all serious, a warm blue eye, an eyebrow finely drawn and excessively arched – an eyebrow which, if ladies wrote sonnets to those of their lovers, might have been made the subject of such a piece of verse – and a light moustache that flourished upwards as if blown that way by the breath of a constant smile. There was something in his physiognomy at once benevolent and picturesque. But, as I have hinted, it was not at all serious. The young man's face was, in this respect, singular; it was not at all serious, and yet it inspired the liveliest confidence.

'Be sure you put in plenty of snow,' said his sister. '*Bonté divine*,[12] what a climate!'

'I shall leave the sketch all white, and I shall put in the little figures in black,' the young man answered, laughing. 'And I shall call it – what is that line in Keats? – Mid-May's Eldest Child!'[13]

'I don't remember,' said the lady, 'that mamma ever told me it was like this.'

'Mamma never told you anything disagreeable. And it's not like this – every day. You will see that tomorrow we shall have a splendid day.'

'*Qu'en savez-vous?*[14] Tomorrow I shall go away.'

'Where shall you go?'

'Anywhere away from here. Back to Silberstadt. I shall write to the Reigning Prince.'

The young man turned a little and looked at her, with his crayon poised. 'My dear Eugenia,' he murmured, 'were you so happy at sea?'

Eugenia got up; she still held in her hand the drawing her brother had given her. It was a bold expressive sketch of a group of miserable people on the deck of a steamer,[15] clinging together and clutching at each other, while the vessel lurched downward, at a terrific angle, into the hollow of a wave. It was extremely clever, and full of a sort of tragi-comical power. Eugenia dropped her eyes upon it and made a sad grimace. 'How can you draw such odious scenes?' she asked. 'I should like to throw it into the fire!' And she tossed the paper away. Her brother watched, quietly, to see where it went. It fluttered down to the floor, where he let it lie. She came toward the window, pinching in her waist.

'Why don't you reproach me – abuse me?' she asked. 'I think I should feel better then. Why don't you tell me that you hate me for bringing you here?'

'Because you would not believe it. I adore you, dear sister! I am delighted to be here, and I am charmed with the prospect.'

'I don't know what had taken possession of me. I had lost my head,' Eugenia went on.

The young man, on his side, went on plying his pencil. 'It is evidently a most curious and interesting country. Here we are, and I mean to enjoy it.'

His companion turned away with an impatient step, but presently came back. 'High spirits are doubtless an excellent thing,' she said; 'but you give one too much of them, and I can't see that they have done you any good.'

The young man stared, with lifted eyebrows, smiling; he tapped his handsome nose with his pencil. 'They have made me happy!'

'That was the least they could do; they have made you nothing else. You have gone through life thanking fortune for such very small favours that she has never put herself to any trouble for you.'

'She must have put herself to a little, I think, to present me with so admirable a sister.'

'Be serious, Felix.[16] You forget that I am your elder.'

'With a sister, then, so elderly!' rejoined Felix, laughing. 'I hoped we had left seriousness in Europe.'

'I fancy you will find it here. Remember that you are nearly thirty years old, and that you are nothing but an obscure Bohemian[17] – a penniless correspondent of an illustrated paper.'

'Obscure as much as you please, but not so much of a Bohemian as you think. And not at all penniless! I have a hundred pounds in my pocket; I have an engagement to make fifty sketches, and I mean to paint the portraits of all our cousins, and of all *their* cousins, at a hundred dollars a head.'

'You are not ambitious,' said Eugenia.

'You are, dear Baroness,' the young man replied.

The Baroness was silent a moment, looking out at the sleet-darkened grave-yard and the bumping horse-cars. 'Yes, I am ambitious,' she said at last. 'And my ambition has brought me to this dreadful place!' She glanced about her – the room had a certain vulgar nudity, the bed and the window were curtainless – and she gave a little passionate sigh. 'Poor old ambition!' she exclaimed. Then she flung herself down upon a sofa which stood near against the wall, and covered her face with her hands.

Her brother went on with his drawing, rapidly and skilfully; and after some moments he sat down beside her and showed her his sketch. 'Now, don't you think that's pretty good for an obscure Bohemian?' he asked. 'I have knocked off another fifty francs.'

Eugenia glanced at the little picture as he laid it on her lap. 'Yes, it is very clever,' she said. And in a moment she added, 'Do you suppose our cousins do that?'

'Do what?'

'Get into those things, and look like that.'

Felix meditated a while. 'I really can't say. It will be interesting to discover.'

'Oh, the rich people can't!' said the Baroness.

'Are you very sure they are rich?' asked Felix lightly.

His sister slowly turned in her place, looking at him. 'Heavenly powers!' she murmured. 'You have a way of bringing out things!'

'It will certainly be much pleasanter if they are rich,' Felix declared.

'Do you suppose if I had not known they were rich I would ever have come?'

The young man met his sister's somewhat peremptory eye with his bright, contented glance. 'Yes it certainly will be pleasanter,' he repeated.

'That is all I expect of them,' said the Baroness. 'I don't count upon their being clever or friendly – at first – or elegant or interesting. But I assure you I insist upon their being rich.'

Felix leaned his head upon the back of the sofa and looked a while at the oblong patch of sky to which the window served as frame. The snow was ceasing; it seemed to him that the sky had begun to brighten. 'I count upon their being rich,' he said at last, 'and powerful, and clever, and friendly, and elegant, and interesting, and generally delightful! *Tu vas voir*.'[18] And he bent forward and kissed his sister. 'Look there!' he went on. 'As a portent, even while I speak, the sky is turning the colour of gold; the day is going to be splendid.'

And indeed, within five minutes the weather had changed. The sun broke out through the snow-clouds and jumped into the Baroness's room. '*Bonté divine*,' exclaimed this lady, 'what a climate!'

'We will go out and see the world,' said Felix.

And after a while they went out. The air had grown warm, as well as brilliant; and sunshine had dried the pavements. They walked about the streets at hazard, looking at the people and the houses, the shops and the vehicles, the blazing blue sky and the muddy crossings, the hurrying men and the slow-strolling maidens, the fresh red bricks and the bright green trees, the extraordinary mixture of smartness and shabbiness. From one hour to another the day had grown vernal; even in the bustling streets there was an odour of earth and blossom. Felix was immensely entertained. He had called it a comical country, and he went about laughing at everything he saw. You would have said that American civilisation expressed itself to his sense in a tissue of capital jokes. The jokes were certainly excellent, and the young man's merriment was very joyous and genial. He possessed what is called the pictorial sense, and this first glimpse of democratic manners stirred the same sort of attention that he would have given to the movements of a lively young person with a bright complexion. Such attention would have been demonstrative and complimentary; and in the present case Felix might have passed for an undispirited young exile revisiting the haunts of his childhood. He kept looking at the violet blue in the sky, at the scintillating air, at the scattered and multiplied patches of colour.

'*Comme c'est bariolé*,[19] eh?' he said to his sister, in that foreign tongue which they both appeared to feel a mysterious prompting occasionally to use.

'Yes, it is *bariolé* indeed,' the Baroness answered. 'I don't like the colouring; it hurts my eyes.'

'It shows how extremes meet,' the young man rejoined. 'Instead of coming to the West we seem to have gone to the East. The way the sky touches the house-tops is just like Cairo; and the red and blue sign-boards patched over the face of everything remind one of Mahometan decoration.'

'The young women are not Mahometan,'[20] said his companion.

'They can't be said to hide their faces. I never saw anything so bold.'

'Thank heaven they don't hide their faces!' cried Felix. 'Their faces are uncommonly pretty.'

'Yes, their faces are often very pretty,' said the Baroness, who was a very clever woman. She was too clever a woman not to be capable of a great deal of just and fine observation. She clung more closely than usual to her brother's arm; she was not exhilarated, as he was; she said very little, but she noted a great many things, and made her reflexions. She was a little excited; she felt that she had indeed come to a strange country, to make her fortune. Superficially, she was conscious of a good deal of irritation and displeasure; the Baroness was a very delicate and fastidious person. Of old, more than once, she had gone, for entertainment's sake and in brilliant company, to a fair in a provincial town. It seemed to her now that she was at an enormous fair – that the entertainment and the *désagréments*[21] were very much the same. She found herself alternately smiling and shrinking; the show was very curious, but it was probable from moment to moment that one would be jostled. The Baroness had never seen so many people walking about before; she had never been so mixed up with people she did not know. But little by little she felt that this fair was a more serious undertaking. She went with her brother into a large public garden,[22] which seemed very pretty, but where she was surprised at seeing no carriages. The afternoon was drawing to a close; the coarse, vivid grass and the slender tree-boles were gilded by the level sunbeams – gilded as with gold that was fresh from the mine. It was the hour at which ladies should come out for an airing and roll past a hedge of pedestrians, holding their parasols askance. Here, however, Eugenia observed no indications of this custom, the absence of which was more anomalous as there was a charming avenue of remarkably graceful arching elms in the most convenient contiguity to a large, cheerful street, in which, evidently, among the more prosperous members of the *bourgeoisie*, a great deal of pedestrianism went forward. Our friends passed out into this well-lighted promenade, and Felix noticed a great many more pretty girls, and called his sister's attention to them. This latter measure, however, was superfluous; for the Baroness had inspected, narrowly, these charming young ladies.

'I feel an intimate conviction that our cousins are like that,' said Felix.

The Baroness hoped so, but this is not what she said. 'They are very pretty,' she said, 'but they are mere little girls. Where are the women – the women of thirty?'

'Of thirty-three, do you mean?' her brother was going to ask; for he understood often both what she said and what she did not say. But he only exclaimed upon the beauty of the sunset, while the Baroness, who had come to seek her fortune, reflected that it would certainly be well for her if the persons against whom she might need to measure herself should all be mere little girls. The sunset was superb; they stopped to look at it; Felix declared that he had never seen such a gorgeous mixture of colours. The Baroness also thought it splendid; and she was perhaps the more easily pleased from the fact that while she stood there she was conscious of much admiring observation on the part of various nice-looking people who passed that way, and to whom a distinguished, strikingly-dressed woman with a foreign air, exclaiming upon the beauties of nature on a Boston street corner in the French tongue, could not be an object of indifference. Eugenia's spirits rose. She surrendered herself to a certain tranquil gaiety. If she had come to seek her fortune, it seemed to her that her fortune would be easy to find. There was a promise of it in the gorgeous purity of the western sky; there was an intimation in the mild unimpertinent gaze of the passers of a certain natural facility in things.

'You will not go back to Silberstadt, eh?' asked Felix.

'Not tomorrow,' said the Baroness.

'Nor write to the Reigning Prince?'

'I shall write to him that they evidently know nothing about him over here.'

'He will not believe you,' said the young man. 'I advise you to let him alone.'

Felix himself continued to be in high good-humour. Brought up among ancient customs and in picturesque cities, he yet found plenty of local colour in the little Puritan[23] metropolis. That evening, after dinner, he told his sister that he would go forth early on the morrow to look up their cousins.

'You are very impatient,' said Eugenia.

'What can be more natural,' he asked, 'after seeing all those pretty girls today? If one's cousins are of that pattern, the sooner one knows them the better.'

'Perhaps they are not,' said Eugenia. 'We ought to have brought some letters[24] – to some other people.'

'The other people would not be our kinsfolk.'

'Possibly they would be none the worse for that,' the Baroness replied.

Her brother looked at her with his eyebrows lifted. 'That was not what you said when you first proposed to me that we should come out here and fraternise with our relatives. You said that it was the prompting of natural affection; and when I suggested some reasons against it you declared that the *voix du sang*[25] should go before everything.'

'You remember all that?' asked the Baroness.

'Vividly! I was greatly moved by it.'

She was walking up and down the room, as she had done in the morning; she stopped in her walk and looked at her brother. She apparently was going to say something, but she checked herself and resumed her walk. Then, in a few moments, she said something different, which had the effect of an explanation of the suppression of her earlier thought. 'You will never be anything but a child, dear brother.'

'One would suppose that you, madam,' answered Felix, laughing, 'were a thousand years old.'

'I am – sometimes,' said the Baroness.

'I will go, then, and announce to our cousins the arrival of a personage so extraordinary. They will immediately come and pay you their respects.'

Eugenia paced the length of the room again, and then she stopped before her brother, laying her hand upon his arm. 'They are not to come and see me,' she said. 'You are not to allow that. That is not the way I shall meet them first.' And in answer to his interrogative glance she went on. 'You will go and examine, and report. You will come back and tell me who they are and what they are; their number, gender, their respective ages – all about them. Be sure you observe everything; be ready to describe to me the locality, the accessories – how shall I say it? – the *mise en scène*.[26] Then, at my own time, at my own hour, under circumstances of my own choosing, I will go to them. I will present myself – I will appear before them!' said the Baroness, this time phrasing her idea with a certain frankness.

'And what message am I to take to them?' asked Felix, who had a lively faith in the justness of his sister's arrangements.

She looked at him a moment – at his expression of agreeable veracity; and, with that justness that he admired, she replied, 'Say what you please. Tell my story in the way that seems to you most – natural.' And she bent her forehead for him to kiss.

CHAPTER 2

THE next day was splendid, as Felix had prophesied; if the winter
had suddenly leaped into spring, the spring had for the moment
as quickly leaped into summer. This was an observation made
by a young girl who came out of a large square house in the
country, and strolled about in the spacious garden which separated
it from a muddy road. The flowering shrubs and the neatly-
disposed plants were basking in the abundant light and warmth;
the transparent shade of the great elms – they were magnificent
trees – seemed to thicken by the hour; and the intensely habitual
stillness offered a submissive medium to the sound of a distant
church-bell. The young girl listened to the church-bell; but she
was not dressed for church. She was bare-headed; she wore a
white muslin waist[1] with an embroidered border, and the skirt
of her dress was of coloured muslin. She was a young lady of
some two or three and twenty years of age, and though a young
person of her sex walking bare-headed in a garden, of a Sunday
morning in spring-time, can, in the nature of things, never be a
displeasing object, you would not have pronounced this innocent
Sabbath-breaker especially pretty. She was tall and pale, thin and
a little awkward; her hair was fair and perfectly straight; her eyes
were dark, and they had the singularity of seeming at once dull
and restless – differing herein, as you see, fatally from the ideal
'fine eyes', which we always imagine to be both brilliant and tranquil. The doors and windows of the large square house were all
wide open, to admit the purifying sunshine, which lay in generous
patches upon the floor of a wide, high, covered piazza[2] adjusted
to two sides of the mansion – a piazza on which several straw-
bottomed rocking-chairs and half a dozen of those small cylindrical
stools in green and blue porcelain, which suggest an affiliation
between the residents and the Eastern trade, were symmetrically

disposed. It was an ancient house – ancient in the sense of being eighty years old; it was built of wood, painted a clean, clear, faded grey, and adorned along the front, at intervals, with flat wooden pilasters, painted white. These pilasters appeared to support a kind of classic pediment, which was decorated in the middle by a large triple window in a boldly-carved frame, and in each of its smaller angles by a glazed circular aperture. A large white door, furnished with a highly-polished brass knocker, presented itself to the rural-looking road, with which it was connected by a spacious pathway, paved with worn and cracked, but very clean, bricks. Behind it there were meadows and orchards, a barn and a pond; and facing it, a short distance along the road, on the opposite side, stood a smaller house, painted white, with external shutters painted green, a little garden on one hand and an orchard on the other. All this was shining in the morning air, through which the simple details of the picture addressed themselves to the eye as distinctly as the items of a 'sum' in addition.

A second young lady presently came out of the house, across the piazza, descended into the garden and approached the young girl of whom I have spoken. This second young lady was also thin and pale; but she was older than the other; she was shorter; she had dark, smooth hair. Her eyes, unlike the other's, were quick and bright; but they were not at all restless. She wore a straw bonnet with white ribbons, and a long red India scarf, which, on the front of her dress, reached to her feet. In her hand she carried a little key.

'Gertrude,' she said, 'are you very sure you had better not go to church?'

Gertrude looked at her a moment, plucked a small sprig from a lilac-bush, smelled it and threw it away. 'I am not very sure of anything!' she answered.

The other young lady looked straight past her, at the distant pond, which lay shining between the long banks of fir trees. Then she said in a very soft voice, 'This is the key of the dining-room closet. I think you had better have it, if any one should want anything.'

'Who is there to want anything?' Gertrude demanded. 'I shall be all alone in the house.'

'Some one may come,' said her companion.

'Do you mean Mr Brand?'

'Yes, Gertrude. He may like a piece of cake.'

'I don't like men that are always eating cake!' Gertrude declared, giving a pull at the lilac-bush.

Her companion glanced at her, and then looked down on the ground. 'I think father expected you would come to church,' she said. 'What shall I say to him?'

'Say I have a bad headache.'

'Would that be true?' asked the elder lady, looking straight at the pond again.

'No, Charlotte,' said the younger one simply.

Charlotte transferred her quiet eyes to her companion's face. 'I am afraid you are feeling restless.'

'I am feeling as I always feel,' Gertrude replied, in the same tone.

Charlotte turned away; but she stood there a moment. Presently she looked down at the front of her dress. 'Doesn't it seem to you, somehow, as if my scarf were too long?' she asked.

Gertrude walked half round her, looking at the scarf. 'I don't think you wear it right,' she said.

'How should I wear it, dear?'

'I don't know; differently from that. You should draw it differently over your shoulders, round your elbows; you should look differently behind.'

'How should I look?' Charlotte inquired.

'I don't think I can tell you,' said Gertrude, plucking out the scarf a little behind. 'I could do it myself, but I don't think I can explain it.'

Charlotte, by a movement of her elbows, corrected the laxity that had come from her companion's touch. 'Well, some day you must do it for me. It doesn't matter now. Indeed, I don't think it matters,' she added, 'how one looks behind.'

'I should say it mattered more,' said Gertrude. 'Then you don't know who may be observing you. You are not on your guard. You can't try to look pretty.'

Charlotte received this declaration with extreme gravity. 'I don't think one should ever try to look pretty,' she rejoined earnestly.

Her companion was silent. Then she said, 'Well, perhaps it's not of much use.'

Charlotte looked at her a little, and then kissed her. 'I hope you will be better when we come back.'

'My dear sister, I am very well!' said Gertrude.

Charlotte went down the large brick walk to the garden gate; her companion strolled slowly toward the house. At the gate Charlotte met a young man, who was coming in – a tall, fair young man, wearing a high hat and a pair of thread gloves.[3] He was handsome, but rather too stout. He had a pleasant smile. 'Oh, Mr Brand!' exclaimed the young lady.

'I came to see whether your sister was not going to church,' said the young man.

'She says she is not going; but I am very glad you have come. I think if you were to talk to her a little' ... and Charlotte lowered her voice. 'It seems as if she were restless.'

Mr Brand smiled down on the young lady from his great height. 'I shall be very glad to talk to her. For that I should be willing to absent myself from almost any occasion of worship, however attractive.'

'Well, I suppose you know,' said Charlotte softly, as if positive acceptance of this proposition might be dangerous. 'But I am afraid I shall be late.'

'I hope you will have a pleasant sermon,' said the young man.

'Oh, Mr Gilman is always pleasant,' Charlotte answered. And she went on her way.

Mr Brand went into the garden, where Gertrude, hearing the gate close behind him, turned and looked at him. For a moment she watched him coming; then she turned away. But almost immediately she corrected this movement, and stood still, facing him. He took off his hat and wiped his forehead, as he approached. Then he put on his hat again and held out his hand. His hat being removed, you would have perceived that his forehead was very large and smooth, and his hair abundant but rather colourless. His nose was too large, and his mouth and eyes were too small; but for all this he was, as I have said, a young man of striking appearance. The expression of his little clean-coloured blue eyes was irresistibly gentle and serious; he looked, as the phrase is, as good as gold. The young girl, standing in the garden path, glanced, as he came up, at his thread gloves.

'I hoped you were going to church,' he said. 'I wanted to walk with you.'

'I am very much obliged to you,' Gertrude answered. 'I am not going to church.'

She had shaken hands with him; he held her hand a moment. 'Have you any special reason for not going?'

'Yes, Mr Brand,' said the young girl.

'May I ask what it is?'

She looked at him, smiling; and in her smile, as I have intimated, there was a certain dullness. But mingled with this dullness was something sweet and suggestive. 'Because the sky is so blue!' she said.

He looked at the sky, which was magnificent, and then said, smiling too, 'I have heard of young ladies staying at home for bad weather, but never for good. Your sister, whom I met at the gate, tells me you are depressed,' he added.

'Depressed? I am never depressed.'

'Oh, surely, sometimes,' replied Mr Brand, as if he thought this a regrettable account of one's self.

'I am never depressed,' Gertrude repeated. 'But I am sometimes wicked. When I am wicked I am in high spirits. I was wicked just now to my sister.'

'What did you do to her?'

'I said things that puzzled her – on purpose.'

'Why did you do that, Miss Gertrude?' asked the young man.

She began to smile again. 'Because the sky is so blue!'

'You say things that puzzle *me*,' Mr Brand declared.

'I always know when I do it,' proceeded Gertrude. 'But people puzzle me more, I think. And they don't seem to know!'

'This is very interesting,' Mr Brand observed, smiling.

'You told me to tell you about my – my struggles,' the young girl went on.

'Let us talk about them. I have so many things to say.'

Gertrude turned away a moment; and then, turning back, 'You had better go to church,' she said.

'You know,' the young man urged, 'that I have always one thing to say.'

Gertrude looked at him a moment. 'Please don't say it now!'

'We are all alone,' he continued, taking off his hat; 'all alone in this beautiful Sunday stillness.'

Gertrude looked around her, at the breaking buds, the shining distance, the blue sky to which she had referred as a pretext for her irregularities. 'That's the reason,' she said, 'why I don't want you to speak. Do me a favour; go to church.'

'May I speak when I come back?' asked Mr Brand.

'If you are still disposed,' she answered.

'I don't know whether you are wicked,' he said, 'but you are certainly puzzling.'

She had turned away; she raised her hands to her ears. He looked at her a moment, and then he slowly walked to church.

She wandered for a while about the garden, vaguely and without purpose. The church-bell had stopped ringing; the stillness was complete. This young lady relished highly, on occasions, the sense of being alone – the absence of the whole family, and the emptiness of the house. Today, apparently, the servants had also gone to church: there was never a figure at the open windows; behind the house there was no stout negress in a red turban, lowering the bucket into the great shingle-hooded well. And the front door of the big, unguarded home stood open, with the trustfulness of the golden age;[4] or, what is more to the purpose, with that of New England's silvery prime.[5] Gertrude slowly passed through it, and went from one of the empty rooms to the other – large, clear-coloured rooms, with white wainscots, ornamented with thin-legged mahogany furniture, and, on the walls, with old-fashioned engravings, chiefly of Scriptural subjects, hung very high. This agreeable sense of solitude, of having the house to herself, of which I have spoken, always excited Gertrude's imagination; she could not have told you why, and neither can her humble historian. It always seemed to her that she must do something particular – that she must honour the occasion; and while she roamed about, wondering what she could do, the occasion usually came to an end. Today she wondered more than ever. At last she took down a book; there was no library in the house, but there were books in all the rooms. None of them were forbidden books,[6] and Gertrude had not stopped at home for the sake of a chance to climb to the inaccessible shelves. She possessed herself of a very obvious volume – one of the series of the *Arabian Nights*[7] – and she brought it out into the portico and sat down with it in her lap. There, for a quarter of an hour, she read the history of the loves of the Prince Camaralzaman and the Princess Badoura.[8] At last, looking up, she beheld, as it seemed to her, the Prince Camaralzaman standing before her. A beautiful young man was making her a very low bow – a magnificent bow, such as she had never seen before. He appeared to have dropped from the clouds; he was wonderfully handsome; he smiled – smiled as if he were smiling on purpose. Extreme surprise, for a moment, kept Gertrude sitting still; then she rose, without even keeping her finger in her book. The young man, with his hat in his hand, still looked at her, smiling and smiling. It was very strange.

'Will you kindly tell me,' said the mysterious visitor, at last, 'whether I have the honour of speaking to Miss Wentworth?'

'My name is Gertrude Wentworth,' murmured the young woman.

'Then – then – I have the honour – the pleasure – of being your cousin.'

The young man had so much the character of an apparition that this announcement seemed to complete his unreality. 'What cousin? Who are you?' said Gertrude.

He stepped back a few paces and looked up at the house; then glanced round him at the garden and the distant view. After this he burst out laughing. 'I see it must seem to you very strange,' he said. There was, after all, something substantial in his laughter. Gertrude looked at him from head to foot. Yes, he was remarkably handsome; but his smile was almost a grimace. 'It is very still,' he went on, coming nearer again. And as she only looked at him for reply, he added, 'Are you all alone?'

'Everyone has gone to church,' said Gertrude.

'I was afraid of that!' the young man exclaimed. 'But I hope you are not afraid of me.'

'You ought to tell me who you are,' Gertrude answered.

'I am afraid of you!' said the young man. 'I had a different plan. I expected the servant would take in my card, and that you would put your heads together, before admitting me, and make out my identity.'

Gertrude had been wondering with a quick intensity which brought its result; and the result seemed an answer – a wondrous, delightful answer – to her vague wish that something would befall her. 'I know – I know,' she said. 'You come from Europe.'

'We came two days ago You have heard of us, then – you believe in us?'

'We have known, vaguely,' said Gertrude, 'that we had relations in France.'

'And have you ever wanted to see us?' asked the young man.

Gertrude was silent a moment. 'I have wanted to see you.'

'I am glad, then, it is you I have found. We wanted to see you, so we came.'

'On purpose?' asked Gertrude.

The young man looked round him, smiling still. 'Well, yes; on purpose. Does that sound as if we should bore you?' he added. 'I don't think we shall – I really don't think we shall. We are rather fond of wandering, too; and we were glad of a pretext.'

'And you have just arrived?'

'In Boston, two days ago. At the inn I asked for Mr Wentworth. He must be your father. They found out for me where he lived; they seemed often to have heard of him. I determined to come, without ceremony. So, this lovely morning, they set my face in the right direction and told me to walk straight before me, out of town. I came on foot because I wanted to see the country. I walked and walked, and here I am! It's a good many miles.'

'It is seven miles and a half,' said Gertrude softly. Now that this handsome young man was proving himself a reality she found herself vaguely trembling; she was deeply excited. She had never in her life spoken to a foreigner, and she had often thought it would be delightful to do so. Here was one who had suddenly been engendered by the Sabbath stillness for her private use; and such a brilliant, polite smiling one! She found time and means to compose herself, however; to remind herself that she must exercise a sort of official hospitality. 'We are very – very glad to see you,' she said. 'Won't you come into the house?' And she moved toward the open door.

'You are not afraid of me, then?' asked the young man again, with his light laugh.

She wondered a moment, and then, 'We are not afraid – here,' she said.

'*Ah, comme vous devez avoir raison!*'[9] cried the young man, looking all round him, appreciatively. It was the first time that Gertrude had heard so many words of French spoken. They gave her something of a sensation. Her companion followed her, watching, with a certain excitement of his own, this tall, interesting-looking girl, dressed in her clear, crisp muslin. He paused in the hall, where there was a broad white staircase with a white balustrade. 'What a pleasant house!' he said. 'It's lighter inside than it is out.'

'It's pleasanter here,' said Gertrude, and she led the way into the parlour – a high, clean, rather empty-looking room. Here they stood looking at each other – the young man smiling more than ever; Gertrude, very serious, trying to smile.

'I don't believe you know my name,' he said. 'I am called Felix Young. Your father is my uncle. My mother was his half-sister, and older than he.'

'Yes,' said Gertrude, 'and she turned Roman Catholic and married in Europe.'

'I see you know,' said the young man. 'She married, and she died. Your father's family didn't like her husband. They called him a foreigner; but he was not. My poor father was born in Sicily, but his parents were American.'

'In Sicily?' Gertrude murmured.

'It is true,' said Felix Young, 'that they had spent their lives in Europe. But they were very patriotic. And so are we.'

'And you are Sicilian,' said Gertrude.

'Sicilian, no! Let's see. I was born at a little place – a dear little place – in France. My sister was born at Vienna.'

'So you are French,' said Gertrude.

'Heaven forbid!' cried the young man. Gertrude's eyes were fixed upon him almost insistently. He began to laugh again. 'I can easily be French, if that will please you.'

'You are a foreigner of some sort,' said Gertrude.

'Of some sort – yes; I suppose so. But who can say of what sort? I don't think we have ever had occasion to settle the question. You know there are people like that. About their country, their religion, their profession, they can't tell.'

Gertrude stood there gazing; she had not asked him to sit down. She had never heard of people like that; she wanted to hear. 'Where do you live?' she asked.

'They can't tell that either!' said Felix. 'I am afraid you will think we are little better than vagabonds. I have lived anywhere – everywhere. I really think I have lived in every city in Europe.' Gertrude gave a little long, soft exhalation. It made the young man smile at her again; and his smile made her blush a little. To take refuge from blushing she asked him if, after his long walk, he was not hungry or thirsty. Her hand was in her pocket; she was fumbling with the little key that her sister had given her. 'Ah, my dear young lady,' he said, clasping his hands a little, 'if you could give me, in charity, a glass of wine!'

Gertrude gave a smile and a little nod, and went quickly out of the room. Presently she came back with a very large decanter in one hand and a plate in the other, on which was placed a big round cake with a frosted top. Gertrude, in taking the cake from the closet, had had a moment of acute consciousness that it composed the refection of which her sister had thought that Mr Brand would like to partake. Her kinsman from across the seas was looking at the pale high-hung engravings. When she came in he turned and smiled at her, as if they had been old friends meeting after a separation. 'You wait upon me yourself?' he asked. 'I am served like the gods!' She had waited upon a great many people, but none of them had ever told her that. The observation added a certain lightness to the step with which she went to a little table where there were some curious red glasses – glasses covered with little gold sprigs, which Charlotte used to dust every morning with her own hands. Gertrude thought the glasses very handsome, and it was a pleasure to her to know that the wine was good; it was her father's famous madeira. Felix Young thought it excellent; he wondered why he had been told that there was no wine in America. She cut him an immense triangle out of the cake, and again she thought of Mr Brand. Felix sat there, with his glass in one hand and his huge morsel of cake in the other – eating, drinking, smiling, talking. 'I am very hungry,' he said. 'I am not at all tired; I am never tired. But I am very hungry.'

'You must stay to dinner,' said Gertrude. 'At two o'clock.[10]

They will all have come back from church; you will see the others.'

'Who are the others?' asked the young man. 'Describe them all.'

'You will see for yourself. It is you that must tell me; now, about your sister.'

'My sister is the Baroness Münster,' said Felix.

On hearing that his sister was a Baroness, Gertrude got up and walked about slowly, in front of him. She was silent a moment. She was thinking of it. 'Why didn't she come, too?' she asked.

'She did come; she is in Boston, at the hotel.'

'We will go and see her,' said Gertrude, looking at him.

'She begs you will not!' the young man replied. 'She sends you her love; she sent me to announce her. She will come and pay her respects to your father.'

Gertrude felt herself trembling again. A Baroness Münster, who sent a brilliant young man to 'announce' her; who was coming, as the Queen of Sheba came to Solomon,[11] to pay her 'respects' to quiet Mr Wentworth – such a personage presented herself to Gertrude's vision with a most effective unexpectedness. For a moment she hardly knew what to say. 'When will she come?' she asked at last.

'As soon as you will allow her – tomorrow. She is very impatient,' answered Felix, who wished to be agreeable.

'Tomorrow, yes,' said Gertrude. She wished to ask more about her; but she hardly knew what could be predicated of a Baroness Münster. 'Is she – is she – married?'

Felix had finished his cake and wine; he got up, fixing upon the young girl his bright expressive eyes. 'She is married to a German prince – Prince Adolf, of Silberstadt-Schreckenstein.[12] He is not the Reigning Prince; he is a younger brother.'

Gertrude gazed at her informant; her lips were slightly parted. 'Is she a – a *Princess*?' she asked at last.

'Oh no,' said the young man; 'her position is rather a singular one. It's a morganatic marriage.'

'Morganatic?' These were new names and new words to poor Gertrude.

'That's what they call a marriage, you know, contracted between a scion of a ruling house and – and a common mortal. They made Eugenia a Baroness, poor woman; but that was all they could do. Now they want to dissolve the marriage. Prince Adolf, between ourselves, is a ninny; but his brother, who is a clever man, has plans for him. Eugenia, naturally enough, makes difficulties; not, however, that I think she cares much – she's a very clever woman; I'm sure you'll like her – but she wants to bother them. Just now everything is *en l'air*.'[13]

The cheerful off-hand tone in which her visitor related this darkly-romantic tale seemed to Gertrude very strange; but it seemed also to convey a certain flattery to herself, a recognition of her wisdom and dignity. She felt a dozen impressions stirring within her, and presently the one that was uppermost found words. 'They want to dissolve her marriage?' she asked.

'So it appears.'

'And against her will?'

'Against her right.'

'She must be very unhappy!' said Gertrude.

Her visitor looked at her, smiling; he raised his hand to the back of his head and held it there a moment. 'So she says,' he answered. 'That's her story. She told me to tell it you.'

'Tell me more,' said Gertrude.

'No, I will leave that to her; she does it better.'

Gertrude gave a little excited sigh again. 'Well, if she is unhappy,' she said, 'I am glad she has come to us.'

She had been so interested that she failed to notice the sound of a footstep in the portico; and yet it was a footstep that she always recognised. She heard it in the hall, and then she looked out of the window. They were all coming back from church – her father, her sister and brother, and their cousins, who always came to dinner on Sunday. Mr Brand had come in first; he was in advance of the others, because, apparently, he was still disposed to say what she had not wished him to say an hour before. He came into the parlour, looking for Gertrude. He had two little books in his hand. On seeing Gertrude's companion he slowly stopped, looking at him.

'Is this a cousin?' asked Felix.

Then Gertrude saw that she must introduce him; but her ears, and, by sympathy, her lips, were full of all that he had been telling her. 'This is the Prince,' she said – 'the Prince of Silberstadt-Schreckenstein!'

Felix burst out laughing, and Mr Brand stood staring, while the others, who had passed into the house, appeared behind him in the open doorway.

CHAPTER 3

THAT evening, at dinner, Felix Young gave his sister, the Baroness Münster, an account of his impressions. She saw that he had come back in the highest possible spirits; but this fact, to her own mind, was not a reason for rejoicing. She had but a limited confidence in her brother's judgement; his capacity for taking rose-coloured views was such as to vulgarise one of the prettiest of tints. Still, she supposed he could be trusted to give her the mere facts; and she invited him, with some eagerness, to communicate them. 'I suppose, at least, they didn't turn you from the door,' she said. 'You have been away some ten hours.'

'Turn me from the door!' Felix exclaimed. 'They took me to their hearts; they killed the fatted calf.'[1]

'I know what you want to say: they are a collection of angels.'

'Exactly,' said Felix. 'They are a collection of angels – simply.'

'*C'est bien vague,*'[2] remarked the Baroness. 'What are they like?'

'Like nothing you ever saw.'

'I am sure I am much obliged; but that is hardly more definite. Seriously, they were glad to see you?'

'Enchanted. It has been the proudest day of my life. Never, never have I been so lionised![3] I assure you, I was cock of the walk. My dear sister,' said the young man, '*nous n'avons qu'à nous tenir;*[4] we shall be great swells!'[5]

Madame Münster looked at him, and her eye exhibited a slight responsive spark. She touched her lips to a glass of wine, and then she said, 'Describe them. Give me a picture.'

Felix drained his own glass. 'Well, it's in the country, among the meadows and woods; a wild sort of place, and yet not far from here. Only, such a road, my dear! Imagine one of the Alpine glaciers reproduced in mud. But you will not spend much time on it, for they want you to come and stay, once for all.'

'Ah,' said the Baroness, 'they want me to come and stay, once for all? *Bon*.'[6]

'It's intensely rural, tremendously natural; and all overhung with this strange white light, this far-away blue sky. There's a big wooden house – a kind of three-storey bungalow; it looks like a magnified Nuremberg toy. There was a gentleman there that made a speech to me about it and called it a 'venerable mansion'; but it looks as if it had been built last night.'

'Is it handsome – is it elegant?' asked the Baroness.

Felix looked at her a moment, smiling. 'It's very clean! No splendours, no gilding, no troops of servants; rather straight-backed chairs. But you might eat off the floors, and you can sit down on the stairs.'

'That must be a privilege. And the inhabitants are straight-backed too, of course.'

'My dear sister,' said Felix, 'the inhabitants are charming.'

'In what style?'

'In a style of their own. How shall I describe it? It's primitive; it's patriarchal; it's the *ton*[7] of the golden age.'

'And have they nothing golden but their *ton*? Are there no symptoms of wealth?'

'I should say there was wealth without symptoms. A plain, homely way of life; nothing for show, and very little for – what shall I call it? – for the senses; but a great *aisance*,[8] and a lot of money, out of sight, that comes forward very quietly for sub-scriptions to institutions, for repairing tenements, for paying doctor's bills: perhaps even for portioning[9] daughters.'

'And the daughters?' Madame Münster demanded. 'How many are there?'

'There are two, Charlotte and Gertrude.'

'Are they pretty?'

'One of them,' said Felix.

'Which is that?'

The young man was silent, looking at his sister. 'Charlotte,' he said at last.

She looked at him in return. 'I see. You are in love with Gertrude. They must be Puritans to their finger-tips; anything but gay!'

'No, they are not gay,' Felix admitted. 'They are sober; they

60

are even severe. They are of a pensive cast; they take things
hard. I think there is something the matter with them; they have
some melancholy memory or some depressing expectation. It's not
the epicurean[10] temperament. My uncle, Mr Wentworth, is a
tremendously high-toned old fellow; he looks as if he were under-
going martyrdom, not by fire, but by freezing. But we shall cheer
them up; we shall do them good. They will take a good deal of
stirring up; but they are wonderfully kind and gentle. And they
are appreciative. They think one clever; they think one remarkable!'

'That is very fine, so far as it goes,' said the Baroness. 'But
are we to be shut up to these three people, Mr Wentworth and
the two young women – what did you say their names were –
Deborah and Hephzibah?'

'Oh no; there is another little girl, a cousin of theirs, a very
pretty creature; a thorough little American. And then there is the
son of the house.'

'Good,' said the Baroness. 'We are coming to the gentlemen.
What of the son of the house?'

'I am afraid he gets tipsy.'

'He, then, has the epicurean temperament! How old is he?'

'He is a boy of twenty; a pretty young fellow, but I am afraid
he has vulgar tastes. And then there is Mr Brand – a very tall
young man, a sort of lay-priest. They seem to think a good deal
of him, but I don't exactly make him out.'

'And is there nothing,' asked the Baroness, 'between these
extremes – this mysterious ecclesiastic and that intemperate
youth?'

'Oh yes; there is Mr Acton. I think,' said the young man, with
a nod at his sister, 'that you will like Mr Acton.'

'Remember that I am very fastidious,' said the Baroness. 'Has
he very good manners?'

'He will have them with you. He is a man of the world; he
has been to China.'

Madame Münster gave a little laugh. 'A man of the Chinese
world! He must be very interesting.'

'I have an idea that he brought home a fortune,' said Felix.

'That is always interesting. Is he young, good-looking, clever?'

'He is less than forty; he has a baldish head; he says witty things.

I rather think,' added the young man, 'that he will admire the Baroness Münster.'

'It is very possible,' said this lady. Her brother never knew how she would take things: but shortly afterwards she declared that he had made a very pretty description, and that on the morrow she would go and see for herself.

They mounted, accordingly, into a great barouche[11] – a vehicle as to which the Baroness found nothing to criticise but the price that was asked for it and the fact that the coachman wore a straw hat. (At Silberstadt Madame Münster had had liveries of yellow and crimson.) They drove into the country, and the Baroness, leaning far back and swaying her lace-fringed parasol, looked to right and to left and surveyed the wayside objects. After a while she pronounced them *affreux*. Her brother remarked that it was apparently a country in which the foreground was inferior to the *plans reculés*;[12] and the Baroness rejoined that the landscape seemed to be all foreground. Felix had fixed with his new friends the hour at which he should bring his sister; it was four o'clock in the afternoon. The large clean-faced house wore, to his eyes, as the barouche drove up to it, a very friendly aspect; the high, slender elms made lengthening shadows in front of it. The Baroness descended; her American kinsfolk were stationed in the portico. Felix waved his hat to them, and a tall, lean gentleman, with a high forehead and a clean-shaven face, came forward toward the garden gate. Charlotte Wentworth walked at his side; Gertrude came behind, more slowly. Both of these young ladies wore rustling silk dresses. Felix ushered his sister into the gate. 'Be very gracious,' he said to her. But he saw the admonition was superfluous. Eugenia was prepared to be gracious as only Eugenia could be. Felix knew no keener pleasure than to be able to admire his sister unrestrictedly; for if the opportunity was frequent, it was not inveterate. When she desired to please she was to him, as to everyone else, the most charming woman in the world. Then he forgot that she was ever anything else; that she was sometimes hard and perverse; that he was occasionally afraid of her. Now, as she took his arm to pass into the garden, he felt that she desired, that she proposed, to please, and this situation made him very happy. Eugenia would please.

The tall gentleman came to meet her, looking very rigid and grave. But it was a rigidity that had no illiberal meaning. Mr Wentworth's manner was pregnant, on the contrary, with a sense of grand responsibility, of the solemnity of the occasion, of its being difficult to show sufficient deference to a lady at once so distinguished and so unhappy. Felix had observed on the day before his characteristic pallor; and now he perceived that there was something almost cadaverous in his uncle's high-featured white face. But so clever were this young man's quick sympathies and perceptions that he had already learned that in these semi-mortuary manifestations there was no cause for alarm. His light imagination had gained a glimpse of Mr Wentworth's spiritual mechanism, and taught him that, the old man being infinitely conscientious, the special operation of conscience within him announced itself by several of the indications of physical faintness.

The Baroness took her uncle's hand, and stood looking at him with her ugly face and her beautiful smile. 'Have I done right to come?' she asked.

'Very right, very right,' said Mr Wentworth solemnly. He had arranged in his mind a little speech; but now it quite faded away. He felt almost frightened. He had never been looked at in just that way – with just that fixed, intense smile – by any woman; and it perplexed and weighed upon him, now, that the woman who was smiling so, and who had instantly given him a vivid sense of her possessing other unprecedented attributes, was his own niece, the child of his own father's daughter. The idea that his niece should be a German Baroness, married 'morganatically' to a Prince, had already given him much to think about. Was it right, was it just, was it acceptable? He always slept badly, and the night before he had lain awake much more even than usual, asking himself these questions. The strange word 'morganatic' was constantly in his ears; it reminded him of a certain Mrs Morgan[13] whom he had once known, and who had been a bold, unpleasant woman. He had a feeling that it was his duty, so long as the Baroness looked at him, smiling in that way, to meet her glance with his own scrupulously-adjusted, consciously-frigid organs of vision: but on this occasion he failed to perform his duty to the last. He looked away toward his daughters. 'We are very glad to see you,' he had said. 'Allow me to introduce my daughters – Miss Charlotte Wentworth, Miss Gertrude Wentworth.'

The Baroness thought she had never seen people less demonstrative. But Charlotte kissed her and took her hand, looking at her sweetly and solemnly. Gertrude seemed to her most funereal, though Gertrude might have found a source of gaiety in the fact that Felix, with his magnificent smile, had been talking to her; he had greeted her as a very old friend. When she kissed the Baroness she had tears in her eyes. Madame Münster took each of these young women by the hand, and looked at them all over. Charlotte thought her very strange-looking and singularly dressed; she could not have said whether it was well or ill. She was glad, at any rate, that they had put on their silk gowns – especially Gertrude. 'My cousins are very pretty,' said the Baroness, turning her eyes from one to the other. 'Your daughters are very handsome, sir.'

Charlotte blushed quickly; she had never yet heard her personal appearance alluded to in a loud expressive voice. Gertrude looked away – not at Felix; she was extremely pleased. It was not the compliment that pleased her; she did not believe it, she thought herself very plain. She could hardly have told you the source of her satisfaction; it came from something in the way the Baroness spoke, and it was not diminished – it was rather deepened, oddly enough – by the young girl's disbelief. Mr Wentworth was silent; and then he asked, formally, 'Won't you come into the house?'

'These are not all; you have some other children,' said the Baroness.

'I have a son,' Mr Wentworth answered.

'And why doesn't he come to meet me?' Eugenia cried. 'I am afraid he is not so charming as his sisters.'

'I don't know; I will see about it,' the old man declared.

'He is rather afraid of ladies,' Charlotte said softly.

'He is very handsome,' said Gertrude, as loud as she could.

'We will go in and find him. We will draw him out of his *cachette*.'[14] And the Baroness took Mr Wentworth's arm, who was not aware that he had offered it to her, and who, as they walked toward the house, wondered whether he ought to have offered it and whether it was proper for her to take it if it had not been offered. 'I want to know you well,' said the Baroness, interrupting these meditations, 'and I want you to know me.'

'It seems natural that we should know each other,' Mr Wentworth rejoined. 'We are near relatives.'

'Ah, there comes a moment in life when one reverts, irresistibly, to one's natural ties – to one's natural affections. You must have found that!' said Eugenia.

Mr Wentworth had been told the day before by Felix that Eugenia was very clever, very brilliant, and the information had held him in some suspense. This was the cleverness, he supposed; the brilliancy was beginning. 'Yes, the natural affections are very strong,' he murmured.

'In some people,' the Baroness declared. 'Not in all.' Charlotte was walking beside her; she took hold of her hand again, smiling always. 'And you, *cousine*, where did you get that enchanting complexion?' she went on; 'such lilies and roses!' The roses in poor Charlotte's countenance began speedily to predominate over the lilies, and she quickened her step and reached the portico. 'This is the country of complexions,' the Baroness continued, addressing herself to Mr Wentworth. 'I am convinced they are more delicate. There are very good ones in England – in Holland; but they are very apt to be coarse. There is too much red.'

'I think you will find,' said Mr Wentworth, 'that this country is superior in many respects to those you mention. I have been to England and Holland.'

'Ah, you have been to Europe?' cried the Baroness. 'Why didn't you come and see me? But it's better, after all, this way,' she said. They were entering the house; she paused and looked round her. 'I see you have arranged your house – your beautiful house – in the – in the Dutch taste!'

'The house is very old,' remarked Mr Wentworth. 'General Washington[15] once spent a week here.'

'Oh, I have heard of Washington,'[16] cried the Baroness. 'My father used to adore him.'

Mr Wentworth was silent a moment and then, 'I found he was very well known in Europe,' he said.

Felix had lingered in the garden with Gertrude; he was standing before her and smiling, as he had done the day before. What had happened the day before seemed to her a kind of dream. He had been there and he had changed everything; the others had seen him, they had talked with him; but that he should come again, that he should be part of the future, part of her small, familiar, much-meditating life – this needed, afresh, the evidence of her senses. The evidence had come to her senses now; and her senses seemed to rejoice in it. 'What do you think of Eugenia?' Felix asked. 'Isn't she charming?'

'She is very brilliant,' said Gertrude. 'But I can't tell yet. She seems to me like a singer singing an air. You can't tell till the song is done.'

'Ah, the song will never be done!' exclaimed the young man, laughing. 'Don't you think her handsome?'

Gertrude had been disappointed in the beauty of the Baroness Münster; she had expected her, for mysterious reasons, to resemble a very pretty portrait of the Empress Josephine,[17] of which there hung an engraving in one of the parlours, and which the younger Miss Wentworth had always greatly admired. But the Baroness was not at all like that – not at all. Though different, however, she was very wonderful, and Gertrude felt herself most suggestively corrected. It was strange, nevertheless, that Felix should speak in that positive way about his sister's beauty. 'I think I *shall* think her handsome,' Gertrude said. 'It must be very interesting to know her. I don't feel as if I ever could.'

'Ah, you will know her well; you will become great friends,' Felix declared, as if this were the easiest thing in the world.

'She is very graceful,' said Gertrude, looking after the Baroness, suspended to her father's arm. It was a pleasure to her to say that anyone was graceful.

Felix had been looking about him. 'And your little cousin of yesterday,' he said, 'who was so wonderfully pretty – what has become of her?'

'She is in the parlour,' Gertrude answered. 'Yes, she is very pretty.' She felt as if it were her duty to take him straight into the house, to where he might be near her cousin. But after hesitating a moment she lingered still. 'I didn't believe you would come back,' she said.

'Not come back!' cried Felix, laughing. 'You didn't know, then, the impression made upon this susceptible heart of mine.'

She wondered whether he meant the impression her cousin Lizzie had made. 'Well,' she said, 'I didn't think we should ever see you again.'

'And pray, what did you think would become of me?'

'I don't know. I thought you would melt away.'

'That's a compliment to my solidity! I melt very often,' said Felix, 'but there is always something left of me.'

'I came and waited for you by the door because the others did,' Gertrude went on. 'But if you had never appeared I should not have been surprised.'

'I hope,' declared Felix, looking at her, 'that you would have been disappointed.'

She looked at him a little, and shook her head. 'No – no!'

'*Ah, par exemple!*'[18] cried the young man. 'You deserve that I should never leave you.'

Going into the parlour they found Mr Wentworth performing introductions. A young man was standing before the Baroness, blushing a good deal, laughing a little, and shifting his weight from one foot to the other – a slim, mild-faced young man, with neatly arranged features, like those of Mr Wentworth. Two other gentlemen, behind him, had risen from their seats, and a little apart, near one of the windows, stood a remarkably pretty young girl. The young girl was knitting a stocking; but, while her fingers quickly moved, she looked with wide, brilliant eyes at the Baroness.

'And what is your son's name?' said Eugenia, smiling at the young man.

'My name is Clifford Wentworth, ma'am,' he said in a tremulous voice.

'Why didn't you come out to meet me, Mr Clifford Wentworth?' the Baroness demanded, with her beautiful smile.

'I didn't think you would want me,' said the young man, slowly sidling about.

'One always wants a *beau cousin*[19] – if one has one! But if you are very nice to me in future I won't remember it against you.' And Madame Münster transferred her smile to the other persons present. It rested first upon the candid countenance and

67

long-skirted figure of Mr Brand, whose eyes were intently fixed upon Mr Wentworth, as if to beg him not to prolong an anomalous situation. Mr Wentworth pronounced his name; Eugenia gave him a very charming glance, and then looked at the other gentleman.

This latter personage was a man of rather less than the usual stature and the usual weight, with a quick, observant, agreeable dark eye, a small quantity of thin dark hair, and a small moustache. He had been standing with his hands in his pockets; and when Eugenia looked at him he took them out. But he did not, like Mr Brand, look evasively and urgently at their host. He met Eugenia's eyes; he appeared to appreciate the privilege of meeting them. Madame Münster instantly felt that he was, intrinsically, the most important person present. She was not unconscious that this impression was in some degree manifested in the little sympathetic nod with which she acknowledged Mr Wentworth's announcement, 'My cousin, Mr Acton!'

'Your cousin – not mine?' said the Baroness.

'It only depends upon you,' Mr Acton declared, laughing.

The Baroness looked at him a moment, and noticed that he had very white teeth. 'Let it depend upon your behaviour,' she said. 'I think I had better wait. I have cousins enough. Unless I can also claim relationship,' she added, 'with that charming young lady.' And she pointed to the young girl at the window.

'That's my sister,' said Mr Acton. And Gertrude Wentworth put her arm round the young girl and led her forward. It was not, apparently, that she needed much leading. She came toward the Baroness with a light, quick step, and with perfect self-possession, rolling her stocking round its needles. She had dark blue eyes and dark brown hair; she was wonderfully pretty.

Eugenia kissed her, as she had kissed the other young women, and then held her off a little, looking at her. 'Now this is quite another *type*,' she said; she pronounced the word in the French manner. 'This is a different outline, my uncle, a different character, from that of your own daughters. This, Felix,' she went on, 'is very much more what we have always thought of as the American type.'

The young girl, during this exposition, was smiling askance at everyone in turn, and at Felix out of turn. 'I find only one type here!' cried Felix laughing. 'The type adorable!'

This sally was received in perfect silence, but Felix, who learned all things quickly, had already learned that the silences frequently observed among his new acquaintances were not necessarily restrictive or resentful. It was, as one might say, the silence of expectation, of modesty. They were all standing round his sister, as if they were expecting her to acquit herself of the exhibition of some peculiar faculty, some brilliant talent. Their attitude seemed to imply that she was a kind of conversational mountebank, attired, intellectually, in gauze and spangles. This attitude gave a certain ironical force to Madame Münster's next words. 'Now this is your circle,' she said to her uncle. 'This is your *salon*.[20] These are your regular *habitués*,[21] eh? I am so glad to see you all together.'

'Oh,' said Mr Wentworth, 'they are always dropping in and out. You must do the same.'

'Father,' interposed Charlotte Wentworth, 'they must do something more.' And she turned her sweet serious face, that seemed at once timid and placid, upon their interesting visitor. 'What is your name?' she asked.

'Eugenia-Camilla-Dolores,' said the Baroness, smiling. 'But you needn't say all that.'

'I will say Eugenia, if you will let me. You must come and stay with us.'

The Baroness laid her hand upon Charlotte's arm very tenderly; but she reserved herself. She was wondering whether it would be possible to 'stay' with these people. 'It would be very charming – very charming,' she said; and her eyes wandered over the company, over the room. She wished to gain time before committing herself. Her glance fell upon young Mr Brand, who stood there, with his arms folded and his hand on his chin, looking at her. 'The gentleman, I suppose, is a sort of ecclesiastic,' she added to Mr Wentworth, lowering her voice a little.

'He is a minister,' answered Mr Wentworth.

'A Protestant?'[22] asked Eugenia.

'I am a Unitarian,[23] madam,' replied Mr Brand impressively.

'Ah, I see,' said Eugenia. 'Something new.' She had never heard of this form of worship.

Mr Acton began to laugh, and Gertrude looked anxiously at Mr Brand.

'You have come very far,' said Mr Wentworth.

'Very far – very far,' the Baroness replied, with a graceful shake of her head, a shake that might have meant many different things.

'That's a reason why you ought to settle down with us,' said Mr Wentworth, with that dryness of utterance which, as Eugenia was too intelligent not to feel, took nothing from the delicacy of his meaning.

She looked at him, and for an instant, in his cold, still face, she seemed to see a far-away likeness to the vaguely-remembered image of her mother. Eugenia was a woman of sudden emotions, and now, unexpectedly, she felt one rising in her heart. She kept looking round the circle; she knew that there was admiration in all the eyes that were fixed upon her. She smiled at them all.

'I came to look – to try – to ask,' she said. 'It seems to me I have done well. I am very tired; I want to rest.' There were tears in her eyes. The luminous interior, the gentle, tranquil people, the simple, serious life – the sense of these things pressed upon her with an overmastering force, and she felt herself yielding to one of the most genuine emotions she had ever known. 'I should like to stay here,' she said. 'Pray take me in.'

Though she was smiling, there were tears in her voice as well as in her eyes. 'My dear niece,' said Mr Wentworth softly. And Charlotte put out her arms and drew the Baroness toward her; while Robert Acton turned away, with his hands stealing into his pockets.

CHAPTER 4

A FEW days after the Baroness Münster had presented herself to her American kinsfolk she came, with her brother, and took up her abode in that small white house adjacent to Mr Wentworth's own dwelling of which mention has already been made. It was on going with his daughters to return her visit that Mr Wentworth placed this comfortable cottage at her service; the offer being the result of a domestic colloquy, diffused through the ensuing twenty-four hours, in the course of which the two foreign visitors were discussed and analysed with a great deal of earnestness and subtlety. The discussion went forward, as I say, in the family circle; but that circle on the evening following Madame Münster's return to town, as on many other occasions, included Robert Acton and his pretty sister. If you had been present, it would probably not have seemed to you that the advent of these brilliant strangers was treated as an exhilarating occurrence, a pleasure the more in this tranquil household, a prospective source of entertainment. This was not Mr Wentworth's way of treating any human occurrence. The sudden irruption into the well-ordered consciousness of the Wentworths of an element not allowed for in its scheme of usual obligations, required a readjustment of that sense of responsibility which constituted its principal furniture. To consider an event, crudely and baldly, in the light of the pleasure it might bring them, was an intellectual exercise with which Felix Young's American cousins were almost wholly unacquainted, and which they scarcely supposed to be largely pursued in any section of human society. The arrival of Felix and his sister was a satisfaction, but it was a singularly joyless and inelastic satisfaction. It was an extension of duty, of the exercise of the more recondite virtues; but neither Mr Wentworth, nor Charlotte, nor Mr Brand, who, among these excellent people, was a great promoter of reflexion and aspiration, frankly adverted to it as an extension of enjoyment. This function was ultimately assumed by Gertrude Wentworth, who was a peculiar girl, but the full compass of whose peculiarities had not been exhibited before they very ingeniously found their pretext in the presence of these possibly too agreeable foreigners. Gertrude, however, had to struggle with a great accumulation of obstructions, both of the subjective, as the metaphysicians say, and of the objective order; and indeed it is no small part of the purpose of this little history to set forth her struggle. What seemed paramount in this abrupt enlargement of Mr Wentworth's sympathies and those of his daughters was an extension of the field of possible mistakes; and the doctrine, as it may almost be called, of the oppressive gravity of mistakes was one of the most cherished traditions of the Wentworth family.

'I don't believe she wants to come and stay in this house,' said Gertrude; Madame Münster, from this time forward, receiving no other designation than the personal pronoun. Charlotte and Gertrude acquired considerable facility in addressing her, directly, as 'Eugenia'; but in speaking of her to each other they rarely called her anything but 'she'.

'Doesn't she think it good enough for her?' cried little Lizzie Acton, who was always asking unpractical questions that required, in strictness, no answer, and to which indeed she expected no other answer than such as she herself invariably furnished in a small innocently-satirical laugh.

'She certainly expressed a willingness to come,' said Mr Wentworth.

'That was only politeness,' Gertrude rejoined.

'Yes, she is very polite – very polite,' said Mr Wentworth.

'She is too polite,' his son declared, in a softly-growling tone which was habitual to him, but which was an indication of nothing worse than a vaguely humorous intention. 'It is very embarrassing.'

'That is more than can be said of you, sir,' said Lizzie Acton, with her little laugh.

'Well, I don't mean to encourage her,' Clifford went on.

'I'm sure I don't care if you do!' cried Lizzie.

'She will not think of you, Clifford,' said Gertrude gravely.

'I hope not!' Clifford exclaimed.

'She will think of Robert,' Gertrude continued, in the same tone.

Robert Acton began to blush; but there was no occasion for it, for everyone was looking at Gertrude – everyone, at least, save Lizzie, who, with her pretty head on one side, contemplated her brother.

'Why do you attribute motives, Gertrude?' asked Mr Wentworth.

'I don't attribute motives, father,' said Gertrude. 'I only say she will think of Robert; and she will!'

'Gertrude judges by herself!' Acton exclaimed, laughing. 'Don't you, Gertrude? Of course the Baroness will think of me. She will think of me from morning till night.'

'She will be very comfortable here,' said Charlotte, with something of a housewife's pride. 'She can have the large north-east room. And the French bedstead,' Charlotte added, with a constant sense of the lady's foreignness.

'She will not like it,' said Gertrude, 'not even if you pin little tidies all over the chairs.'

'Why not, dear?' asked Charlotte, perceiving a touch of irony here, but not resenting it.

Gertrude had left her chair; she was walking about the room; her stiff silk dress, which she had put on in honour of the Baroness, made a sound upon the carpet. 'I don't know,' she replied. 'She will want something more – more private.'

'If she wants to be private she can stay in her room,' Lizzie Acton remarked.

Gertrude paused in her walk, looking at her. 'That would not be pleasant,' she answered. 'She wants privacy and pleasure together.'

Robert Acton began to laugh again. 'My dear cousin, what a picture!'

Charlotte had fixed her serious eyes upon her sister; she wondered whence she had suddenly derived these strange notions. Mr Wentworth also observed his young daughter.

'I don't know what her manner of life may have been,' he said: 'but she certainly never can have enjoyed a more refined and salubrious home.'

Gertrude stood there looking at them all. 'She is the wife of a Prince,' she said.

'We are all princes here,' said Mr Wentworth; 'and I don't know of any palace in this neighbourhood that is to let.'

'Cousin William,' Robert Acton interposed, 'do you want to do something handsome? Make them a present, for three months, of the little house over the way.'

'You are very generous with other people's things!' cried his sister.

'Robert is very generous with his own things,' Mr Wentworth observed dispassionately, and looking in cold meditation at his kinsman.

'Gertrude,' Lizzie went on, 'I had an idea you were so fond of your new cousin.'

'Which new cousin?' asked Gertrude.

'I don't mean the Baroness!' the young girl rejoined, with her laugh. 'I thought you expected to see so much of him.'

'Of Felix? I hope to see a great deal of him,' said Gertrude simply.

'Then why do you want to keep him out of the house?'

Gertrude looked at Lizzie Acton, and then looked away.

'Should you want me to live in the house with you, Lizzie?' asked Clifford.

'I hope you never will. I hate you!' Such was this young lady's reply.

'Father,' said Gertrude, stopping before Mr Wentworth and smiling, with a smile the sweeter, as her smile always was, for its rarity, 'do let them live in the little house over the way. It will be lovely!'

Robert Acton had been watching her. 'Gertrude is right,' he said. 'Gertrude is the cleverest girl in the world. If I might take the liberty, I would strongly recommend their living there.'

'There is nothing there so pretty as the north-east room,' Charlotte urged.

'She will make it pretty. Leave her alone!' Acton exclaimed.

Gertrude, at his compliment, had blushed and looked at him; it was as if someone less familiar had complimented her. 'I am sure she will make it pretty. It will be very interesting. It will be a place to go to. It will be a foreign house.'

'Are we very sure that we need a foreign house?' Mr Wentworth inquired. 'Do you think it desirable to establish a foreign house – in this quiet place?'

'You speak,' said Acton, laughing, 'as if it were a question of the poor Baroness opening a wine-shop or a gaming-table.'

'It would be too lovely!' Gertrude declared again, laying her hand on the back of her father's chair.

'That she should open a gaming-table?' Charlotte asked, with great gravity.

Gertrude looked at her a moment, and then, 'Yes, Charlotte,' she said simply.

'Gertrude is growing pert,' Clifford Wentworth observed, with his humorous young growl. 'That comes of associating with foreigners.'

Mr Wentworth looked up at his daughter, who was standing beside him; he drew her gently forward. 'You must be careful,' he said. 'You must keep watch. Indeed, we must all be careful. This is a great change; we are to be exposed to peculiar influences. I don't say they are bad; I don't judge them in advance. But they may perhaps make it necessary that we should exercise a great deal of wisdom and self-control. It will be a different tone.'

Gertrude was silent a moment, in deference to her father's speech; then she spoke in a manner that was not in the least an answer to it. 'I want to see how they will live. I am sure they will have different hours. She will do all kinds of little things differently. When we go over there it will be like going to Europe. She will have a boudoir.[1] She will invite us to dinner – very late. She will breakfast in her room.'

Charlotte gazed at her sister again. Gertrude's imagination seemed to her to be fairly running riot. She had always known that Gertrude had a great deal of imagination – she had been very proud of it. But at the same time she had always felt that it was a dangerous and irresponsible faculty; and now, to her sense, for the moment, it seemed to threaten to make her sister a strange person who should come in suddenly, as from a journey, talking of the peculiar and possibly unpleasant things she had observed. Charlotte's imagination took no journeys whatever; she kept it, as it were, in her pocket, with the other furniture of this receptacle – a thimble, a little box of peppermint, and a morsel of court-plaster.[2] 'I don't believe she would have any dinner – or any breakfast,' said Miss Wentworth. 'I don't believe she knows how to do anything herself. I should have to get her ever so many servants, and she wouldn't like them.'

'She has a maid,' said Gertrude; 'a French maid. She mentioned her.'

'I wonder if the maid has a little fluted cap and red slippers,' said Lizzie Acton. 'There was a French maid in that play that Robert took me to see. She had pink stockings; she was very wicked.'

'She was a *soubrette*,'[3] Gertrude announced, who had never seen a play in her life. 'They call that a soubrette. It will be a great chance to learn French.' Charlotte gave a little soft, helpless groan. She had a vision of a wicked theatrical person, clad in pink stockings and red shoes, and speaking, with confounding volubility, an incomprehensible tongue, flitting through the sacred penetralia[4] of that large, clean house. 'That is one reason in favour of their coming here,' Gertrude went on. 'But we can make Eugenia speak French to us, and Felix. I mean to begin – the next time.'

Mr Wentworth had kept her standing near him, and he gave her his earnest, thin, unresponsive glance again. 'I want you to make me a promise, Gertrude,' he said.

'What is it?' she asked, smiling.

'Not to get excited. Not to allow these – these occurrences to be an occasion for excitement.'

She looked down at him a moment, and then she shook her head. 'I don't think I can promise that, father. I am excited already.'

Mr Wentworth was silent a while; they all were silent, as if in recognition of something audacious and portentous.

'I think they had better go to the other house,' said Charlotte quietly.

'I shall keep them in the other house,' Mr Wentworth subjoined more pregnantly.

Gertrude turned away; then she looked across at Robert Acton. Her cousin Robert was a great friend of hers; she often looked at him this way instead of saying things. Her glance on this occasion, however, struck him as a substitute for a larger volume of diffident utterance than usual; inviting him to observe, among other things, the inefficiency of her father's design – if design it was – for diminishing, in the interest of quiet nerves, their occasions of contact with their foreign relatives. But Acton immediately complimented Mr Wentworth upon his liberality. 'That's a very nice thing to do,' he said, 'giving them the little house. You will have treated them handsomely, and whatever happens, you will be glad of it.' Mr Wentworth was liberal, and he knew he was liberal. It gave him pleasure to know it, to feel it, to see it recorded; and this pleasure is the only palpable form of self-indulgence with which the narrator of these incidents will be able to charge him.

'A three days' visit at most, over there, is all I should have found possible,' Madame Münster remarked to her brother, after they had taken possession of the little white house. 'It would have been too *intime*[5] – decidedly too *intime*. Breakfast, dinner, and tea *en famille*[6] – it would have been the end of the world if I could have reached the third day.' And she made the same observation to her maid Augustine, an intelligent person, who enjoyed a liberal share of her confidence. Felix declared that he would willingly spend his life in the bosom of the Wentworth family; that they were the kindest, simplest, most amiable people in the world, and that he had taken a prodigious fancy to them all. The Baroness quite agreed with him that they were simple and kind; they were thoroughly nice people, and she liked them extremely. The girls were perfect ladies; it was impossible to be more of a lady than Charlotte Wentworth, in spite of her little village air. 'But as for thinking them the best company in the world,' said the Baroness, 'that is another thing; and as for wishing to live *porte à porte*[7] with them, I should as soon think of wishing myself back in the convent again, to wear a bombazine apron[8] and sleep in a dormitory.' And yet the Baroness was in high good-humour; she had been very much pleased. With her lively perception and her refined imagination, she was capable of enjoying anything that was characteristic, anything that was good of its kind – the Wentworth household seemed to her very perfect of its kind – wonderfully peaceful and unspotted; pervaded by a sort of dove-coloured freshness that had all the quietude and benevolence of what she deemed to be Quakerism,[9] and yet seemed to be founded upon a degree of material abundance for which, in certain matters of detail, one might have looked in vain at the frugal little court of Silberstadt-Schreckenstein. She perceived immediately that her American relatives thought and talked very little about money; and this of itself made an impression upon Eugenia's imagination. She perceived at the same time that if Charlotte or Gertrude should ask their father for a very considerable sum he would at once place it in their hands; and this made a still greater impression. The greatest impression of all, perhaps, was made by another rapid induction. The Baroness had an immediate conviction that Robert Acton would put his hand into his pocket every day in the week if that rattle-pated little sister of his should bid him. The men in this country, said the Baroness, are evidently very obliging. Her declaration that she was looking for rest and retirement had been by no means wholly untrue; nothing that the Baroness said was wholly untrue. It is but fair to add, perhaps, that nothing that she said was wholly true. She wrote to a friend in Germany that it was a return to nature; it was like drinking new milk, and she was very fond of new milk. She said to herself, of course, that it would be a little dull; but there can be no better proof of her good spirits than the fact that she thought she should not mind its being a little dull. It seemed to her, when from the piazza of her eleemosynary[10] cottage she looked out over the soundless fields, the stony pastures, the clear-faced ponds, the rugged little orchards, that she had never been in the midst of so peculiarly intense a stillness; it was almost a delicate sensual pleasure. It was all very good, very innocent and safe, and out of it something good must come. Augustine, indeed, who had an unbounded faith in her mistress's wisdom and far-sightedness, was a great deal perplexed and depressed. She was always ready to take her cue when she understood it; but she liked to understand it, and on this occasion comprehension failed. What, indeed, was the Baroness doing *dans cette galère*?[11] what fish did she expect to land out of these very stagnant waters? The game was evidently a deep one. Augustine could trust her, but the sense of walking in the dark betrayed itself in the physiognomy of this spare, sober, sallow, middle-aged person, who had nothing in common with Gertrude Wentworth's conception of a soubrette, by the most ironical scowl that had ever rested upon the unpretending tokens of the peace and plenty of the Wentworths. Fortunately, Augustine could quench scepticism in action. She quite agreed with her mistress – or rather she quite outstripped her mistress – in thinking that the little white house was pitifully bare. *'Il faudra,'* said Augustine, *'lui faire un peu de toilette.'*[12] And she began to hang up *portières*[13] in the doorways; to place wax candles,[14] procured after some research, in unexpected situations; to dispose anomalous draperies over the arms of sofas and the backs of chairs. The Baroness had brought with her to the New World a copious provision of the element of costume; and the two Miss Wentworths, when they came over to see her, were somewhat bewildered by the obtrusive distribution of her wardrobe. There were India shawls[15] suspended, curtain-wise, in the parlour door, and curious fabrics, corresponding to Gertrude's metaphysical vision of an opera-cloak, tumbled about in the sitting-places. There were pink silk blinds in the windows, by which the room was strangely bedimmed; and along the chimneypiece was disposed a remarkable band of velvet, covered with coarse, dirty-looking lace. 'I have been making myself a little comfortable,' said the Baroness, much to the confusion of Charlotte, who had been on the point of proposing to come and help her put her superfluous draperies away. But what Charlotte mistook for an almost culpably delayed subsidence Gertrude very presently perceived to be the most ingenious, the most interesting, the most romantic intention. 'What is life, indeed, without curtains?' she secretly asked herself; and she appeared to herself to have been leading hitherto an existence singularly garish and totally devoid of festoons.

Felix was not a young man who troubled himself greatly about anything – least of all about the conditions of enjoyment. His faculty of enjoyment was so large, so unconsciously eager, that it may be said of it that it had a permanent advance upon embarrassment and sorrow. His sentient nature was intrinsically joyous, and novelty and change were in themselves a delight to him. As they had come to him with a great deal of frequency, his life had been more agreeable than appeared. Never was a nature more perfectly fortunate. It was not a restless, apprehensive, ambitious spirit, running a race with the tyranny of fate, but a temper so unsuspicious as to put Adversity off her guard, dodging and evading her with the easy, natural motion of a wind-shifted flower. Felix extracted entertainment from all things, and all his faculties – his imagination, his intelligence, his affections, his senses – had a hand in the game. It seemed to him that Eugenia and he had been very well treated; there was something absolutely touching in that combination of paternal liberality and social considerateness which marked Mr Wentworth's deportment. It was most uncommonly kind of him, for instance, to have given them a house. Felix was positively amused at having a house of his own; for the little white cottage among the apple trees – the chalet, as Madame Münster always called it – was much more sensibly his own than any domiciliary *quatrième*,[16] looking upon a court, with the rent overdue. Felix had spent a good deal of his life in looking into courts, with a perhaps slightly-tattered pair of elbows resting upon the ledge of a high-perched window, and the thin smoke of a cigarette rising into an atmosphere in which street cries died away and the vibration of chimes from ancient belfries became sensible. He had never known anything so infinitely rural as these New England fields; and he took a great fancy to all their pastoral roughness. He had never had a greater sense of luxurious security; and at the risk of making him seem a rather sordid adventurer I must declare that he found an irresistible charm in the fact that he might dine every day at his uncle's. The charm was irresistible, however, because his fancy flung a rosy light over this homely privilege. He appreciated highly the fare that was set before him. There was a kind of fresh-looking abundance about it which made him think that people must have lived so in the mythological era, when they spread their tables upon the grass, replenished them from cornucopias,[17] and had no particular need of kitchen stoves. But the great thing that Felix enjoyed was having found a family – sitting in the midst of gentle, generous people whom he might call by their first names. He had never known anything more charming than the attention they paid to what he said. It was like a large sheet of clean, fine-grained drawing-paper, all ready to be washed over with effective splashes of watercolour. He had never had any cousins, and he had never before found himself in contact so unrestricted with young unmarried ladies.[18] He was extremely fond of the society of ladies, and it was new to him that it might be enjoyed in just this manner. At first he hardly knew what to make of his state of mind. It seemed to him that he was in love, indiscriminately, with three girls at once. He saw that Lizzie Acton was more brilliantly pretty than Charlotte and Gertrude; but this was scarcely a superiority. His pleasure came from something they had in common – a part of which was, indeed, that physical delicacy which seemed to make it proper that they should always dress in thin materials and clear colours. But they were delicate in other ways, and it was most agreeable to him to feel that these latter delicacies were appreciable by contact, as it were. He had known, fortunately, many virtuous gentlewomen, but it now appeared to him that in his relations with them (especially when they were unmarried) he had been looking at pictures under glass. He perceived at present what a nuisance the glass had been – how it perverted and interfered, how it caught the reflexion of other objects and kept you walking from side to side. He had no need to ask himself whether Charlotte and Gertrude, and Lizzie Acton, were in the right light; they were always in the right light. He liked everything about them; he was, for instance, not at all above liking the fact that they had very slender feet and high insteps. He liked their pretty noses; he liked their surprised eyes and their hesitating, not at all positive, way of speaking; he liked so much knowing that he was perfectly at liberty to be alone for hours, anywhere, with either of them, that preference for one to the other, as a companion of solitude, remained a minor affair. Charlotte Wentworth's sweetly severe features were as agreeable as Lizzie Acton's wonderfully expressive blue eyes; and Gertrude's air of being always ready to walk about and listen was as charming as anything else, especially as she walked very gracefully. After a while Felix began to distinguish; but even then he would often wish, suddenly, that they were not all so sad. Even Lizzie Acton, in spite of her fine little chatter and laughter, appeared sad. Even Clifford Wentworth, who had extreme youth in his favour and kept a buggy[19] with enormous wheels and a little sorrel mare with the prettiest legs in the world – even this fortunate lad was apt to have an averted, uncomfortable glance, and to edge away from you at times, in the manner of a person with a bad conscience. The only person in the circle with no sense of oppression of any kind was, to Felix's perception, Robert Acton.

It might perhaps have been feared that after the completion of those graceful domiciliary embellishments which have been mentioned Madame Münster would have found herself confronted with alarming possibilities of *ennui*.[20] But as yet she had not taken the alarm. The Baroness was a restless soul, and she projected her restlessness, as it may be said, into any situation that lay before her. Up to a certain point her restlessness might be counted upon to entertain her. She was always expecting something to happen, and, until it was disappointed, expectancy itself was a delicate pleasure. What the Baroness expected just now it would take some ingenuity to set forth; it is enough that while she looked about her she found something to occupy her imagination. She assured herself that she was enchanted with her new relatives; she professed to herself that, like her brother, she felt it a sacred satisfaction to have found a family. It is certain that she enjoyed to the utmost the gentleness of her kinsfolk's deference. She had, first and last, received a great deal of admiration, and her experience of well-turned compliments was very considerable; but she knew that she had never been so real a power, never counted for so much, as now when, for the first time, the standard of comparison of her little circle was a prey to vagueness. The sense, indeed, that the good people about her had, as regards her remarkable self, no standard of comparison at all, gave her a feeling of almost illimitable power. It was true, as she said to herself, that if for this reason they would be able to discover nothing against her, so they would perhaps neglect to perceive some of her superior points; but she always wound up her reflexions by declaring that she would take care of that.

Charlotte and Gertrude were in some perplexity between their desire to show all proper attention to Madame Münster and their fear of being importunate. The little house in the orchard had hitherto been occupied during the summer months by intimate friends of the family, or by poor relations who found in Mr Wentworth a landlord attentive to repairs and oblivious of quarter-day. Under these circumstances the open door of the small house and that of the large one, facing each other across their homely gardens, levied no tax upon hourly visits. But the Misses Wentworth received an impression that Eugenia was no friend to the primitive custom of 'dropping-in'; she evidently had no idea of living without a door-keeper. 'One goes into your house as into an inn – except that there are no servants rushing forward,' she said to Charlotte. And she added that that was very charming. Gertrude explained to her sister that she meant just the reverse; she didn't like it at all. Charlotte inquired why she should tell an untruth, and Gertrude answered that there was probably some very good reason for it which they should discover when they knew her better. 'There can surely be no good reason for telling an untruth,' said Charlotte. 'I hope she does not think so.'

They had, of course, desired, from the first, to do everything in the way of helping her to arrange herself. It had seemed to Charlotte that there would be a great many things to talk about; but the Baroness was apparently inclined to talk about nothing.

'Write her a note, asking her leave to come and see her. I think that is what she will like,' said Gertrude.

'Why should I give her the trouble of answering me?' Charlotte asked. 'She will have to write a note and send it over.'

'I don't think she will take any trouble,' said Gertrude profoundly.

'What, then, will she do?'

'That is what I am curious to see,' said Gertrude, leaving her sister with an impression that her curiosity was morbid.

They went to see the Baroness without preliminary correspondence; and in the little salon which she had already created, with its becoming light and its festoons, they found Robert Acton.

Eugenia was intensely gracious, but she accused them of neglecting her cruelly. 'You see Mr Acton has had to take pity upon me,' she said. 'My brother goes off sketching, for hours; I can never depend upon him. So I was to send Mr Acton to beg you to come and give me the benefit of your wisdom.'

Gertrude looked at her sister. She wanted to say, '*That* is what she would have done.' Charlotte said that they hoped the Baroness would always come and dine with them; it would give them so much pleasure; and, in that case, she would spare herself the trouble of having a cook.

'Ah, but I must have a cook!' cried the Baroness. 'An old negress in a yellow turban. I have set my heart upon that. I want to look out of my window and see her sitting there on the grass, against the background of those crooked, dusky little apple trees, pulling the husks off a lapful of Indian corn. That will be local colour,[21] you know. There isn't much of it here – you don't mind my saying that, do you? – so one must make the most of what one can get. I shall be most happy to dine with you whenever you will let me; but I want to be able to ask you sometimes. And I want to be able to ask Mr Acton,' added the Baroness.

'You must come and ask me at home,' said Acton. 'You must come and see me; you must dine with me first. I want to show you my place; I want to introduce you to my mother.' He called again upon Madame Münster, two days later. He was constantly at the other house; he used to walk across the fields from his own place, and he appeared to have fewer scruples than his cousins with regard to dropping in. On this occasion he found that Mr Brand had come to pay his respects to the charming stranger; but after Acton's arrival the young theologian said nothing. He sat in his chair with his two hands clasped, fixing upon his hostess a grave, fascinated stare. The Baroness talked to Robert Acton, but, as she talked, she turned and smiled at Mr Brand, who never took his eyes off her. The two men walked away together; they were going to Mr Wentworth's. Mr Brand still said nothing; but after they had passed into Mr Wentworth's garden he stopped and looked back for some time at the little white house. Then, looking at his companion, with his head bent a little to one side and his eyes somewhat contracted, 'Now, I suppose that's what is called conversation,' he said; 'real conversation.'

'It's what I call a very clever woman,' said Acton, laughing.

'It is most interesting,' Mr Brand continued. 'I only wish she would speak French; it would seem more in keeping. It must be quite the style that we have heard about, that we have read about – the style of conversation of Madame de Staël,[22] of Madame Récamier.'[23]

Acton also looked at Madame Münster's residence among its hollyhocks and apple trees. 'What I should like to know,' he said, smiling, 'is just what has brought Madame Récamier to live in that place!'

CHAPTER 5

MR WENTWORTH, with his cane and his gloves in his hand, went every afternoon to call upon his niece. A couple of hours later she came over to the great house to tea. She had let the proposal that she should regularly dine there fall to the ground; she was in the enjoyment of whatever satisfaction was to be derived from the spectacle of an old negress in a crimson turban shelling peas under the apple trees. Charlotte, who had provided the ancient negress, thought it must be a strange household, Eugenia having told her that Augustine managed everything, the ancient negress included – Augustine, who was naturally devoid of all acquaintance with the expurgatory English tongue. By far the most immoral sentiment which I shall have occasion to attribute to Charlotte Wentworth was a certain emotion of disappointment at finding that in spite of these irregular conditions the domestic arrangements at the small house were apparently not – from Eugenia's peculiar point of view – strikingly offensive. The Baroness found it amusing to go to tea;[1] she dressed as if for dinner. The tea-table offered an anomalous and picturesque repast; and on leaving it they all sat and talked in the large piazza, or wandered about the garden in the starlight, with their ears full of those sounds of strange insects which, though they are supposed to be, all over the world, a part of the magic of summer nights, seemed to the Baroness to have, beneath these western skies, an incomparable resonance.

Mr Wentworth, though, as I say, he went punctiliously to call upon her, was not able to feel that he was getting used to his niece. It taxed his imagination to believe that she was really his half-sister's child. His sister was a figure of his early years; she had been only twenty when she went abroad, never to return, making in foreign parts a wilful and undesirable marriage. His aunt, Mrs Whiteside, who had taken her to Europe for the benefit of the tour, gave, on her return, so lamentable an account of Mr Adolphus Young, to whom the headstrong girl had united her destiny, that it operated as a chill upon family feeling – especially in the case of the half-brothers. Catherine had done nothing subsequently to propitiate her family; she had not even written to them in a way that indicated a lucid appreciation of their suspended sympathy; so that it had become a tradition in Boston circles that the highest charity, as regards this young lady, was to think it well to forget her, and to abstain from conjecture as to the extent to which her aberrations were reproduced in her descendants. Over these young people – a vague report of their existence had come to his ears – Mr Wentworth had not, in the course of years, allowed his imagination to hover. It had plenty of occupation nearer home, and, though he had many cares upon his conscience, the idea that he had been an unnatural uncle was very properly never among the number. Now that his nephew and niece had come before him, he perceived that they were the fruit of influences and circumstances very different from those under which his own familiar progeny had reached a vaguely-qualified maturity. He felt no provocation to say that these influences had been exerted for evil; but he was sometimes afraid that he should not be able to like his distinguished, delicate, lady-like niece. He was paralysed and bewildered by her foreignness. She spoke, somehow, a different language. There was something strange in her words. He had a feeling that another man, in his place, would accommodate himself to her tone; would ask her questions and joke with her, reply to those pleasantries of her own which sometimes seemed startling as addressed to an uncle. But Mr Wentworth could not do these things. He could not even bring himself to attempt to measure her position in the world. She was the wife of a foreign nobleman who desired to repudiate her. This had a singular sound, but the old man felt himself destitute of the materials for a judgement. It seemed to him that he ought to find them in his own experience, as a man of the world and an almost public character; but they were not there, and he was ashamed to confess to himself – much more to reveal to Eugenia by interrogations possibly too innocent – the unfurnished condition of this repository.

It appeared to him that he could get much nearer, as he would have said, to his nephew; though he was not sure that Felix was altogether safe. He was so bright and handsome and talkative that it was impossible not to think well of him; and yet it seemed as if there were something almost impudent, almost vicious – or as if there ought to be – in a young man being at once so joyous and so positive. It was to be observed that while Felix was not at all a serious young man there was somehow more of him – he had more weight and volume and resonance – than a number of young men who were distinctly serious. While Mr Wentworth meditated upon this anomaly his nephew was admiring him unrestrictedly. He thought him a most delicate, generous, high-toned old gentleman, with a very handsome head, of the ascetic type, which he promised himself the profit of sketching. Felix was far from having made a secret of the fact that he wielded the paintbrush, and it was not his own fault if it failed to be generally understood that he was prepared to execute the most striking likenesses on the most reasonable terms. 'He is an artist – my cousin is an artist,' said Gertrude; and she offered this information to everyone who would receive it. She offered it to herself, as it were, by way of admonition and reminder; she repeated to herself at odd moments, in lonely places, that Felix was invested with this sacred character. Gertrude had never seen an artist before; she had only read about such people. They seemed to her a romantic and mysterious class, whose life was made up of those agreeable accidents that never happened to other persons. And it merely quickened her meditations on this point that Felix should declare, as he repeatedly did, that he was really not an artist. 'I have never gone into the thing seriously,' he said. 'I have never studied; I have had no training. I do a little of everything, and nothing well. I am only an amateur.'

It pleased Gertrude even more to think that he was an amateur than to think that he was an artist; the former word, to her fancy, had an even subtler connotation. She knew, however, that it was a word to use more soberly. Mr Wentworth used it freely; for though he had not been exactly familiar with it, he found it convenient as a help toward classifying Felix, who, as a young man extremely clever and active and apparently respectable and yet not engaged in any recognised business, was an importunate anomaly. Of course the Baroness and her brother – she was always spoken of first – were a welcome topic of conversation between Mr Wentworth and his daughters and their occasional visitors.

'And the young man, your nephew, what is his profession?' asked an old gentleman – Mr Broderip, of Salem – who had been Mr Wentworth's class-mate at Harvard College in the year 1809, and who came into his office in Devonshire Street. (Mr Wentworth, in his later years, used to go but three times a week to his office, where he had a large amount of highly confidential trust-business to transact.)

'Well, he's an amateur,' said Felix's uncle, with folded hands, and with a certain satisfaction in being able to say it. And Mr Broderip had gone back to Salem with a feeling that this was probably a 'European' expression for a broker or a grain-exporter.

'I should like to do your head, sir,' said Felix to his uncle one evening, before them all – Mr Brand and Robert Acton being also present. 'I think I should make a very fine thing of it. It's an interesting head; it's very mediaeval.'

Mr Wentworth looked grave; he felt awkwardly, as if all the company had come in and found him standing before the looking-glass. 'The Lord made it,' he said. 'I don't think it is for man to make it over again.'

'Certainly the Lord made it,' replied Felix, laughing, 'and He made it very well. But life has been touching up the work. It is a very interesting type of head. It's delightfully wasted and emaciated. The complexion is wonderfully bleached.' And Felix looked round at the circle, as if to call their attention to these interesting points. Mr Wentworth grew visibly paler. 'I should like to do you as an old prelate, an old cardinal, or the prior of an order.'

'A prelate, a cardinal?' murmured Mr Wentworth. 'Do you refer to the Roman Catholic priesthood?'

'I mean an old ecclesiastic who should have led a very pure, abstinent life. Now I take it that has been the case with you, sir; one sees it in your face,' Felix proceeded. 'You have been very – a – very moderate. Don't you think one always sees that in a man's face?'

'You see more in a man's face than I should think of looking for,' said Mr Wentworth coldly.

The Baroness rattled her fan and gave her brilliant laugh. 'It is a risk to look so close!' she exclaimed. 'My uncle has some peccadilloes on his conscience.' Mr Wentworth looked at her, painfully at a loss; and in so far as the signs of a pure and abstinent life were visible in his face they were then probably peculiarly manifest. 'You are a *beau vieillard*,[2] dear uncle,' said Madame Münster, smiling with her foreign eyes.

'I think you are paying me a compliment,' said the old man.

'Surely, I am not the first woman that ever did so!' cried the Baroness.

'I think you are,' said Mr Wentworth gravely. And turning to Felix he added, in the same tone, 'Please don't take my likeness. My children have my daguerreotype.[3] That is quite satisfactory.'

'I won't promise,' said Felix, 'not to work your head into something!'

Mr Wentworth looked at him and then at all the others; and then he got up and slowly walked away.

'Felix,' said Gertrude, in the silence that followed, 'I wish you would paint my portrait.'

Charlotte wondered whether Gertrude was right in wishing this; and she looked at Mr Brand as the most legitimate way of ascertaining. Whatever Gertrude did or said, Charlotte always looked at Mr Brand. It was a standing pretext for looking at Mr Brand – always, as Charlotte thought, in the interest of Gertrude's welfare. It is true that she felt a tremulous interest in Gertrude being right; for Charlotte, in her small, still way, was an heroic sister.

'We should be glad to have your portrait, Miss Gertrude,' said Mr Brand.

'I should be delighted to paint so charming a model,' Felix declared.

'Do you think you are so lovely, my dear?' asked Lizzie Acton, with her little inoffensive pertness, biting off a knot in her knitting.

'It is not because I think I am beautiful,' said Gertrude, looking all round. 'I don't think I am beautiful at all.' She spoke with a sort of conscious deliberateness; and it seemed very strange to Charlotte to hear her discussing this question so publicly. 'It is because I think it would be amusing to sit and be painted. I have always thought that.'

'I am sorry you have not had better things to think about, my daughter,' said Mr Wentworth.

'You are very beautiful, cousin Gertrude,' Felix declared.

'That's a compliment,' said Gertrude. 'I put all the compliments I receive into a little money-jug that has a slit in the side. I shake them up and down, and they rattle. There are not many yet – only two or three.'

'No, it's not a compliment,' Felix rejoined. 'See; I am careful not to give it the form of a compliment. I did not think you were beautiful at first. But you have come to seem so little by little.'

'Take care, now, your jug doesn't burst!' exclaimed Lizzie.

'I think sitting for one's portrait is only one of the various forms of idleness,' said Mr Wentworth. 'Their name is legion.'

'My dear sir,' cried Felix, 'you can't be said to idle when you are making a man work so!'

'One might be painted while one is asleep,' suggested Mr Brand, as a contribution to the discussion.

'Ah, do paint me while I am asleep,'[4] said Gertrude to Felix, smiling. And she closed her eyes a little. It had by this time become a matter of almost exciting anxiety to Charlotte what Gertrude would say or would do next.

She began to sit for her portrait on the following day – in the open air, on the north side of the piazza. 'I wish you would tell me what you think of us – how we seem to you,' she said to Felix, as he sat before his easel.

'You seem to me the best people in the world,' said Felix.

'You say that,' Gertrude resumed, 'because it saves you the trouble of saying anything else.'

The young man glanced at her over the top of his canvas. 'What else should I say? It would certainly be a great deal of trouble to say anything different.'

'Well,' said Gertrude, 'you have seen people before that you have liked, have you not?'

'Indeed I have, thank Heaven!'

'And they have been very different from us,' Gertrude went on.

'That only proves,' said Felix, 'that there are a thousand different ways of being good company.'

'Do you think us good company?' asked Gertrude.

'Company for a king!'

Gertrude was silent a moment; and then, 'There must be a thousand different ways of being dreary,' she said; 'and sometimes I think we make use of them all.'

Felix stood up quickly, holding up his hand. 'If you could only keep that look on your face for half an hour – while I catch it!' he said. 'It is uncommonly handsome.'

'To look handsome for half an hour – that is a great deal to ask of me,' she answered.

'It would be the portrait of a young woman who has taken some vow, some pledge, that she repents of,' said Felix, 'and who is thinking it over at leisure.'

'I have taken no vow, no pledge,' said Gertrude very gravely. 'I have nothing to repent of.'

'My dear cousin, that was only a figure of speech. I am very sure that no one in your excellent family has anything to repent of.'

'And yet we are always repenting!' Gertrude exclaimed. 'That is what I mean by our being dreary. You know it perfectly well; you only pretend that you don't.'

Felix gave a quick laugh. 'The half-hour is going on, and yet you are handsomer than ever. One must be careful what one says, you see.'

'To me,' said Gertrude, 'you can say anything.'

Felix looked at her, as an artist might, and painted for some time in silence. 'Yes, you seem to me different from your father and sister – from most of the people you have lived with,' he observed.

'To say that one's self,' Gertrude went on, 'is like saying – by implication, at least – that one is better. I am not better; I am much worse. But they say themselves that I am different. It makes them unhappy.'

'Since you accuse me of concealing my real impressions, I may admit that I think the tendency – among you generally – is to be made unhappy too easily.'

'I wish you would tell that to my father,' said Gertrude.

'It might make him more unhappy!' Felix exclaimed, laughing.

'It certainly would. I don't believe you have seen people like that.'

'Ah, my dear cousin, how do you know what I have seen?' Felix demanded. 'How can I tell you?'

'You might tell me a great many things, if you only would. You have seen people like yourself – people who are bright and gay and fond of amusement. We are not fond of amusement.'

'Yes,' said Felix, 'I confess that rather strikes me. You don't seem to me to get all the pleasure out of life that you might. You don't seem to me to enjoy ... Do you mind my saying this?' he asked, pausing.

'Please go on,' said the girl earnestly.

'You seem to me very well placed, for enjoying. You have money and liberty and what is called in Europe a "position". But you take a painful view of life, as one may say.'

'One ought to think it bright and charming and delightful, eh?' asked Gertrude.

'I should say so – if one can. It is true it all depends upon that,' Felix added.

'You know there is a great deal of misery in the world,' said his model.

'I have seen a little of it,' the young man rejoined. 'But it was all over there – beyond the sea. I don't see any here. This is a paradise.'

Gertrude said nothing; she sat looking at the dahlias and the currant-bushes in the garden, while Felix went on with his work. 'To "enjoy",' she began at last, 'to take life – not painfully, must one do something wrong?'

Felix gave his long light laugh again. 'Seriously, I think not. And for this reason, among others: you strike me as very capable of enjoying, if the chance were given you, and yet at the same time as incapable of wrong-doing.'

'I am sure,' said Gertrude, 'that you are very wrong in telling a person that she is incapable of that. We are never nearer to evil than when we believe that.'

'You are handsomer than ever,' observed Felix irrelevantly.

Gertrude had got used to hearing him say this. There was not so much excitement in it as at first. 'What ought one to do?' she continued. 'To give parties, to go to the theatre, to read novels, to keep late hours?'

'I don't think it's what one does or one doesn't do that promotes enjoyment,' her companion answered. 'It is the general way of looking at life.'

'They look at it as a discipline – that is what they do here. I have often been told that.'

'Well, that's very good. But there is another way,' added Felix, smiling: 'to look at it as an opportunity.'

'An opportunity – yes,' said Gertrude. 'One would get more pleasure that way.'

'I don't attempt to say anything better for it than that it has been my own way – and that is not saying much!' Felix had laid down his palette and brushes; he was leaning back, with his arms folded, to judge the effect of his work. 'And you know,' he said, 'I am a very petty personage.'

'You have a great deal of talent,' said Gertrude.

'No – no,' the young man rejoined, in a tone of cheerful impartiality, 'I have not a great deal of talent. It is nothing at all remarkable. I assure you I should know if it were. I shall always be obscure. The world will never hear of me.' Gertrude looked at him with a strange feeling. She was thinking of the great world which he knew and which she did not, and how full of brilliant talents it must be, since it could afford to make light of his abilities. 'You needn't in general attach much importance to anything I tell you,' he pursued; 'but you may believe me when I say this – that I am little better than a good-natured feather-head.'

'A feather-head?' she repeated.

'I am a species of Bohemian.'

'A Bohemian?' Gertrude had never heard this term before, save as a geographical denomination; and she quite failed to understand the figurative meaning which her companion appeared to attach to it. But it gave her pleasure.

Felix had pushed back his chair and risen to his feet; he slowly came toward her, smiling. 'I am a sort of adventurer,' he said, looking down at her.

She got up, meeting his smile. 'An adventurer?' she repeated. 'I should like to hear your adventures.'

For an instant she believed that he was going to take her hand; but he dropped his own hands suddenly into the pockets of his painting jacket. 'There is no reason why you shouldn't,' he said. 'I have been an adventurer, but my adventures have been very innocent. They have all been happy ones; I don't think there are any I shouldn't tell. They were very pleasant and very pretty; I should like to go over them in memory. Sit down again, and I will begin,' he added in a moment, with his naturally persuasive smile.

Gertrude sat down again on that day, and she sat down on several other days. Felix, while he plied his brush, told her a great many stories, and she listened with charmed avidity. Her eyes rested upon his lips; she was very serious; sometimes, from her air of wondering gravity, he thought she was displeased. But Felix never believed for more than a single moment in any displeasure of his own producing. This would have been fatuity if the optimism it expressed had not been much more a hope than a prejudice. It is beside the matter to say that he had a good conscience; for the best conscience is a sort of self-reproach, and this young man's brilliantly healthy nature spent itself in objective good intentions which were ignorant of any test save exactness in hitting their mark. He told Gertrude how he had walked over France and Italy with a painter's knapsack on his back, paying his way often by knocking off a flattering portrait of his host or hostess. He told her how he had played the violin in a little band of musicians – not of high celebrity – who travelled through foreign lands giving provincial concerts. He told her also how he had been a momentary ornament of a troupe of strolling actors, engaged in the arduous task of interpreting Shakespeare to French and German, Polish and Hungarian audiences.

While this periodical recital was going on Gertrude lived in a fantastic world; she seemed to herself to be reading a romance that came out in daily numbers. She had known nothing so delightful since the perusal of *Nicholas Nickleby*.[5] One afternoon she went to see her cousin, Mrs Acton, Robert's mother, who was a great invalid, never leaving the house. She came back alone, on foot, across the fields – this being a short way which they often used. Felix had gone to Boston with her father, who desired to take the young man to call upon some of his friends, old gentlemen who remembered his mother – remembered her, but said nothing about her – and several of whom, with the gentle ladies their wives, had driven out from town to pay their respects at the little house among the apple trees, in vehicles which reminded the Baroness, who received her visitors with discriminating civility, of the large, light, rattling barouche in which she herself had made her journey to this neighbourhood. The afternoon was waning; in the western sky the great picture of a New England sunset, painted in crimson and silver, was suspended from the zenith; and the stony pastures, as Gertrude traversed them, thinking intently to herself, were covered with a light, clear glow. At the open gate of one of the fields she saw from the distance a man's figure; he stood there as if he were waiting for her, and as she came nearer she recognised Mr Brand. She had a feeling as of not having seen him for some time; she could not have said for how long, for it yet seemed to her that he had been very lately at the house.

'May I walk back with you?' he asked. And when she had said that he might if he wanted, he observed that he had seen her and recognised her half a mile away.

'You must have very good eyes,' said Gertrude.

'Yes, I have very good eyes, Miss Gertrude,' said Mr Brand. She perceived that he meant something; but for a long time past Mr Brand had constantly meant something, and she had almost got used to it. She felt, however, that what he meant had now a renewed power to disturb her, to perplex and agitate her. He walked beside her in silence for a moment, and then he added, 'I have had no trouble in seeing that you are beginning to avoid me. But perhaps,' he went on, 'one needn't have had very good eyes to see that.'

'I have not avoided you,' said Gertrude, without looking at him.

'I think you have been unconscious that you were avoiding me,' Mr Brand replied. 'You have not even known that I was there.'

'Well, you are here now, Mr Brand!' said Gertrude, with a short laugh. 'I know that very well.'

He made no rejoinder. He simply walked beside her, slowly, as they were obliged to walk over the soft grass. Presently they came to another gate, which was closed. Mr Brand laid his hand upon it, but he made no movement to open it; he stood and looked at his companion. 'You are very much interested – very much absorbed,' he said.

Gertrude glanced at him; she saw that he was pale, and that he looked excited. She had never seen Mr Brand excited before, and she felt that the spectacle, if fully carried out, would be impressive, almost painful. 'Absorbed in what?' she asked. Then she looked away, at the illuminated sky. She felt guilty and uncomfortable, and yet she was vexed with herself for feeling so. But Mr Brand, as he stood there looking at her with his small, kind, persistent eyes, represented an immense body of half-obliterated obligations that were rising again into a certain distinctness.

'You have new interests, new occupations,' he went on. 'I don't know that I can say that you have new duties. We have always old ones, Gertrude,' he added.

'Please open the gate, Mr Brand,' she said; and she felt as if, in saying so, she were cowardly and petulant. But he opened the gate, and allowed her to pass; then he closed it behind himself. Before she had time to turn away he put out his hand and held her an instant by the wrist.

'I want to say something to you,' he answered. And she was on the point of adding, 'And I know just how you will say it'; but these words she kept back.

'I love you, Gertrude,' he said. 'I love you very much; I love you more than ever.'

He had said the words just as she had known he would; she had heard them before. They had no charm for her; she had said to herself before that it was very strange. It was supposed to be delightful for a woman to listen to such words; but these seemed to her flat and mechanical. 'I wish you would forget that,' she declared.

'How can I – why should I?' he asked.

'I have made you no promise – given you no pledge,' she said, looking at him, with her voice trembling a little.

'You have let me feel that I have an influence over you. You have opened your mind to me.'

'I never opened my mind to you, Mr Brand!' Gertrude cried with some vehemence.

'Then you were not so frank as I thought – as we all thought.'

'I don't see what anyone else had to do with it!' cried the girl.

'I mean your father and your sister. You know it makes them happy to think you will listen to me.'

She gave a little laugh. 'It doesn't make them happy,' she said. 'Nothing makes them happy. No one is happy here.'

'I think your cousin is very happy – Mr Young,' rejoined Mr Brand, in a soft, almost timid tone.

'So much the better for him!' And Gertrude gave her little laugh again.

The young man looked at her a moment. 'You are very much changed,' he said.

'I am glad to hear it,' Gertrude declared.

'I am not. I have known you a long time, and I have loved you as you were.'

'I am much obliged to you,' said Gertrude. 'I must be going home.'

He, on his side, gave a little laugh. 'You certainly do avoid me – you see!'

'Avoid me, then,' said the girl.

He looked at her again; and then, very gently, 'No, I will not avoid you,' he replied; 'but I will leave you, for the present, to yourself. I think you will remember – after a while – some of the things you have forgotten. I think you will come back to me; I have great faith in that.'

This time his voice was very touching; there was a strong reproachful force in what he said, and Gertrude could answer nothing. He turned away and stood there, leaning his elbows on the gate and looking at the beautiful sunset. Gertrude left him and took her way home again; but when she reached the middle of the next field she suddenly burst into tears. Her tears seemed to her to have been a long time gathering, and for some moments it was a kind of glee to shed them. But they presently passed away. There was something a little hard in Gertrude; and she never wept again.

CHAPTER 6

GOING of an afternoon to call upon his niece, Mr Wentworth more than once found Robert Acton sitting in her little drawing-room. This was in no degree, to Mr Wentworth, a perturbing fact, for he had no sense of competing with his young kinsman for Eugenia's good graces. Madame Münster's uncle had the highest opinion of Robert Acton, who, indeed, in the family at large, was the object of a great deal of undemonstrative appreciation. They were all proud of him, in so far as the charge of being proud may be brought against people who were, habitually, distinctly guiltless of the misdemeanour known as 'taking credit'. They never boasted of Robert Acton, nor indulged in vainglorious reference to him; they never quoted the clever things he had said, nor mentioned the generous things he had done. But a sort of frigidly-tender faith in his unlimited goodness was a part of their personal sense of right; and there can, perhaps, be no better proof of the high esteem in which he was held than the fact that no explicit judgement was ever passed upon his actions. He was no more praised than he was blamed; but he was tacitly felt to be an ornament to his circle. He was the man of the world of the family. He had been to China and brought home a collection of curiosities; he had made a fortune – or rather he had quintupled a fortune already considerable; he was distinguished by that combination of celibacy, 'property', and good-humour which appeals to even the most subdued imaginations; and it was taken for granted that he would presently place these advantages at the disposal of some well-regulated young woman of his own 'set'. Mr Wentworth was not a man to admit to himself that – his paternal duties apart – he liked any individual much better than all other individuals; but he thought Robert Acton extremely judicious; and this was perhaps as near an approach as he was

98

capable of to the eagerness of preference, which his temperament repudiated as it would have disengaged itself from something slightly unchaste. Acton was, in fact, very judicious – and something more beside; and indeed it must be claimed for Mr Wentworth that in the more illicit parts of his preference there hovered the vague adumbration of a belief that his cousin's final merit was a certain enviable capacity for whistling, rather gallantly, at the sanctions of mere judgement – for showing a larger courage, a finer quality of pluck, than common occasion demanded. Mr Wentworth would never have risked the intimation that Acton was made, in the smallest degree, of the stuff of a hero; but this is small blame to him, for Robert would certainly never have risked it himself. Acton certainly exercised great discretion in all things – beginning with his estimate of himself. He knew that he was by no means so much of a man of the world as he was supposed to be in local circles; but it must be added that he knew also that his natural shrewdness had a reach of which he had never quite given local circles the measure. He was addicted to taking the humorous view of things, and he had discovered that even in the narrowest circles such a disposition may find frequent opportunities. Such opportunities had formed for some time – that is, since his return from China, a year and a half before – the most active element in this gentleman's life, which had just now a rather indolent air. He was perfectly willing to get married. He was very fond of books, and he had a handsome library; that is, his books were much more numerous than Mr Wentworth's. He was also very fond of pictures; but it must be confessed, in the fierce light of contemporary criticism, that his walls were adorned with several rather abortive masterpieces. He had got his learning – and there was more of it than commonly appeared – at Harvard College; and he took a pleasure in old associations which made it a part of his daily contentment to live so near this institution that he often passed it in driving to Boston. He was extremely interested in the Baroness Münster.

She was very frank with him; or at least she intended to be. 'I am sure you find it very strange that I should have settled down in this out-of-the-way part of the world!' she said to him three or four weeks after she had installed herself. 'I am certain you are wondering about my motives. They are very pure.' The Baroness by this time was an old inhabitant; the best society in Boston had called upon her, and Clifford Wentworth had taken her several times to drive in his buggy.

Robert Acton was seated near her, playing with a fan; there were always several fans lying about her drawing-room, with long ribbons of different colours attached to them, and Acton was always playing with one. 'No, I don't find it at all strange,' he said slowly, smiling. 'That a clever woman should turn up in Boston, or its suburbs – that doesn't require so much explanation. Boston is a very nice place.'

'If you wish to make me contradict you,' said the Baroness, '*vous vous y prenez mal*.[1] In certain moods there is nothing I am not capable of agreeing to. Boston is a paradise, and we are in the suburbs of Paradise.'

'Just now I am not at all in the suburbs; I am in the place itself,' rejoined Acton, who was lounging a little in his chair. He was, however, not always lounging; and when he was he was not quite so relaxed as he pretended. To a certain extent, he sought refuge from shyness in this appearance of relaxation; and, like many persons in the same circumstances, he somewhat exaggerated the appearance. Beyond this, the air of being much at his ease was a cover for vigilant observation. He was more than interested in this clever woman, who, whatever he might say, was clever not at all after the Boston fashion; she plunged him into a kind of excitement, held him in vague suspense. He was obliged to admit to himself that he had never yet seen a woman just like this – not even in China. He was ashamed, for inscrutable reasons, of the vivacity of his emotion, and he carried it off, superficially, by taking, still superficially, the humorous view of Madame Münster. It was not at all true that he thought it very natural of her to have made this pious pilgrimage. It might have been said of him in advance that he was too good a Bostonian to regard in the light of an eccentricity the desire of even the remotest alien to visit the New England metropolis. This was an impulse for which, surely, no apology was needed; and Madame Münster was the fortunate possessor of several New England cousins. In fact, however, Madame Münster struck him as out of keeping with her little circle; she was at the best a very agreeable, a gracefully mystifying, anomaly. He knew very well that it would not do to address these reflexions too crudely to Mr Wentworth; he would never have remarked to the old gentleman that he wondered what the Baroness was up to. And indeed he had no great desire to share his vague mistrust with anyone. There was a personal pleasure in it; the greatest pleasure he had known at least since he had come from China. He would keep the Baroness, for better or worse, to himself; he had a feeling that he deserved to enjoy a monopoly of her, for he was certainly the person who had most adequately gauged her capacity for social intercourse. Before long it became apparent to him that the Baroness was disposed to lay no tax upon such a monopoly.

One day (he was sitting there again and playing with a fan) she asked him to apologise, should the occasion present itself, to certain people in Boston for her not having returned their calls. 'There are half a dozen places,' she said; 'a formidable list. Charlotte Wentworth has written it out for me, in a terrifically distinct hand. There is no ambiguity on the subject; I know perfectly where I must go. Mr Wentworth informs me that the carriage is always at my disposal, and Charlotte offers to go with me, in a pair of tight gloves and a very stiff petticoat. And yet for three days I have been putting it off. They must think me horribly vicious.'

'You ask me to apologise, said Acton, 'but you don't tell me what excuse I can offer.'

'That is more,' the Baroness declared, 'than I am held to. It would be like my asking you to buy me a bouquet and giving you the money. I have no reason except that – somehow – it's too violent an effort. It is not inspiring. Wouldn't that serve as an excuse, in Boston? I am told they are very sincere; they don't tell fibs. And then Felix ought to go with me, and he is never in readiness. I don't see him. He is always roaming about the fields and sketching old barns, or taking ten-mile walks, or painting someone's portrait, or rowing on the pond, or flirting with Gertrude Wentworth.'

'I should think it would amuse you to go and see a few people,' said Acton. 'You are having a very quiet time of it here. It's a dull life for you.'

'Ah, the quiet – the quiet!' the Baroness exclaimed. 'That's what I like. It's rest. That's what I came here for. Amusement? I have had amusement. And as for seeing people – I have already seen a great many in my life. If it didn't sound ungracious I should say that I wish very humbly your people here would leave me alone!'

Acton looked at her a moment, and she looked at him. She was a woman who took being looked at remarkably well. 'So you have come here for rest?' he asked.

'So I may say. I came for many of those reasons that are no reasons – don't you know? – and yet that are really the best: to come away, to change, to break with everything. When once one comes away one must arrive somewhere, and I asked myself why I shouldn't arrive here.'

'You certainly had time, on the way!' said Acton, laughing.

Madame Münster looked at him again; and then, smiling, 'And I have certainly had time, since I got here, to ask myself why I came. However, I never ask myself idle questions. Here I am, and it seems to me you ought only to thank me.'

'When you go away you will see the difficulties I shall put in your path.'

'You mean to put difficulties in my path?' she asked, rearranging the rosebud in her corsage.[2]

'The greatest of all – that of having been so agreeable –'

'That I shall be unable to depart? Don't be too sure. I have left some very agreeable people over there.'

'Ah,' said Acton, 'but it was to come here, where I am!'

'I didn't know of your existence. Excuse me for saying anything so rude; but, honestly speaking, I did not. No,' the Baroness pursued, 'it was precisely not to see you – such people as you – that I came.'

'Such people as me?' cried Acton.

'I had a sort of longing to come into those natural relations which I knew I should find here. Over there I had only, as I may say, artificial relations. Don't you see the difference?'

'The difference tells against me,' said Acton. 'I suppose I am an artificial relation.'

'Conventional,' declared the Baroness; 'very conventional.'

'Well, there is one way in which the relation of a lady and a gentleman may always become natural,' said Acton.

'You mean by their becoming lovers? That may be natural or not. And at any rate,' rejoined Eugenia, *'nous n'en sommes pas là!'*[3]

They were not, as yet; but a little later, when she began to go with him to drive, it might almost have seemed that they were. He came for her several times, alone, in his high 'wagon', drawn by a pair of charming light-limbed horses. It was different, her having gone with Clifford Wentworth, who was her cousin and so much younger. It was not to be imagined that she should have a flirtation with Clifford, who was a mere shame-faced boy, and whom a large section of Boston society supposed to be 'engaged' to Lizzie Acton. Not indeed that it was to be conceived that the Baroness was a possible party to any flirtation whatever; for she was undoubtedly a married lady. It was generally known that her matrimonial condition was of the 'morganatic' order; but in its natural aversion to suppose that this meant anything less than absolute wedlock, the conscience of the community took refuge in the belief that it implied something even more.

Acton wished her to think highly of American scenery, and he drove her to great distances, picking out the prettiest roads and the largest points of view. If we are good when we are contented, Eugenia's virtues should now certainly have been uppermost; for she found a charm in the rapid movement through a wild country, and in a companion who from time to time made the vehicle dip, with a motion like a swallow's flight, over roads of primitive construction, and who, as she felt, would do a great many things that she might ask him. Sometimes, for a couple of hours together, there were almost no houses; there were nothing but woods and rivers and lakes and horizons adorned with bright-looking mountains. It seemed to the Baroness very wild, as I have said, and lovely; but the impression added something to that sense of the enlargement of opportunity which had been born of her arrival in the New World.

One day – it was late in the afternoon – Acton pulled up his horses on the crest of a hill which commanded a beautiful prospect. He let them stand a long time to rest, while he sat there and

talked with Madame Münster. The prospect was beautiful in spite
of there being nothing human within sight. There was a wilderness
of woods, and the gleam of a distant river, and a glimpse of half
the hill-tops in Massachusetts. The road had a wide, grassy margin,
on the farther side of which there flowed a deep, clear brook;
there were wild flowers in the grass, and beside the brook lay
the trunk of a fallen tree. Acton waited a while; at last a rustic
wayfarer came trudging along the road. Acton asked him to hold
the horses – a service he consented to render, as a friendly turn
to a fellow-citizen. Then he invited the Baroness to descend, and
the two wandered away, across the grass, and sat down on the
log beside the brook.

'I imagine it doesn't remind you of Silberstadt,' said Acton.
It was the first time that he had mentioned Silberstadt to her,
for particular reasons. He knew she had a husband there, and
this was disagreeable to him; and, furthermore, it had been repeated
to him that this husband wished to put her away – a state of
affairs to which even indirect reference was to be deprecated. It
was true, nevertheless, that the Baroness herself had often alluded
to Silberstadt; and Acton had often wondered why her husband
wished to get rid of her. It was a curious position for a lady –
this being known as a repudiated wife; and it is worthy of observation that the Baroness carried it off with exceeding grace and
dignity. She had made it felt, from the first, that there were two
sides to the question, and that her own side, when she should
choose to present it, would be replete with touching interest.

'It does not remind me of the town, of course,' she said: 'of
the sculptured gables and the Gothic churches, of the wonderful
Schloss,[4] with its moat and its clustering towers. But it has a little
look of some other parts of the principality. One might fancy
one's self among those grand old German forests, those legendary
mountains; the sort of country one sees from the windows at
Schreckenstein.'

'What is Schreckenstein?' asked Acton.

'It is a great castle – the summer residence of the Reigning
Prince.'

'Have you ever lived there?'

'I have stayed there,' said the Baroness. Acton was silent; he looked a while at the uncastled landscape before him. 'It is the first time you have ever asked me about Silberstadt,' she said. 'I should think you would want to know about my marriage; it must seem to you very strange.'

Acton looked at her a moment. 'Now you wouldn't like me to say that!'

'You Americans have such odd ways!' the Baroness declared 'You never ask anything outright; there seem to be so many things you can't talk about.'

'We Americans are very polite,' said Acton, whose national consciousness had been complicated by a residence in foreign lands, and who yet disliked to hear Americans abused. 'We don't like to tread upon people's toes,' he said. 'But I should like very much to hear about your marriage. Now tell me how it came about.'

'The Prince fell in love with me,' replied the Baroness simply. 'He pressed his suit very hard. At first he didn't wish me to marry him; on the contrary. But on that basis I refused to listen to him. So he offered me marriage – in so far as he might. I was young, and I confess I was rather flattered. But if it were to be done again now, I certainly should not accept him.'

'How long ago was this?' asked Acton.

'Oh – several years,' said Eugenia. 'You should never ask a woman for dates.'

'Why I should think that when a woman was relating history . . .' Acton answered. 'And now he wants to break it off?'

'They want him to make a political marriage. It is his brother's idea. His brother is very clever.'

'They must be a precious pair!' cried Robert Acton.

The Baroness gave a little philosophic shrug. '*Que voulez-vous!*[5] They are princes. They think they are treating me very well. Silberstadt is a perfectly despotic little state, and the Reigning Prince may annul the marriage by a stroke of his pen. But he has promised me, nevertheless, not to do so without my formal consent.'

'And this you have refused?'

'Hitherto. It is an indignity, and I have wished at least to make it difficult for them. But I have a little document in my writing-desk which I have only to sign and send back to the Prince.'

'Then it will be all over?'

The Baroness lifted her hand and dropped it again. 'Of course I shall keep my title; at least, I shall be at liberty to keep it if I choose. And I suppose I shall keep it. One must have a name. And I shall keep my pension. It is very small – it is wretchedly small; but it is what I live on.'

'And you have only to sign that paper?' Acton asked.

The Baroness looked at him a moment. 'Do you urge it?'

He got up slowly, and stood with his hands in his pockets. 'What do you gain by not doing it?'

'I am supposed to gain this advantage – that if I delay, or temporise, the Prince may come back to me, may make a stand against his brother. He is very fond of me, and his brother has pushed him only little by little.'

'If he were to come back to you,' said Acton, 'would you – would you take him back?'

The Baroness met his eyes; she coloured just a little. Then she rose. 'I should have the satisfaction of saying, "Now it is my turn. I break with your Serene Highness!"'

They began to walk toward the carriage. 'Well,' said Robert Acton, 'it's a curious story! How did you make his acquaintance?'

'I was staying with an old lady – an old Countess – in Dresden. She had been a friend of my father's. My father was dead; I was very much alone. My brother was wandering about the world in a theatrical troupe.'

'Your brother ought to have stayed with you,' Acton observed, 'and kept you from putting your trust in princes.'[6]

The Baroness was silent a moment, and then, 'He did what he could,' she said. 'He sent me money. The old Countess encouraged the Prince; she was even pressing. It seems to me,' Madame Münster added gently, 'that – under the circumstances – I behaved very well.'

Acton glanced at her, and made the observation – he had made it before – that a woman looks the prettier for having unfolded her wrongs or her sufferings. 'Well,' he reflected audibly, 'I should like to see you send his Serene Highness – somewhere!'

Madame Münster stooped and picked a daisy from the grass. 'And not sign my renunciation?'

'Well, I don't know – I don't know,' said Acton.

'In one case I should have my revenge; in another case I should have my liberty.'

Acton gave a little laugh as he helped her into the carriage. 'At any rate,' he said, 'take good care of that paper.'

A couple of days afterward he asked her to come and see his house. The visit had already been proposed, but it had been put off in consequence of his mother's illness. She was a constant invalid, and she had passed these recent years, very patiently, in a great flowered arm-chair at her bedroom window. Lately, for some days, she had been unable to see anyone; but now she was better, and she sent the Baroness a very civil message. Acton had wished their visitor to come to dinner; but Madame Münster preferred to begin with a simple call. She had reflected that if she should go to dinner Mr Wentworth and his daughters would also be asked, and it had seemed to her that the peculiar character of the occasion would be best preserved in a *tête-à-tête*[7] with her host. Why the occasion should have a peculiar character she explained to no one. As far as anyone could see, it was simply very pleasant. Acton came for her and drove her to his door, an operation which was rapidly performed. His house the Baroness mentally pronounced a very good one; more articulately, she declared that it was enchanting. It was large and square and painted brown; it stood in a well-kept shrubbery, and was approached, from the gate, by a short drive. It was, moreover, a much more modern dwelling than Mr Wentworth's, and was more redundantly upholstered and expensively ornamented. The Baroness perceived that her entertainer had analysed material comfort to a sufficiently fine point. And then he possessed the most delightful *chinoiseries*[8] – trophies of his sojourn in the Celestial Empire:[9] pagodas of ebony and cabinets of ivory; sculptured monsters, grinning and leering on chimney-pieces, in front of beautifully-figured hand-screens; porcelain dinner-sets, gleaming behind the glass doors of mahogany buffets; large screens, in corners, covered with tense silk and embroidered with mandarins and dragons. These things were scattered all over the house, and they gave Eugenia a pretext for a complete domiciliary visit. She liked it, she enjoyed it; she thought it a very nice place. It had a mixture of the homely and the liberal, and though it was almost a museum, the large, little-used rooms were as fresh and clean as a well-kept dairy. Lizzie Acton told her that she dusted all the pagodas and other curiosities every day with her own hands; and the Baroness answered that she was evidently a household fairy. Lizzie had not at all the look of a young lady who dusted things; she wore such pretty dresses and had such delicate fingers that it was difficult to imagine her immersed in sordid cares. She came to meet Madame Münster on her arrival, but she said nothing, or almost nothing, and the Baroness again reflected – she had had occasion to do so before – that American girls had no manners. She disliked this little American girl, and she was quite prepared to learn that she had failed to commend herself to Miss Acton. Lizzie struck her as positive and explicit almost to pertness; and the idea of her combining the apparent incongruities of a taste for housework and the wearing of fresh Parisian-looking dresses suggested the possession of a dangerous energy. It was a source of irritation to the Baroness that in this country it should seem to matter whether a little girl were a trifle less or a trifle more of a nonentity; for Eugenia had hitherto been conscious of no moral pressure as regards the appreciation of diminutive virgins. It was perhaps an indication of Lizzie's pertness that she very soon retired and left the Baroness on her brother's hands. Acton talked a great deal about his *chinoiseries*; he knew a good deal about porcelain and bric-à-brac.[10] The Baroness, in her progress through the house, made, as it were, a great many stations. She sat down everywhere, confessed to being a little tired, and asked about the various objects with a curious mixture of alertness and inattention. If there had been anyone to say it to, she would have declared that she was positively in love with her host; but she could hardly make this declaration – even in the strictest confidence – to Acton himself. It gave her, nevertheless, a pleasure that had some of the charm of unwontedness to feel, with that admirable keenness with which she was capable of feeling things, that he had a disposition without any edges; that even his humorous irony always expanded toward the point. One's impression of his honesty was almost like carrying a bunch of flowers; the perfume was most agreeable, but they were occasionally an inconvenience. One could trust him, at any rate, round all the corners of the world; and, withal, he was not absolutely simple, which would have been excess; he was only relatively simple, which was quite enough for the Baroness.

Lizzie reappeared, to say that her mother would now be happy to receive Madame Münster; and the Baroness followed her to Mrs Acton's apartment. Eugenia reflected, as she went, that it was not the affectation of impertinence that made her dislike this young lady, for on that ground she could easily have beaten her. It was not an aspiration on the girl's part to rivalry, but a kind of laughing, childishly-mocking indifference to the results of comparison. Mrs Acton was an emaciated, sweet-faced woman of five-and-fifty, sitting with pillows behind her and looking out on a clump of hemlocks. She was very modest, very timid, and very ill; she made Eugenia feel grateful that she herself was not like that – neither so ill, nor, possibly, so modest. On a chair, beside her, lay a volume of Emerson's[11] Essays. It was a great occasion for poor Mrs Acton, in her helpless condition, to be confronted with a clever foreign lady, who had more manner than any lady – any dozen ladies – that she had ever seen.

'I have heard a great deal about you,' she said softly, to the Baroness.

'From your son, eh?' Eugenia asked. 'He has talked to me immensely of you. Oh, he talks of you as you would like,' the Baroness declared; 'as such a son *must* talk of such a mother!'

Mrs Acton sat gazing; this was part of Madame Münster's 'manner'. But Robert Acton was gazing too, in vivid consciousness that he had barely mentioned his mother to their brilliant guest. He never talked of this still maternal presence – a presence refined to such delicacy that it had almost resolved itself, with him, simply into the subjective emotions of gratitude. And Acton rarely talked of his emotion. The Baroness turned her smile toward him, and she instantly felt that she had been observed to be fibbing. She had struck a false note. But who were these people to whom such fibbing was not pleasing? If they were annoyed, the Baroness was equally so; and after the exchange of a few civil inquiries and low-voiced responses she took leave of Mrs Acton. She begged Robert not to come home with her; she would get into the carriage alone; she preferred that. This was imperious, and she thought he looked disappointed. While she stood before the door with him – the carriage was turning in the gravel walk – this thought restored her serenity.

When she had given him her hand in farewell she looked at him a moment. 'I have almost decided to despatch that paper,' she said.

He knew that she alluded to the document that she had called her renunciation; and he assisted her into the carriage without saying anything. But just before the vehicle began to move he said, 'Well, when you have in fact despatched it, I hope you will let me know!'

CHAPTER 7

FELIX YOUNG finished Gertrude's portrait, and he afterwards transferred to canvas the features of many members of that circle of which it may be said that he had become, for the time, the pivot and the centre. I am afraid it must be confessed that he was a decidedly flattering painter, and that he imparted to his models a romantic grace which seemed easily and cheaply acquired by the payment of a hundred dollars to a young man who made 'sitting' so entertaining. For Felix was paid for his pictures, making, as he did, no secret of the fact that in guiding his steps to the Western world affectionate curiosity had gone hand in hand with a desire to better his condition. He took his uncle's portrait quite as if Mr Wentworth had never averted himself from the experiment; and as he compassed his end only by the exercise of gentle violence it is but fair to add that he allowed the old man to give him nothing but his time. He passed his arm into Mr Wentworth's one summer morning – very few arms, indeed, had ever passed into Mr Wentworth's – and led him across the garden and along the road into the studio which he had extemporised in the little house among the apple trees. The grave gentleman felt himself more and more fascinated by his clever nephew, whose fresh, demonstrative youth seemed a compendium of experiences so strangely numerous. It appeared to him that Felix must know a great deal; he would like to learn what he thought about some of those things as regards which his own conversation had always been formal but his knowledge vague. Felix had a confident, gaily trenchant way of judging human actions which Mr Wentworth grew little by little to envy; it seemed like criticism made easy. Forming an opinion – say on a person's conduct – was with Mr Wentworth a good deal like fumbling in a lock with a key chosen at hazard. He seemed to himself to go about the world with a big bunch of these ineffectual instruments at his girdle. His nephew, on the other hand, with a single turn of the wrist, opened any door as adroitly as a house thief. He felt obliged to keep up the convention that an uncle is always wiser than a nephew, even if he could keep it up no otherwise than by listening in serious silence to Felix's quick, light, constant discourse. But there came a day when he lapsed from consistency and almost asked his nephew's advice.

'Have you ever entertained the idea of settling in the United States?' he asked one morning, while Felix brilliantly plied his brush.

'My dear uncle,' said Felix, 'excuse me if your question makes me smile a little. To begin with, I have never entertained an idea. Ideas often entertain *me*; but I am afraid I have never seriously made a plan. I know what you are going to say; or rather, I know what you think, for I don't think you will say it – that this is very frivolous and loose-minded on my part. So it is; but I am made like that; I take things as they come, and somehow there is always some new thing to follow the last. In the second place, I should never propose to *settle*. I can't settle, my dear uncle; I am not a settler. I know that is what strangers are supposed to do here; they always settle. But I haven't – to answer your question – entertained that idea.'

'You intend to return to Europe and resume your irregular manner of life?' Mr Wentworth inquired.

'I can't say I intend. But it's very likely I shall go back to Europe. After all, I am a European. I feel that, you know. It will depend a good deal upon my sister. She's even more of a European than I; here, you know, she's a picture out of her setting. And as for "resuming", dear uncle, I really have never given up my irregular manner of life. What, for me, could be more irregular than this?'

'Than what?' asked Mr Wentworth, with his pale gravity.

'Well, than everything! Living in the midst of you, this way; this charming, quiet, serious family life; fraternising with Charlotte and Gertrude; calling upon twenty young ladies, and going out to walk with them; sitting with you in the evening on the piazza and listening to the crickets, and going to bed at ten o'clock.'

'Your description is very animated,' said Mr Wentworth; 'but I see nothing improper in what you describe.'

'Neither do I, dear uncle. It is extremely delightful; I shouldn't like it if it were improper. I assure you I don't like improper things; though I daresay you think I do,' Felix went on, painting away.

'I have never accused you of that.'

'Pray don't,' said Felix; 'because, you see, at bottom I am a terrible Philistine.'[1]

'A Philistine?' repeated Mr Wentworth.

'I mean, as one may say, a plain, God-fearing man.' Mr Wentworth looked at him reservedly, like a mystified sage, and Felix continued, 'I trust I shall enjoy a venerable and venerated old age. I mean to live long. I can hardly call that a plan, perhaps; but it's a keen desire – a rosy vision. I shall be a lively, perhaps even a frivolous, old man!'

'It is natural,' said his uncle sententiously, 'that one should desire to prolong an agreeable life. We have perhaps a selfish indisposition to bring our pleasure to a close. But I presume,' he added, 'that you expect to marry.'

'That too, dear uncle, is a hope, a desire, a vision,' said Felix. It occurred to him for an instant that this was possibly a preface to the offer of the hand of one of Mr Wentworth's admirable daughters. But in the name of decent modesty and a proper sense of the hard realities of this world, Felix banished the thought. His uncle was the incarnation of benevolence, certainly; but from that to accepting – much more postulating – the idea of a union between a young lady with a dowry presumptively brilliant, and a penniless artist with no prospect of fame, there was a very long way. Felix had lately become conscious of a luxurious preference for the society – if possible, unshared with others – of Gertrude Wentworth; but he had relegated this young lady, for the moment, to the coldly brilliant category of unattainable possessions. She was not the first woman for whom he had entertained an unpractical admiration. He had been in love with duchesses and countesses, and he had made, once or twice, a perilously near approach to cynicism in declaring that the disinterestedness of women had been overrated. On the whole, he had tempered audacity with modesty; and it is but fair to him, now, to say explicitly that he would have been incapable of taking advantage of his present large allowance of familiarity to make love to the younger of his handsome cousins. Felix had grown up among traditions in the light of which such a proceeding looked like a grievous breach of hospitality. I have said that he was always happy, and it may be counted among the present sources of happiness that he had, as regards this matter of his relations with Gertrude, a deliciously good conscience. His own deportment seemed to him suffused with the beauty of virtue – a form of beauty that he admired with the same vivacity with which he admired all other forms.

'I think that if you marry,' said Mr Wentworth presently, 'it will conduce to your happiness.'

'*Sicurissimo!*'[2] Felix exclaimed; and then, arresting his brush, he looked at his uncle with a smile. 'There is something I feel tempted to say to you. May I risk it?'

Mr Wentworth drew himself up a little. 'I am very safe; I don't repeat things.' But he hoped Felix would not risk too much.

Felix was laughing at his answer. 'It's odd to hear you telling me how to be happy. I don't think you know yourself, dear uncle. Now, does that sound brutal?'

The old man was silent a moment, and then, with a dry dignity that suddenly touched his nephew, 'We may sometimes point out a road we are unable to follow.'

'Ah, don't tell me you have had any sorrows,' Felix rejoined. 'I didn't suppose it, and I didn't mean to allude to them. I simply meant that you all don't amuse yourselves.'

'Amuse ourselves? We are not children.'

'Precisely not. You have reached the proper age. I was saying that, the other day, to Gertrude,' Felix added. 'I hope it was not indiscreet.'

'If it was,' said Mr Wentworth, with a keener irony than Felix would have thought him capable of, 'it was but your way of amusing yourself. I am afraid you never had a trouble.'

'Oh yes, I have!' Felix declared, with some spirit; 'before I knew better. But you don't catch me at it again.'

Mr Wentworth maintained for a while a silence more expressive than a deep-drawn sigh. 'You have no children,' he said at last.

'Don't tell me,' Felix exclaimed, 'that your charming young people are a source of grief to you!'

'I don't speak of Charlotte.' And then, after a pause, Mr Wentworth continued, 'I don't speak of Gertrude. But I feel considerable anxiety about Clifford. I will tell you another time.'

The next time he gave Felix a sitting his nephew reminded him that he had taken him into his confidence. 'How is Clifford today?' Felix asked. 'He has always seemed to me a young man of remarkable discretion. Indeed, he is only too discreet; he seems on his guard against me – as if he thought me rather light company. The other day he told his sister – Gertrude repeated it to me – that I was always laughing at him. If I laugh it is simply from the impulse to try and inspire him with confidence. That is the only way I have.'

'Clifford's situation is no laughing matter,' said Mr Wentworth. 'It is very peculiar, as I suppose you have guessed.'

'Ah, you mean his love affair with his cousin?'

Mr Wentworth stared, blushing a little. 'I mean his absence from college. He has been suspended. We have decided not to speak of it unless we are asked.'

'Suspended?' Felix repeated.

'He has been requested by the Harvard authorities to absent himself for six months. Meanwhile he is studying with Mr Brand. We think Mr Brand will help him; at least we hope so.'

'What befell him at college?' Felix asked. 'He was too fond of pleasure? Mr Brand certainly will not teach him any of those secrets!'

'He was too fond of something of which he should not have been fond. I suppose it is considered a pleasure.'

Felix gave his light laugh. 'My dear uncle, is there any doubt about its being a pleasure? C'est de son âge,[3] as they say in France.'

'I should have said rather it was a vice of later life – of disappointed old age.'

Felix glanced at his uncle, with his lifted eyebrows, and then, 'Of what are you speaking?' he demanded, smiling.

'Of the situation in which Clifford was found.'

'Ah, he was found – he was caught?'

'Necessarily, he was caught. He couldn't walk; he staggered.'

'Oh,' said Felix, 'he drinks! I rather suspected that, from something I observed the first day I came here. I quite agree with you that it is a low taste. It is not a vice for a gentleman. He ought to give it up.'

'We hope for a good deal from Mr Brand's influence,' Mr Wentworth went on. 'He has talked to him from the first. And he never touches anything himself.'

'I will talk to him – I will talk to him!' Felix declared gaily.

'What will you say to him?' asked his uncle, with some apprehension.

Felix for some moments answered nothing. 'Do you mean to marry him to his cousin?' he asked at last.

'Marry him?' echoed Mr Wentworth. 'I shouldn't think his cousin would want to marry him.'

'You have no understanding, then, with Mrs Acton?'

Mr Wentworth stared, almost blankly. 'I have never discussed such subjects with her.'

'I should think it might be time,' said Felix. 'Lizzie Acton is admirably pretty, and if Clifford is dangerous –'

'They are not engaged,' said Mr Wentworth. 'I have no reason to suppose they are engaged.'

'*Par exemple!*' cried Felix. 'A clandestine engagement? Trust me, Clifford, as I say, is a charming boy. He is incapable of that. Lizzie Acton, then, would not be jealous of another woman.'

'I certainly hope not,' said the old man, with a vague sense of jealousy being an even lower vice than a love of liquor.

'The best thing for Clifford, therefore,' Felix propounded, 'is to become interested in some clever, charming woman.' And he paused in his painting, and, with his elbows on his knees, looked with bright communicativeness at his uncle. 'You see, I believe greatly in the influence of women. Living with women helps to make a man a gentleman. It is very true, Clifford has his sisters, who are so charming. But there should be a different sentiment in play from the fraternal, you know. He has Lizzie Acton; but she, perhaps, is rather immature.'

'I suspect Lizzie has talked to him, reasoned with him,' said Mr Wentworth.

'On the impropriety of getting tipsy – on the beauty of temperance? That is dreary work for a pretty young girl. No,' Felix continued; 'Clifford ought to frequent some agreeable woman, who, without ever mentioning such unsavoury subjects, would give him a sense of its being very ridiculous to be fuddled. If he could fall in love with her a little, so much the better. The thing would operate as a cure.'

'Well, now, what lady should you suggest?' asked Mr Wentworth.

'There is a clever woman under your hand. My sister.'

'Your sister – under my hand?' Mr Wentworth repeated.

'Say a word to Clifford. Tell him to be bold. He is well disposed already; he has invited her two or three times to drive. But I don't think he comes to see her. Give him a hint to come – to come often. He will sit there of an afternoon, and they will talk. It will do him good.'

Mr Wentworth meditated. 'You think she will exercise a helpful influence?'

'She will exercise a civilising – I may call it a sobering – influence. A charming, witty woman always does – especially if she is a little of a coquette. My dear uncle, the society of such women has been half my education. If Clifford is suspended, as you say, from college, let Eugenia be his preceptress.'

Mr Wentworth continued thoughtful. 'You think Eugenia is a coquette?' he asked.

'What pretty woman is not?' Felix demanded in turn. But this, for Mr Wentworth, could at the best have been no answer, for he did not think his niece pretty. 'With Clifford,' the young man pursued, 'Eugenia will simply be enough of a coquette to be a little ironical. That's what he needs. So you recommend him to be nice with her, you know. The suggestion will come best from you.'

'Do I understand,' asked the old man, 'that I am to suggest to my son to make a – a profession of – of affection to Madame Münster?'

'Yes, yes – a profession!' cried Felix sympathetically.

'But, as I understand it, Madame Münster is a married woman.'

'Ah,' said Felix, smiling, 'of course she can't marry him. But she will do what she can.'

Mr Wentworth sat for some time with his eyes on the floor; at last he got up. 'I don't think,' he said, 'that I can undertake to recommend to my son any such course.' And without meeting Felix's surprised glance he broke off his sitting, which was not resumed for a fortnight.

Felix was very fond of the little lake which occupied so many of Mr Wentworth's numerous acres, and of a remarkable grove of pines which lay upon the farther side of it, planted upon a steep embankment and haunted by the summer breeze. The murmur of the air in the far-off tree-tops had a strange distinctness; it was almost articulate. One afternoon the young man came out of his painting-room and passed the open door of Eugenia's little salon. Within, in the cool dimness, he saw his sister, dressed in white, buried in her arm-chair and holding to her face an immense bouquet. Opposite to her sat Clifford Wentworth, twirling his hat. He had evidently just presented the bouquet to the Baroness, whose fine eyes, as she glanced at him over the big roses and geraniums, wore a conversational smile. Felix, standing on the threshold of the cottage, hesitated for a moment as to whether he should retrace his steps and enter the parlour. Then he went his way and passed into Mr Wentworth's garden. That civilising process to which he had suggested that Clifford should be subjected appeared to have come on of itself. Felix was very sure, at least, that Mr Wentworth had not adopted his ingenious device for stimulating the young man's aesthetic consciousness. 'Doubtless he supposes,' he said to himself, after the conversation that has been narrated, 'that I desire, out of fraternal benevolence, to procure for Eugenia the amusement of a flirtation – or, as he probably calls it, an intrigue – with the too susceptible Clifford. It must be admitted – and I have noticed it before – that nothing exceeds the license occasionally taken by the imagination of very rigid people.' Felix, on his own side, had of course said nothing to Clifford; but he had observed to Eugenia that Mr Wentworth was much mortified at his son's low tastes. 'We ought to do something to help them, after all their kindness to us,' he had added. 'Encourage Clifford to come and see you, and inspire him with a taste for conversation. That will supplant the other, which only comes from his puerility, from his not taking his position in the world – that of a rich young man of ancient stock – seriously enough. Make him a little more serious. Even if he makes love to you it is no great matter.'

'I am to offer myself as a superior form of intoxication – a substitute for a brandy bottle, eh?' asked the Baroness. 'Truly, in this country one comes to strange uses.'

But she had not positively declined to undertake Clifford's higher education, and Felix, who had not thought of the matter again, being haunted with visions of more personal profit, now reflected that the work of redemption had fairly begun. The idea, in prospect, had seemed of the happiest, but in operation it made him a trifle uneasy. 'What if Eugenia – what if Eugenia – ?' he asked himself softly, the question dying away in his sense of Eugenia's undetermined capacity. But before Felix had time either to accept or to reject its admonition, even in this vague form, he saw Robert Acton turn out of Mr Wentworth's enclosure by a distant gate and come toward the cottage in the orchard. Acton had evidently walked from his own house along a shady by-way, and he was intending to pay a visit to Madame Münster. Felix watched him a moment; then he turned away. Acton could be left to play the part of Providence and interrupt – if interruption were needed – Clifford's entanglement with Eugenia.

Felix passed through the garden toward the house and toward a postern gate which opened upon a path leading across the fields, beside a little wood, to the lake. He stopped and looked up at the house; his eyes rested more particularly upon a certain open window, on the shady side. Presently Gertrude appeared there, looking out into the summer light. He took off his hat to her and bade her good-day; he remarked that he was going to row across the pond, and begged that she would do him the honour to accompany him. She looked at him a moment; then, without saying anything, she turned away. But she soon reappeared, below, in one of those quaint and charming Leghorn hats,[4] tied with white satin bows, that were worn at that period; she also carried a green parasol. She went with him to the edge of the lake, where a couple of boats were always moored; they got into one of them, and Felix with gentle strokes propelled it to the opposite shore. The day was the perfection of summer weather; the little lake was the colour of sunshine; the plash of the oars was the only sound, and they found themselves listening to it. They disembarked, and by a winding path ascended the pine-crested mound which overlooked the water, whose white expanse glittered between the trees. The place was delightfully cool, and had the added charm that – in the softly-sounding pine-boughs – you seemed to hear the coolness as well as feel it. Felix and Gertrude sat down on the rust-coloured carpet of pine-needles and talked of many things. Felix spoke at last, in the course of talk, of his going away; it was the first time he had alluded to it.

'You are going away?' said Gertrude, looking at him.

'Some day – when the leaves begin to fall. You know I can't stay for ever.'

Gertrude transferred her eyes to the outer prospect, and then, after a pause, she said, 'I shall never see you again.'

'Why not?' asked Felix. 'We shall probably both survive my departure.'

But Gertrude only repeated, 'I shall never see you again. I shall never hear of you,' she went on. 'I shall know nothing about you. I knew nothing about you before, and it will be the same again.'

'I knew nothing about you then, unfortunately,' said Felix. 'But now I shall write to you.'

'Don't write to me. I shall not answer you,' Gertrude declared.

'I should of course burn your letters,' said Felix.

Gertrude looked at him again. 'Burn my letters? You sometimes say strange things.'

'They are not strange in themselves,' the young man answered. 'They are only strange as said to you. You will come to Europe.'

'With whom shall I come?' She asked this question simply; she was very much in earnest. Felix was interested in her earnestness; for some moments he hesitated. 'You can't tell me that,' she pursued. 'You can't say that I shall go with my father and my sister; you don't believe that.'

'I shall keep your letters,' said Felix presently, for all answer.

'I never write. I don't know how to write.' Gertrude, for some time, said nothing more; and her companion, as he looked at her, wished it had not been 'disloyal' to make love to the daughter of an old gentleman who had offered one hospitality. The afternoon waned; the shadows stretched themselves; and the light grew deeper in the western sky. Two persons appeared on the opposite side of the lake, coming from the house and crossing the meadow. 'It is Charlotte and Mr Brand,' said Gertrude. 'They are coming over here.' But Charlotte and Mr Brand only came down to the edge of the water and stood there, looking across; they made no motion to enter the boat that Felix had left at the mooring-place. Felix waved his hat to them; it was too far to call. They made no visible response, and they presently turned away and walked along the shore.

'Mr Brand is not demonstrative,' said Felix. 'He is never demonstrative to me. He sits silent, with his chin in his hand, looking at me. Sometimes he looks away. Your father tells me he is so eloquent; and I should like to hear him talk. He looks like such a noble young man. But with me he will never talk. And yet I am so fond of listening to brilliant imagery!'

'He is very eloquent,' said Gertrude; 'but he has no brilliant imagery. I have heard him talk a great deal. I knew that when they saw us they would not come over here.'

'Ah, he is making *la cour*,[5] as they say, to your sister? They desire to be alone?'

'No,' said Gertrude gravely, 'they have no such reason as that for being alone.'

'But why doesn't he make *la cour* to Charlotte?' Felix inquired. 'She is so pretty, so gentle, so good.'

Gertrude glanced at him, and then she looked at the distantly-seen couple they were discussing. Mr Brand and Charlotte were walking side by side. They might have been a pair of lovers, and yet they might not. 'They think I should not be here,' said Gertrude.

'With me? I thought you didn't have those ideas.'

'You don't understand. There are a great many things you don't understand.'

'I understand my stupidity. But why, then, do not Charlotte and Mr Brand, who, as an elder sister and a clergyman, are free to walk about together, come over and make me wiser by breaking up the unlawful interview into which I have lured you?'

'That is the last thing they would do,' said Gertrude.

Felix stared at her a moment, with his lifted eyebrows. *'Je n'y comprends rien!'*[6] he exclaimed; then his eyes followed for a while the retreating figures of this critical pair. 'You may say what you please,' he declared; 'it is evident to me that your sister is not indifferent to her clever companion. It is agreeable to her to be walking there with him. I can see that from here.' And in the excitement of observation Felix rose to his feet.

Gertrude rose also, but she made no attempt to emulate her companion's discovery; she looked rather in another direction. Felix's words had struck her; but a certain delicacy checked her. 'She is certainly not indifferent to Mr Brand; she has the highest opinion of him.'

'One can see it – one can see it,' said Felix in a tone of amused contemplation, with his head on one side. Gertrude turned her back to the opposite shore; it was disagreeable to her to look, but she hoped Felix would say something more. 'Ah, they have wandered away into the wood,' he added.

Gertrude turned round again. 'She is *not* in love with him,' she said; it seemed her duty to say that.

'Then he is in love with her; or if he is not, he ought to be. She is such a perfect little woman of her kind. She reminds me of a pair of old-fashioned silver sugar-tongs; you know I am very fond of sugar. And she is very nice with Mr Brand; I have noticed that; very gentle and gracious.'

Gertrude reflected a moment. Then she took a great resolution. 'She wants him to marry me,' she said. 'So of course she is nice.'

Felix's eyebrows rose higher than ever. 'To marry you! Ah, ah, this is interesting. And you think one must be very nice with a man to induce him to do that?'

Gertrude had turned a little pale, but she went on, 'Mr Brand wants it himself.'

Felix folded his arms and stood looking at her. 'I see – I see,' he said quickly. 'Why did you never tell me this before?'

'It is disagreeable to me to speak of it even now. I wished simply to explain to you about Charlotte.'

'You don't wish to marry Mr Brand, then?'

'No,' said Gertrude gravely.

'And does your father wish it?'

'Very much ˙

'And you don't like him – you have refused him?'

'I don't wish to marry him.'

'Your father and sister think you ought to, eh?'

'It is a long story,' said Gertrude. 'They think there are good reasons. I can't explain it. They think I have obligations, and that I have encouraged him.'

Felix smiled at her, as if she had been telling him an amusing story about someone else. 'I can't tell you how this interests me,' he said. 'Now you don't recognise these reasons – these obligations?'

'I am not sure; it is not easy.' And she picked up her parasol and turned away, as if to descend the slope.

'Tell me this,' Felix went on, going with her; 'are you likely to give in – to let them persuade you?'

Gertrude looked at him with the serious face that she had constantly worn in opposition to his almost eager smile.

'I shall never marry Mr Brand,' she said.

'I see!' Felix rejoined. And they slowly descended the hill together, saying nothing till they reached the margin of the pond. 'It is your own affair,' he then resumed; 'but do you know, I am not altogether glad? If it were settled that you were to marry Mr Brand I should take a certain comfort in the arrangement, I should feel more free. I have no right to make love to you myself, eh?' And he paused, lightly pressing his argument upon her.

'None whatever,' replied Gertrude quickly – too quickly.

'Your father would never hear of it; I haven't a penny. Mr Brand, of course, has property of his own, eh?'

'I believe he has some property; but that has nothing to do with it.'

'With you, of course not; but with your father and sister it must have. So, as I say, if this were settled, I should feel more at liberty.'

'More at liberty?' Gertrude repeated. 'Please unfasten the boat.'

Felix untwisted the rope and stood holding it. 'I should be able to say things to you that I can't give myself the pleasure of saying now,' he went on. 'I could tell you how much I admire you, without seeming to pretend to that which I have no right to pretend to.

I should make violent love to you,' he added, laughing, 'if I thought you were so placed as not to be offended by it.'

'You mean if I were engaged to another man? That is strange reasoning!' Gertrude exclaimed.

'In that case you would not take me seriously.'

'I take everyone seriously!' said Gertrude. And without his help she stepped lightly into the boat.

Felix took up the oars and sent it forward. 'Ah, this is what you have been thinking about? It seemed to me you had something on your mind. I wish very much,' he added, 'that you would tell me some of these so-called reasons – these obligations.'

'They are not real reasons – good reasons,' said Gertrude, looking at the pink and yellow gleams in the water.

'I can't understand that! Because a handsome girl has had a spark of coquetry, that is no reason.'

'If you mean me, it's not that. I have not done that.'

'It is something that troubles you, at any rate,' said Felix.

'Not so much as it used to,' Gertrude rejoined.

He looked at her, smiling always. 'That is not saying much, eh?' But she only rested her eyes, very gravely, on the lighted water. She seemed to him to be trying to hide the signs of the trouble of which she had just told him. Felix felt, at all times, much the same impulse to dissipate visible melancholy that a good housewife feels to brush away dust. There was something he wished to brush away now; suddenly he stopped rowing and poised his oars. 'Why should Mr Brand have addressed himself to you, and not to your sister?' he asked. 'I am sure she would listen to him.'

Gertrude, in her family, was thought capable of a good deal of levity; but her levity had never gone so far as this. It moved her greatly, however, to hear Felix say that he was sure of something; so that, raising her eyes toward him, she tried intently, for some moments, to conjure up this wonderful image of a love affair between her own sister and her own suitor. We know that Gertrude had an imaginative mind; so that it is not impossible that this effort should have been partially successful. But she only murmured, 'Ah, Felix! ah, Felix!'

'Why shouldn't they marry? Try and make them marry!' cried Felix.

'Try and make them?'

'Turn the tables on them. Then they will leave you alone. I will help you as far as I can.'

Gertrude's heart began to beat; she was greatly excited: she had never had anything so interesting proposed to her before. Felix had begun to row again, and he now sent the boat home with long strokes. 'I believe she *does* care for him!' said Gertrude, after they had disembarked.

'Of course she does, and we will marry them off. It will make them happy: it will make everyone happy. We shall have a wedding, and I will write an epithalamium.'[7]

'It seems as if it would make *me* happy,' said Gertrude.

'To get rid of Mr Brand, eh? To recover your liberty?'

Gertrude walked on. 'To see my sister married to so good a man.'

Felix gave his light laugh. 'You always put things on those grounds: you will never say anything for yourself. You are all so afraid, here, of being selfish. I don't think you know how,' he went on. 'Let me show you! It will make me happy for myself, and for just the reverse of what I told you a while ago. After that, when I make love to you, you will have to think I mean it.'

'I shall never think you mean anything,' said Gertrude. 'You are too fantastic.'

'Ah,' cried Felix, 'that's a license to say everything! Gertrude, I adore you!'

CHAPTER 8

CHARLOTTE and Mr Brand had not returned when they reached the house; but the Baroness had come to tea, and Robert Acton also, who now regularly asked for a place at this generous repast, or made his appearance later in the evening. Clifford Wentworth, with his juvenile growl, remarked upon it.

'You are always coming to tea nowadays, Robert,' he said. 'I should think you had drunk enough tea in China.'

'Since when is Mr Acton more frequent?' asked the Baroness.

'Since you came,' said Clifford. 'It seems as if you were a kind of attraction.'

'I suppose I am a curiosity,' said the Baroness. 'Give me time and I will make you a salon.'

'It would fall to pieces after you go!' exclaimed Acton.

'Don't talk about her going in that familiar way,' Clifford said. 'It makes me feel gloomy.'

Mr Wentworth glanced at his son, and, taking note of these words, wondered if Felix had been teaching him, according to the programme he had sketched out, to make love to the wife of a German prince.

Charlotte came in late with Mr Brand; but Gertrude, to whom, at least, Felix had taught something, looked in vain, in her face, for the traces of a guilty passion. Mr Brand sat down by Gertrude, and she presently asked him why they had not crossed the pond to join Felix and herself.

'It is cruel of you to ask me that,' he answered, very softly. He had a large morsel of cake before him; but he fingered it without eating it. 'I sometimes think you are growing cruel,' he added.

Gertrude said nothing; she was afraid to speak. There was a kind of rage in her heart; she felt as if she could easily persuade herself that she was persecuted. She said to herself that it was quite

126

right that she should not allow him to make her believe she was wrong. She thought of what Felix had said to her; she wished, indeed, Mr Brand would marry Charlotte. She looked away from him and spoke no more. Mr Brand ended by eating his cake, while Felix sat opposite, describing to Mr Wentworth the students' duels at Heidelberg. After tea they all dispersed themselves, as usual, upon the piazza and in the garden; and Mr Brand drew near to Gertrude again.

'I didn't come to you this afternoon because you were not alone,' he began; 'because you were with a newer friend.'

'Felix? He is an old friend by this time.'

Mr Brand looked at the ground for some moments. 'I thought I was prepared to hear you speak in that way,' he resumed. 'But I find it very painful.'

'I don't see what else I can say,' said Gertrude.

Mr Brand walked beside her for a while in silence; Gertrude wished he would go away. 'He is certainly very accomplished. But I think I ought to advise you.'

'To advise me?'

'I think I know your nature.'

'I think you don't,' said Gertrude, with a soft laugh.

'You make yourself out worse than you are – to please him,' Mr Brand said sadly.

'Worse – to please him? What do you mean?' asked Gertrude, stopping.

Mr Brand stopped also, and with the same soft straightforwardness. 'He doesn't care for the things you care for – the great questions of life.'

Gertrude, with her eyes on his, shook her head. 'I don't care for the great questions of life. They are much beyond me.'

'There was a time when you didn't say that,' said Mr Brand.

'Oh,' rejoined Gertrude, 'I think you made me talk a great deal of nonsense. And it depends,' she added, 'upon what you call the great questions of life. There are some things I care for.'

'Are they the things you talk about with your cousin?'

'You should not say things to me against my cousin, Mr Brand,' said Gertrude. 'That is dishonourable.'

He listened to this respectfully; then he answered, with a little vibration of the voice, 'I should be very sorry to do anything dishonourable. But I don't see why it is dishonourable to say that your cousin is frivolous.'

'Go and say it to himself!'

'I think he would admit it,' said Mr Brand. 'That is the tone he would take. He would not be ashamed of it.'

'Then I am not ashamed of it!' Gertrude declared. 'That is probably what I like him for. I am frivolous myself.'

'You are trying, as I said just now, to lower yourself.'

'I am trying for once to be natural!' cried Gertrude passionately. 'I have been pretending, all my life; I have been dishonest; it is you that have made me so!' Mr Brand stood gazing at her, and she went on, 'Why shouldn't I be frivolous, if I want? One has a right to be frivolous, if it's one's nature. No, I don't care for the great questions. I care for pleasure – for amusement. Perhaps I am fond of wicked things; it is very possible!'

Mr Brand remained staring; he was even a little pale, as if he had been frightened. 'I don't think you know what you are saying!' he exclaimed.

'Perhaps not. Perhaps I am talking nonsense. But it is only with you that I talk nonsense. I never do so with my cousin.'

'I will speak to you again, when you are less excited,' said Mr Brand.

'I am always excited when you speak to me. I must tell you that – even if it prevents you altogether, in future. Your speaking to me irritates me. With my cousin it is very different. That seems quiet and natural.'

He looked at her, and then he looked away, with a kind of helpless distress, at the dusky garden and the faint summer stars. After which, suddenly turning back, 'Gertrude, Gertrude!' he softly groaned. 'Am I really losing you?'

She was touched – she was pained; but it had already occurred to her that she might do something better than say so. It would not have alleviated her companion's distress to perceive, just then, whence she had sympathetically borrowed this ingenuity. 'I am not sorry for you,' Gertrude said; 'for in paying so much attention to me you are following a shadow – you are wasting something precious. There is something else you might have that you don't look at – something better than I am. That is a reality!' And then, with intention, she looked at him and tried to smile a little. He thought this smile of hers very strange; but she turned away and left him.

She wandered about alone in the garden wondering what Mr Brand would make of her words, which it had been a singular pleasure for her to utter. Shortly after, passing in front of the house, she saw, at a distance, two persons standing near the garden gate. It was Mr Brand going away and bidding good-night to Charlotte, who had walked down with him from the house. Gertrude saw that the parting was prolonged; then she turned her back upon it. She had not gone very far, however, when she heard her sister slowly following her. She neither turned round nor waited for her; she knew what Charlotte was going to say. Charlotte, who at last overtook her, in fact presently began; she had passed her arm into Gertrude's.

'Will you listen to me, dear, if I say something very particular?'

'I know what you are going to say,' said Gertrude. 'Mr Brand feels very badly.'

'Oh, Gertrude, how can you treat him so?' Charlotte demanded. And as her sister made no answer she added, 'After all he has done for you!'

'What has he done for me?'

'I wonder you can ask, Gertrude. He has helped you so. You told me so yourself, a great many times. You told me that he helped you to struggle with your – your peculiarities. You told me that he had taught you how to govern your temper.'

For a moment Gertrude said nothing. Then, 'Was my temper very bad?' she asked.

'I am not accusing you, Gertrude,' said Charlotte.

'What are you doing, then?' her sister demanded, with a little laugh.

'I am pleading for Mr Brand – reminding you of all you owe him.'

'I have given it all back,' said Gertrude, still with her little laugh. 'He can take back the virtue he imparted! I want to be wicked again.'

Her sister made her stop in the path, and fixed upon her in

the darkness a sweet reproachful gaze. 'If you talk this way I shall almost believe it. Think of all we owe Mr Brand. Think of how he has always expected something of you. Think how much he has been to us. Think of his beautiful influence upon Clifford.'

'He is very good,' said Gertrude, looking at her sister. 'I know he is very good. But he shouldn't speak against Felix.'

'Felix is good,' Charlotte answered, softly but promptly. 'Felix is very wonderful. Only he is so different. Mr Brand is much nearer to us. I should never think of going to Felix with a trouble – with a question. Mr Brand is much more to us, Gertrude.'

'He is very – very good,' Gertrude repeated. 'He is more to you; yes, much more. Charlotte,' she added suddenly, 'you are in love with him!'

'Oh, Gertrude!' cried poor Charlotte; and her sister saw her blushing in the darkness.

Gertrude put her arm around her. 'I wish he would marry you!' she went on.

Charlotte shook herself free. 'You must not say such things!' she exclaimed, beneath her breath.

'You like him more than you say, and he likes you more than he knows.'

'This is very cruel of you!' Charlotte Wentworth murmured.

But if it was cruel Gertrude continued pitiless. 'Not if it's true,' she answered; 'I wish he would marry you.'

'Please don't say that.'

'I mean to tell him so!' said Gertrude.

'Oh, Gertrude, Gertrude!' her sister almost moaned.

'Yes, if he speaks to me again about myself. I will say, "Why don't you marry Charlotte? She's a thousand times better than I."'

'You *are* wicked; you *are* changed!' cried her sister.

'If you don't like it you can prevent it,' said Gertrude. 'You can prevent it by keeping him from speaking to me!' And with this she walked away, very conscious of what she had done; measuring it and finding a certain joy and a quickened sense of freedom in it.

Mr Wentworth was rather wide of the mark in suspecting that Clifford had begun to pay unscrupulous compliments to his brilliant cousin; for the young man had really more scruples than he received credit for in his family. He had a certain transparent shamefacedness which was in itself a proof that he was not at his ease in dissipation. His collegiate peccadilloes had aroused a domestic murmur as disagreeable to the young man as the creaking of his boots would have been to a house-breaker. Only, as the house-breaker would have simplified matters by removing his *chaussures*,[1] it had seemed to Clifford that the shortest cut to comfortable relations with people – relations which should make him cease to think that when they spoke to him they meant something improving – was to renounce all ambition toward a nefarious development. And, in fact, Clifford's ambition took the most commendable form. He thought of himself in the future as the well-known and much-liked Mr Wentworth, of Boston, who should, in the natural course of prosperity, have married his pretty cousin, Lizzie Acton; should live in a wide-fronted house, in view of the Common,[2] and should drive, behind a light wagon, over the damp autumn roads, a pair of beautifully-matched sorrel horses. Clifford's vision of the coming years was very simple; its most definite features were this element of familiar matrimony and the duplication of his resources for trotting. He had not yet asked his cousin to marry him; but he meant to do so as soon as he should have taken his degree. Lizzie was serenely conscious of his intention, and she had made up her mind that he would improve. Her brother, who was very fond of this light, quick, competent little Lizzie, saw, on his side, no reason to interpose. It seemed to him a graceful social law that Clifford and his sister should become engaged: he himself was not engaged, but everyone else, fortunately, was not such a fool as he. He was fond of Clifford, as well, and had his own way – of which it must be confessed he was a little ashamed – of looking at those aberrations which had led to the young man's compulsory retirement from the neighbouring seat of learning. Acton had seen the world, as he said to himself; he had been to China and had knocked about among men. He had learned the essential difference between a nice young fellow and a mean young fellow, and he was satisfied that there was no harm in Clifford. He believed – although it must be added that he had not quite the courage to declare it – in the doctrine of wild oats,[3] which he thought a useful preventive of superfluous fears. If Mr Wentworth and Charlotte and Mr Brand would only apply it in Clifford's case, they would be happier; and Acton thought it a pity they should not be happier. They took the boy's misdemeanours too much to heart; they talked to him too solemnly; they frightened and bewildered him. Of course there was the great standard of morality, which forbade that a man should get tipsy, play at billiards for money, or cultivate his sensual consciousness; but what fear was there that poor Clifford was going to run a tilt at any great standard? It had, however, never occurred to Acton to dedicate the Baroness Münster to the redemption of a refractory collegian. The instrument, here, would have seemed to him quite too complex for the operation. Felix, on the other hand, had spoken in obedience to the belief that the more charming a woman is, the more numerous, literally, are her definite social uses.

Eugenia herself, as we know, had plenty of leisure to enumerate her uses. As I have had the honour of intimating, she had come four thousand miles to seek her fortune; and it is not to be supposed that after this great effort she could neglect any apparent aid to advancement. It is my misfortune that in attempting to describe in a short compass the deportment of this remarkable woman I am obliged to express things rather brutally. I feel this to be the case, for instance, when I say that she had primarily detected such an aid to advancement in the person of Robert Acton, but that she had afterwards remembered that a prudent archer has always a second bowstring. Eugenia was a woman of finely-mingled motive, and her intentions were never sensibly gross. She had a sort of aesthetic ideal for Clifford which seemed to her a disinterested reason for taking him in hand. It was very well for a fresh-coloured young gentleman to be ingenuous; but Clifford, really, was crude. With such a pretty face he ought to have prettier manners. She would teach him that, with a beautiful name, the expectation of a large property, and, as they said in Europe, a social position, an only son should know how to carry himself.

Once Clifford had begun to come and see her by himself and for himself, he came very often. He hardly knew why he should come; he saw her almost every evening at his father's house; he had nothing particular to say to her. She was not a young girl, and fellows of his age called only upon young girls. He exaggerated her age; she seemed to him an old woman; it was happy that the Baroness, with all her intelligence, was incapable of guessing this. But gradually it struck Clifford that visiting old women might be, if not a natural, at least, as they say of some articles of diet, an acquired taste. The Baroness was certainly a very amusing old woman; she talked to him as no lady – and indeed no gentleman – had ever talked to him before.

'You should go to Europe and make the tour,'[4] she said to him one afternoon. 'Of course, on leaving college, you will go.'

'I don't want to go,' Clifford declared. 'I know some fellows who have been to Europe. They say you can have better fun here.'

'That depends. It depends upon your idea of fun. Your friends probably were not introduced.'

'Introduced?' Clifford demanded.

'They had no opportunity of going into society; they formed no *relations*.'[5] This was one of a certain number of words that the Baroness often pronounced in the French manner.

'They went to a ball, in Paris; I know that,' said Clifford.

'Ah, there are balls and balls; especially in Paris. No, you must go, you know; it is not a thing from which you can dispense yourself. You need it.'

'Oh, I'm very well,' said Clifford. 'I'm not sick.'

'I don't mean for your health, my poor child. I mean for your manners.'

'I haven't got any manners!' growled Clifford.

'Precisely. You don't mind my assenting to that, eh?' asked the Baroness with a smile. 'You must go to Europe and get a few. You can get them better there. It is a pity you might not have come while I was living in – in Germany. I would have introduced you; I had a charming little circle. You would perhaps have been rather young; but the younger one begins, I think, the better. Now, at any rate, you have no time to lose, and when I return you must immediately come to me.'

All this, to Clifford's apprehension, was a great mixture – his beginning young, Eugenia's return to Europe, his being introduced to her charming little circle. What was he to begin, and what was her little circle? His ideas about her marriage had a good deal of vagueness; but they were in so far definite as that he felt it to be a matter not to be freely mentioned. He sat and looked all round the room: he supposed she was alluding in some way to her marriage.

'Oh, I don't want to go to Germany,' he said; it seemed to him the most convenient thing to say.

She looked at him a while, smiling with her lips, but not with her eyes. 'You have scruples?' she asked.

'Scruples?' said Clifford.

'You young people, here, are very singular; one doesn't know where to expect you. When you are not extremely improper you are so terribly proper. I daresay you think that, owing to my irregular marriage, I live with loose people. You were never more mistaken. I have been all the more particular.'

'Oh no,' said Clifford, honestly distressed. 'I never thought such a thing as that.'

'Are you very sure? I am convinced that your father does, and your sisters. They say to each other that, here, I am on my good behaviour, but that over there – married by the left hand[6] – I associate with light women.'

'Oh no,' cried Clifford energetically, 'they don't say such things as that to each other!'

'If they think them they had better say them,' the Baroness rejoined. 'Then they can be contradicted. Please contradict that whenever you hear it, and don't be afraid of coming to see me on account of the company I keep. I have the honour of knowing more distinguished men, my poor child, than you are likely to see in a lifetime. I see very few women; but those are women of rank. So, my dear young Puritan, you needn't be afraid. I am not in the least one of those who think that the society of women who have lost their place in the *vrai monde*[7] is necessary to form a young man. I have never taken that tone. I have kept my place myself, and I think we are a much better school than the others. Trust me, Clifford, and I will prove that to you,' the Baroness continued, while she made the agreeable reflexion that she could not, at least, be accused of perverting her young kinsman. 'So if you ever fall among thieves don't go about saying I sent you to them.'

Clifford thought it so comical that he should know – in spite of her figurative language – what she meant, and that she should mean what he knew, that he could hardly help laughing a little, although he tried hard. 'Oh no! oh no!' he murmured.

'Laugh out, laugh out, if I amuse you!' cried the Baroness. 'I am here for that!' And Clifford thought her a very amusing person indeed. 'But remember,' she said on this occasion, 'that you are coming – next year – to pay me a visit over there.'

About a week afterward she said to him, point-blank, 'Are you seriously making love to your little cousin?'

'Seriously making love' – these words, on Madame Münster's lips, had to Clifford's sense a portentous and embarrassing sound; he hesitated about assenting, lest he should commit himself to more than he understood. 'Well, I shouldn't say it if I was!' he exclaimed.

'Why wouldn't you say it?' the Baroness demanded. 'Those things ought to be known.'

'I don't care whether it is known or not,' Clifford rejoined. 'But I don't want people looking at me.'

'A young man of your importance ought to learn to bear observation – to carry himself as if he were quite indifferent to it. I won't say, exactly, unconscious,' the Baroness explained. 'No, he must seem to know he is observed, and to think it natural he should be; but he must appear perfectly used to it. Now you haven't that, Clifford; you haven't that at all. You must have that, you know. Don't tell me you are not a young man of importance,' Eugenia added. 'Don't say anything so flat as that.'

'Oh no, you don't catch me saying that!' cried Clifford.

'Yes, you must come to Germany,' Madame Münster continued. 'I will show you how people can be talked about and yet not seem to know it. You will be talked about, of course, with me; it will be said you are my lover. I will show you how little one may mind that – how little I shall mind it.'

Clifford sat staring, blushing, and laughing. 'I shall mind it a good deal!' he declared.

'Ah, not too much, you know; that would be uncivil. But I give you leave to mind it a little; especially if you have a passion for Miss Acton. *Voyons*; as regards that, you either have, or you have not. It is very simple to say it.'

'I don't see why you want to know,' said Clifford.

'You ought to want me to know. If one is arranging a marriage, one tells one's friends.'

'Oh, I'm not arranging anything,' said Clifford.

'You don't intend to marry your cousin?'

'Well, I expect I shall do as I choose!'

The Baroness leaned her head upon the back of her chair and closed her eyes, as if she were tired. Then opening them again, 'Your cousin is very charming,' she said.

'She is the prettiest girl in this place,' Clifford rejoined.

' "In this place" is saying little; she would be charming anywhere. I am afraid you are entangled.'

'Oh no, I'm not entangled.'

'Are you engaged? At your age that is the same thing.'

Clifford looked at the Baroness with some audacity. 'Will you tell no one?'

'If it's as sacred as that – no.'

'Well, then – we are not!' said Clifford.

'That's the great secret – that you are not, eh?' asked the Baroness, with a quick laugh. 'I am very glad to hear it. You are altogether too young. A young man in your position must choose and compare; he must see the world first. Depend upon it,' she added, 'you should not settle that matter before you have come abroad and paid me that visit. There are several things I should like to call your attention to first.'

'Well, I am rather afraid of that visit,' said Clifford. 'It seems to me it will be rather like going to school again.'

The Baroness looked at him a moment. 'My dear child,' she said, 'there is no agreeable man who has not, at some moment, been to school to a clever woman – probably a little older than himself. And you must be thankful when you get your instruction gratis. With me you would get it gratis.'

The next day Clifford told Lizzie Acton that the Baroness thought her the most charming girl she had ever seen.

Lizzie shook her head. 'No, she doesn't!' she said.

'Do you think everything she says,' asked Clifford, 'is to be taken the opposite way?'

'I think that is!' said Lizzie.

Clifford was going to remark that in this case the Baroness must desire greatly to bring about a marriage between Mr Clifford Wentworth and Miss Elizabeth Acton; but he resolved, on the whole, to suppress this observation.

CHAPTER 9

It seemed to Robert Acton, after Eugenia had come to his house, that something had passed between them which made them a good deal more intimate. It was hard to say exactly what, except her telling him that she had taken her resolution with regard to the Prince Adolf; for Madame Münster's visit had made no difference in their relations. He came to see her very often; but he had come to see her very often before. It was agreeable to him to find himself in her little drawing-room; but this was not a new discovery. There was a change, however, in this sense; that if the Baroness had been a great deal in Acton's thoughts before, she was now never out of them. From the first she had been personally fascinating; but the fascination now had become intellectual as well. He was constantly pondering her words and motions; they were as interesting as the factors in an algebraic problem. This is saying a good deal; for Acton was extremely fond of mathematics. He asked himself whether it could be that he was in love with her, and then hoped he was not; hoped it not so much for his own sake as for that of the amatory passion itself. If this was love, love had been overrated. Love was a poetic impulse, and his own state of feeling with regard to the Baroness was largely characterised by that eminently prosaic sentiment – curiosity. It was true, as Acton with his quietly cogitative habit observed to himself, that curiosity, pushed to a given point, might become a romantic passion; and he certainly thought enough about this charming woman to make him restless and even a little melancholy. It puzzled and vexed him at times to feel that he was not more ardent. He was not in the least bent upon remaining a bachelor. In his younger years he had been – or he had tried to be – of the opinion that it would be a good deal 'jollier' not to marry, and he had flattered himself that his single condition was something of a citadel. It was a citadel, at all events, of which he had long since levelled the outworks. He had removed the guns from the ramparts; he had lowered the drawbridge across the moat. The drawbridge had swayed lightly under Madame Münster's step; why should he not cause it to be raised again, so that she might be kept prisoner? He had an idea that she would become – in time at least, and on learning the conveniences of the place for making a lady comfortable – a tolerably patient captive. But the drawbridge was never raised, and Acton's brilliant visitor was as free to depart as she had been to come. It was part of his curiosity to know why the deuce so susceptible a man was *not* in love with so charming a woman. If her various graces were, as I have said, the factors in an algebraic problem, the answer to this question was the indispensable unknown quantity. The pursuit of the unknown quantity was extremely absorbing; for the present it taxed all Acton's faculties.

Toward the middle of August he was obliged to leave home for some days; an old friend, with whom he had been associated in China, had begged him to come to Newport,[1] where he lay extremely ill. His friend got better, and at the end of a week Acton was released. I use the word 'released' advisedly; for in spite of his attachment to his Chinese comrade he had been but a half-hearted visitor. He felt as if he had been called away from the theatre during the progress of a remarkably interesting drama. The curtain was up all this time, and he was losing the fourth act; that fourth act which would be so essential to a just appreciation of the fifth. In other words, he was thinking about the Baroness, who, seen at this distance, seemed a truly distinguished figure. He saw at Newport a great many pretty women, who certainly were figures as distinguished as beautiful light dresses could make them; but though they talked a great deal – and the Baroness's strong point was perhaps also her conversation – Madame Münster appeared to lose nothing by the comparison. He wished she too had come to Newport. Would it not be possible to make up, as they said, a party for visiting the famous watering-place and invite Eugenia to join it? It was true that the complete satisfaction would be to spend a fortnight at Newport with Eugenia alone. It would be a great pleasure to see her, in society, carry everything before her, as he was sure she would do. When Acton caught himself thinking these thoughts he began to walk up and down, with his hands in his pockets, frowning a little and looking at the floor. What did it prove – for it certainly proved something – this lively disposition to be 'off' somewhere with Madame Münster, away from all the rest of them? Such a vision, certainly, seemed a refined implication of matrimony, after the Baroness should have formally got rid of her informal husband. At any rate, Acton, with his characteristic discretion, forbore to give expression to whatever else it might imply, and the narrator of these incidents is not obliged to be more definite.

He returned home rapidly, and, arriving in the afternoon, lost as little time as possible in joining the familiar circle at Mr Wentworth's. On reaching the house, however, he found the piazzas empty. The doors and windows were open, and their emptiness was made clear by the shafts of lamp-light from the parlours. Entering the house, he found Mr Wentworth sitting alone in one of these apartments, engaged in the perusal of the *North American Review*.[2] After they had exchanged greetings and his cousin had made discreet inquiry about his journey, Acton asked what had become of Mr Wentworth's companions.

'They are scattered about, amusing themselves as usual,' said the old man. 'I saw Charlotte, a short time since, seated, with Mr Brand, upon the piazza. They were conversing with their customary animation. I suppose they have joined her sister, who, for the hundredth time, was doing the honours of the garden to her foreign cousin.'

'I suppose you mean Felix,' said Acton. And on Mr Wentworth's assenting, he said, 'And the others?'

'Your sister has not come this evening. You must have seen her at home,' said Mr Wentworth.

'Yes. I proposed to her to come. She declined.'

'Lizzie, I suppose, was expecting a visitor,' said the old man, with a kind of solemn slyness.

'If she was expecting Clifford, he had not turned up.'

Mr Wentworth, at this intelligence, closed the *North American Review* and remarked that he understood Clifford to say that he was going to see his cousin. Privately, he reflected that if Lizzie Acton had had no news of his son, Clifford must have gone to

Boston for the evening; an unnatural course of a summer night, especially when accompanied with disingenuous representations.

'You must remember that he has two cousins,' said Acton, laughing. And then, coming to the point, 'If Lizzie is not here,' he added, 'neither apparently is the Baroness.'

Mr Wentworth stared a moment, and remembered that queer proposition of Felix's. For a moment he did not know whether it was not to be wished that Clifford, after all, might have gone to Boston. 'The Baroness has not honoured us tonight,' he said. 'She has not come over for three days.'

'Is she ill?' Acton asked.

'No; I have been to see her.'

'What is the matter with her?'

'Well,' said Mr Wentworth, 'I infer she is tired of us.'

Acton pretended to sit down, but he was restless; he found it impossible to talk with Mr Wentworth. At the end of ten minutes he took up his hat and said that he thought he would 'go off'. It was very late; it was ten o'clock.

His quiet-faced kinsman looked at him a moment. 'Are you going home?' he asked.

Acton hesitated, and then answered that he proposed to go over and take a look at the Baroness.

'Well, *you* are honest, at least,' said Mr Wentworth sadly.

'So are you, if you come to that!' cried Acton, laughing. 'Why shouldn't I be honest?'

The old man opened the *North American* again, and read a few lines. 'If we have ever had any virtue amongst us, we had better keep hold of it now,' he said. He was not quoting.[3]

'We have a Baroness amongst us,' said Acton. 'That's what we must keep hold of!' He was too impatient to see Madame Münster again to wonder what Mr Wentworth was talking about. Nevertheless, after he had passed out of the house and traversed the garden and the little piece of road that separated him from Eugenia's provisional residence, he stopped a moment. He stood in her little garden; the long window of her parlour was open, and he could see the white curtains, with the lamp-light shining through them, swaying softly to and fro in the warm night wind. There was a sort of excitement in the idea of seeing Madame Münster again;

he became aware that his heart was beating rather faster than usual. It was this that made him stop, with a half-amused surprise. But in a moment he went along the piazza and, approaching the open window, tapped upon its lintel with his stick. He could see the Baroness within; she was standing in the middle of the room. She came to the window and pulled aside the curtain; then she stood looking at him a moment. She was not smiling; she seemed serious.

'*Mais entrez donc!*'[4] she said at last. Acton passed in across the window-sill; he wondered, for an instant, what was the matter with her. But the next moment she had begun to smile and had put out her hand. 'Better late than never,' she said. 'It is very kind of you to come at this hour.'

'I have just returned from my journey,' said Acton.

'Ah, very kind, very kind,' she repeated, looking about her where to sit.

'I went first to the big house,' Acton continued. 'I expected to find you there.'

She had sunk into her usual chair; but she got up again and began to move about the room. Acton had laid down his hat and stick; he was looking at her, conscious that there was in fact a great charm in seeing her again. 'I don't know whether I ought to tell you to sit down,' she said. 'It is too late to begin a visit.'

'It is too early to end one,' Acton declared; 'and we needn't mind the beginning.'

She looked at him again, and, after a moment, dropped once more into her low chair, while he took a place near her. 'We are in the middle, then?' she asked. 'Was that where we were when you went away? No, I haven't been to the other house.'

'Not yesterday, nor the day before, eh?'

'I don't know how many days it is.'

'You are tired of it?' said Acton.

She leaned back in her chair; her arms were folded. 'That is a terrible accusation, but I have not the courage to defend myself.'

'I am not attacking you,' said Acton. 'I expected something of this kind.'

'It's a proof of extreme intelligence. I hope you enjoyed your journey.'

'Not at all,' Acton declared. 'I would much rather have been here with you.'

'Now you *are* attacking me,' said the Baroness. 'You are contrasting my inconstancy with your own fidelity.'

'I confess I never get tired of people I like.'

'Ah, you are not a poor, wicked, foreign woman, with irritable nerves and a sophisticated mind!'

'Something has happened to you since I went away,' said Acton, changing his place.

'Your going away – that is what has happened to me.'

'Do you mean to say that you have missed me?' he asked.

'If I had meant to say it, it would not be worth your making a note of. I am very dishonest, and my compliments are worthless.'

Acton was silent for some moments. 'You have broken down,' he said at last.

Madame Münster left her chair and began to move about.

'Only for a moment. I shall pull myself together again.'

'You had better not take it too hard. If you are bored, you needn't be afraid to say so – to me at least.'

'You shouldn't say such things as that,' the Baroness answered. 'You should encourage me.'

'I admire your patience; that is encouraging.'

'You shouldn't even say that. When you talk of my patience you are disloyal to your own people. Patience implies suffering; and what have I had to suffer?'

'Oh, not hunger, not unkindness, certainly,' said Acton, laughing. 'Nevertheless, we all admire your patience.'

'You all detest me!' cried the Baroness, with a sudden vehemence, turning her back toward him.

'You make it hard,' said Acton, getting up, 'for a man to say something tender to you.' This evening there was something particularly striking and touching about her; an unwonted softness and a look of suppressed emotion. He felt himself suddenly appreciating the fact that she had behaved very well. She had come to this quiet corner of the world under the weight of a cruel indignity, and she had been so gracefully, modestly thankful for the rest she found there. She had joined that simple circle over the way; she had mingled in its plain provincial talk; she had shared its meagre and savourless pleasures. She had set herself a task, and she had rigidly performed it. She had conformed to the angular conditions of New England life, and she had had the tact and pluck to carry it off as if she liked them. Acton felt a more downright need than he had ever felt before to tell her that he admired her and that she struck him as a very superior woman. All along, hitherto, he had been on his guard with her; he had been cautious, observant, suspicious. But now a certain light tumult in his blood seemed to intimate that a finer degree of confidence in this charming woman would be its own reward. 'We don't detest you,' he went on. 'I don't know what you mean. At any rate, I speak for myself; I don't know anything about the others. Very likely you detest them for the dull life they make you lead. Really, it would give me a sort of pleasure to hear you say so.'

Eugenia had been looking at the door on the other side of the room; now she slowly turned her eyes toward Robert Acton. 'What can be the motive,' she asked, 'of a man like you – an honest man, a *galant homme*⁵ – in saying so base a thing as that?'

'Does it sound very base?' asked Acton candidly. 'I suppose it does, and I thank you for telling me so. Of course I don't mean it literally.'

The Baroness stood looking at him. 'How do you mean it?' she asked.

This question was difficult to answer, and Acton, feeling the least bit foolish, walked to the open window and looked out. He stood there, thinking a moment, and then he turned back. 'You know that document that you were to send to Germany,' he said. 'You called it your "renunciation". Did you ever send it?'

Madame Münster's eyes expanded: she looked very grave. 'What a singular answer to my question!'

'Oh, it isn't an answer,' said Acton. 'I have wished to ask you, many times. I thought it probable you would tell me yourself. The question, on my part, seems abrupt now; but it would be abrupt at any time.'

The Baroness was silent a moment; and then, 'I think I have told you too much!' she said.

This declaration appeared to Acton to have a certain force; he had indeed a sense of asking more of her than he offered her.

He returned to the window and watched, for a moment, a little star that twinkled through the lattice of the piazza. There were at any rate offers enough he could make; perhaps he had hitherto not been sufficiently explicit in doing so. 'I wish you would ask something of me,' he presently said. 'Is there nothing I can do for you? If you can't stand this dull life any more, let me amuse you!'

The Baroness had sunk once more into a chair, and she had taken up a fan which she held, with both hands, to her mouth. Over the top of the fan her eyes were fixed on him. 'You are very strange tonight,' she said with a laugh.

'I will do anything in the world,' he rejoined, standing in front of her. 'Shouldn't you like to travel about and see something of the country? Won't you go to Niagara? You ought to see Niagara, you know.'

'With you, do you mean?'

'I should be delighted to take you.'

'You alone?'

Acton looked at her, smiling, and yet with a serious air. 'Well, yes; we might go alone,' he said.

'If you were not what you are,' she answered, 'I should feel insulted.'

'How do you mean – what I am?'

'If you were one of the gentlemen I have been used to all my life. If you were not a queer Bostonian.'

'If the gentlemen you have been used to have taught you to expect insults,' said Acton, 'I am glad I am what I am. You had much better come to Niagara.'

'If you wish to "amuse" me,' the Baroness declared, 'you need go to no further expense. You amuse me very effectually.'

He sat down opposite to her; she still held her fan up to her face, with her eyes only showing above it. There was a moment's silence, and then he said, returning to his former question, 'Have you sent that document to Germany?'

Again there was a moment's silence. The expressive eyes of Madame Münster seemed, however, half to break it. 'I will tell you – at Niagara!' she said.

She had hardly spoken when the door at the farther end of the room opened – the door upon which, some minutes previous, Eugenia had fixed her gaze. Clifford Wentworth stood there, blushing and looking rather awkward. The Baroness rose, quickly, and Acton, more slowly, did the same. Clifford gave him no greeting; he was looking at Eugenia.

'Ah, you were here?' exclaimed Acton.

'He was in Felix's studio,' said Madame Münster. 'He wanted to see his sketches.'

Clifford looked at Robert Acton, but he said nothing; he only fanned himself with his hat. 'You chose a bad moment,' said Acton; 'you hadn't much light.'

'I hadn't any!' said Clifford, laughing.

'Your candle went out?' Eugenia asked. 'You should have come back here and lighted it again.'

Clifford looked at her a moment. 'So I have – come back. But I have left the candle!'

Eugenia turned away. 'You are very stupid, my poor boy. You had better go home.'

'Well,' said Clifford, 'good-night!'

'Haven't you a word to throw to a man when he has safely returned from a dangerous journey?' Acton asked.

'How do you do?' said Clifford. 'I thought – I thought you were –' And he paused, looking at the Baroness again.

'You thought I was at Newport, eh? So I was – this morning.'

'Good-night, clever child!' said Madame Münster, over her shoulder.

Clifford stared at her – not at all like a clever child; and then, with one of his little facetious growls, took his departure.

'What is the matter with him?' asked Acton, when he was gone. 'He seemed rather in a muddle.'

Eugenia, who was near the window, glanced out, listening a moment. 'The matter – the matter' – she answered. 'But you don't say such things here.'

'If you mean that he had been drinking a little, you can say that.'

'He doesn't drink any more. I have cured him. And in return he is in love with me.'

It was Acton's turn to stare. He instantly thought of his sister;

146

but he said nothing about her. He began to laugh. 'I don't wonder at his passion! But I wonder at his forsaking your society for that of your brother's paint-brushes.'

Eugenia was silent a minute. 'He had not been in the studio. I invented that – at the moment.'

'Invented it? For what purpose?'

'He has an idea of being romantic. He has adopted the habit of coming to see me at midnight – passing only through the orchard and through Felix's painting-room, which has a door opening that way. It seems to amuse him,' added Eugenia, with a little laugh.

Acton felt more surprise than he confessed to, for this was a new view of Clifford, whose irregularities had hitherto been quite without the romantic element. He tried to laugh again, but he felt rather too serious, and after a moment's hesitation his seriousness explained itself. 'I hope you don't encourage him,' he said. 'He must not be inconstant to poor Lizzie.'

'To your sister?'

'You know they are decidedly intimate,' said Acton.

'Ah,' cried Eugenia, smiling, 'has she – has she –'

'I don't know,' Acton interrupted, 'what she has. But I always supposed that Clifford had a desire to make himself agreeable to her.'

'Ah, *par exemple!*' the Baroness went on. 'The little monster! The next time he becomes sentimental I will tell him that he ought to be ashamed of himself.'

Acton was silent a moment. 'You had better say nothing about it.'

'I had told him as much already, on general grounds,' said the Baroness. 'But in this country, you know, the relations of young people are so extraordinary that one is quite at sea. They are not engaged when you would quite say they ought to be. Take Charlotte Wentworth, for instance, and that young ecclesiastic. If I were her father I should insist upon his marrying her; but it appears to be thought there is no urgency. On the other hand, you suddenly learn that a boy of twenty and a little girl who is still with her governess – your sister has no governess? Well, then, who is never away from her mamma – a young couple, in short, between whom you have noticed nothing beyond an exchange of the childish pleasantries characteristic of their age, are on the point of setting up as man and wife.' The Baroness spoke with a certain exaggerated volubility which was in contrast with the languid grace that had characterised her manner before Clifford made his appearance. It seemed to Acton that there was a spark of irritation in her eye – a note of irony (as when she spoke of Lizzie being never away from her mother) in her voice. If Madame Münster was irritated, Robert Acton was vaguely mystified; she began to move about the room again, and he looked at her without saying anything. Presently she took out her watch, and, glancing at it, declared that it was three o'clock in the morning, and that he must go.

'I have not been here an hour,' he said, 'and they are still sitting up at the big house. You can see the lights. Your brother has not come in.'

'Oh, at the big house,' cried Eugenia, 'they are terrible people! I don't know what they may do over there. I am a quiet little humdrum woman; I have rigid rules, and I keep them. One of them is not to have visitors in the small hours – especially clever men like you. So good-night!'

Decidedly the Baroness was incisive; and though Acton bade her good-night and departed, he was still a good deal mystified.

The next day Clifford Wentworth came to see Lizzie, and Acton, who was at home and saw him pass through the garden, took note of the circumstance. He had a natural desire to make it tally with Madame Münster's account of Clifford's disaffection; but his ingenuity, finding itself unequal to the task, resolved at last to ask help of the young man's candour. He waited till he saw him going away, and then he went out and overtook him in the grounds.

'I wish very much you would answer me a question,' Acton said. 'What were you doing last night at Madame Münster's?'

Clifford began to laugh and to blush, by no means like a young man with a romantic secret. 'What did she tell you?' he asked.

'That is exactly what I don't want to say.'

'Well, I want to tell you the same,' said Clifford; 'and unless I know it perhaps I can't.'

They had stopped in a garden path; Acton looked hard at his rosy young kinsman. 'She said she couldn't fancy what had got into you; you appeared to have taken a violent dislike to her.'

Clifford stared, looking a little alarmed. 'Oh, come,' he growled, 'you don't mean that!'

'And that when – for common civility's sake – you came occasionally to the house, you left her alone and spent your time in Felix's studio, under pretext of looking at his sketches.'

'Oh, come!' growled Clifford, again.

'Did you ever know me to tell an untruth?'

'Yes, lots of them!' said Clifford, seeing an opening out of the discussion for his sarcastic powers. 'Well,' he presently added, 'I thought you were my father.'

'You knew someone was there?'

'We heard you coming in.'

Acton meditated. 'You had been with the Baroness, then?'

'I was in the parlour. We heard your step outside. I thought it was my father.'

'And on that,' asked Acton, 'you ran away?'

'She told me to go – to go out by the studio.'

Acton meditated more intensely; if there had been a chair at hand he would have sat down. 'Why should she wish you not to meet your father?'

'Well,' said Clifford, 'father doesn't like to see me there.'

Acton looked askance at his companion, and forbore to make any comment upon this assertion. 'Has he said so,' he asked, 'to the Baroness?'

'Well, I hope not,' said Clifford. 'He hasn't said so – in so many words – to me. But I know it worries him; and I want to stop worrying him. The Baroness knows it, and she wants me to stop too.'

'To stop coming to see her?'

'I don't know about that; but to stop worrying father. Eugenia knows everything,' Clifford added, with an air of knowingness of his own.

'Ah,' said Acton interrogatively, 'Eugenia knows everything?'

'She knew it was not father coming in.'

'Then why did you go?'

Clifford blushed and laughed afresh. 'Well, I was afraid it was. And besides, she told me to go at any rate.'

'Did she think it was I?' Acton asked.

'She didn't say so.'

Again Robert Acton reflected. 'But you didn't go,' he presently said; 'you came back.'

'I couldn't get out of the studio,' Clifford rejoined. 'The door was locked, and Felix has nailed some planks across the lower half of the confounded windows, to make the light come in from above. So they were no use. I waited there a good while, and then suddenly I felt ashamed. I didn't want to be hiding away from my own father. I couldn't stand it any longer. I bolted out, and when I found it was you I was a little flurried. But Eugenia carried it off, didn't she?' Clifford added, in the tone of a young humourist whose perception had not been permanently clouded by the sense of his own discomfort.

'Beautifully!' said Acton. 'Especially,' he continued, 'when one remembers that you were very imprudent and that she must have been a good deal annoyed.'

'Oh,' cried Clifford, with the indifference of a young man who feels that however he may have failed of felicity in behaviour, he is extremely just in his impressions, 'Eugenia doesn't care for anything!'

Acton hesitated a moment. 'Thank you for telling me this,' he said at last. And then, laying his hand on Clifford's shoulder, he added, 'Tell me one thing more: are you by chance the least bit sweet on the Baroness?'

'No, sir!' said Clifford, almost shaking off his hand.

CHAPTER 10

THE first Sunday that followed Robert Acton's return from Newport witnessed a change in the brilliant weather that had long prevailed. The rain began to fall and the day was cold and dreary. Mr Wentworth and his daughters put on overshoes and went to church, and Felix Young, without overshoes, went also, holding an umbrella over Gertrude. It is to be feared that, in the whole observance, this was the privilege he most highly valued. The Baroness remained at home; she was in neither a cheerful nor a devotional mood. She had, however, never been, during her residence in the United States, what is called a regular attendant at divine service; and on this particular Sunday morning of which I began with speaking she stood at the window of her little drawing-room, watching the long arm of a rose tree that was attached to her piazza, but a portion of which had disengaged itself, sway to and fro, shake and gesticulate, against the dusky drizzle of the sky. Every now and then, in a gust of wind, the rose tree scattered a shower of water-drops against the window-pane; it appeared to have a kind of human movement – a menacing, warning intention. The room was very cold; Madame Münster put on a shawl and walked about. Then she determined to have some fire; and summoning her ancient negress, the contrast of whose polished ebony and whose crimson turban had been at first a source of satisfaction to her, she made arrangements for the production of a crackling flame. This old woman's name was Azarina. The Baroness had begun by thinking that there would be a savoury wildness in her talk, and, for amusement, she had encouraged her to chatter. But Azarina was dry and prim; her conversation was anything but African; she reminded Eugenia of the tiresome old ladies she met in society. She knew, however, how to make a fire; so that after she had laid the logs, Eugenia, who was terribly bored, found a quarter of an hour's entertainment in sitting and watching them blaze and sputter. She had thought it very likely Robert Acton would come and see her; she had not met him since that infelicitous evening. But the morning waned without his coming; several times she thought she heard his step on the piazza, but it was only a window-shutter shaking in a rain-gust. The Baroness, since the beginning of that episode in her career of which a slight sketch has been attempted in these pages, had had many moments of irritation. But today her irritation had a peculiar keenness; it appeared to feed upon itself. It urged her to do something; but it suggested no particularly profitable line of action. If she could have done something at the moment, on the spot, she would have stepped upon a European steamer and turned her back, with a kind of rapture, upon that profoundly mortifying failure, her visit to her American relations. It is not exactly apparent why she should have termed this enterprise a failure, inasmuch as she had been treated with the highest distinction for which allowance had been made in American institutions. Her irritation came, at bottom, from the sense, which, always present, had suddenly grown acute, that the social soil on this big, vague continent was somehow not adapted for growing those plants whose fragrance she especially inclined to inhale, and by which she liked to see herself surrounded – a species of vegetation for which she carried a collection of seed-lings, as we may say, in her pocket. She found her chief happiness in the sense of exerting a certain power and making a certain impression; and now she felt the annoyance of a rather wearied swimmer who, on nearing shore, to land, finds a smooth straight wall of rock when he had counted upon a clean firm beach. Her power, in the American air, seemed to have lost its prehensile attributes; the smooth wall of rock was insurmountable. 'Surely *je n'en suis pas là*,'[1] she said to herself, 'that I let it make me uncomfortable that a Mr Robert Acton shouldn't honour me with a visit!' Yet she was vexed that he had not come; and she was vexed at her vexation.

Her brother, at least, came in, stamping in the hall and shaking the wet from his coat. In a moment he entered the room, with a glow in his cheek and half a dozen rain-drops glistening on his moustache. 'Ah, you have a fire,' he said.

'*Les beaux jours sont passés,*'[2] replied the Baroness.

'Never, never! They have only begun,' Felix declared, planting himself before the hearth. He turned his back to the fire, placed his hands behind him, extended his legs and looked away through the window with an expression of face which seemed to denote the perception of rose-colour even in the tints of a wet Sunday.

His sister, from her chair, looked up at him, watching him; and what she saw in his face was not grateful to her present mood. She was not puzzled by many things, but her brother's disposition was a frequent source of wonder to her. I say frequent, and not constant, for there were long periods during which she gave her attention to other problems. Sometimes she had said to herself that his happy temper, his eternal gaiety, was an affectation, a *pose*; but she was vaguely conscious that during the present summer he had been a highly successful comedian. They had never yet had an explanation; she had not known the need of one. Felix was presumably following the bent of his disinterested genius, and she felt that she had no advice to give him that he would understand. With this, there was always a certain element of comfort about Felix – the assurance that he would not interfere. He was very delicate, this pure-minded Felix; in effect, he was her brother, and Madame Münster felt that there was a great propriety, every way, in that. It is true that Felix was delicate; he was not fond of explanations with his sister; this was one of the very few things in the world about which he was uncomfortable. But now he was not thinking of anything uncomfortable.

'Dear brother,' said Eugenia at last, 'do stop making *les yeux doux*[3] at the rain.'

'With pleasure. I will make them at you!' answered Felix.

'How much longer,' asked Eugenia, in a moment, 'do you propose to remain in this lovely spot?'

Felix stared. 'Do you want to go away – already?'

'"Already" is delicious. I am not so happy as you.'

Felix dropped into a chair, looking at the fire. 'The fact is I *am* happy,' he said, in his light, clear tone.

'And do you propose to spend your life in making love to Gertrude Wentworth?'

'Yes!' said Felix, smiling sidewise at his sister.

The Baroness returned his glance, much more gravely; and then, 'Do you like her?' she asked.

'Don't you?' Felix demanded.

The Baroness was silent a moment. 'I will answer you in the words of the gentleman who was asked if he liked music: *"Je ne la crains pas!"'*[4]

'She admires you immensely,' said Felix.

'I don't care for that. Other women should not admire one.'

'They should dislike you?'

Again Madame Münster hesitated. 'They should hate me! It's a measure of the time I have been losing here that they don't.'

'No time is lost in which one has been happy!' said Felix, with a bright sententiousness which may well have been a little irritating.

'And in which,' rejoined his sister, with a harsher laugh, 'one has secured the affections of a young lady with a fortune!'

Felix explained very candidly and seriously. 'I have secured Getrude's affection, but I am by no means sure that I have secured her fortune. That may come – or it may not.'

'Ah, well, it *may*! That's the great point.'

'It depends upon her father. He doesn't smile upon our union. You know he wants her to marry Mr Brand.'

'I know nothing about it!' cried the Baroness. 'Please to put on a log.' Felix complied with her request and sat watching the quickening of the flame. Presently his sister added, 'And you propose to elope with mademoiselle?'

'By no means. I don't wish to do anything that's disagreeable to Mr Wentworth. He has been far too kind to us.'

'But you must choose between pleasing yourself and pleasing him.'

'I want to please everyone!' exclaimed Felix joyously. 'I have a good conscience. I made up my mind at the outset that it was not my place to make love to Gertrude.'

'So, to simplify matters, she made love to you?'

Felix looked at his sister with sudden gravity. 'You say you are not afraid of her,' he said. 'But perhaps you ought to be – a little. She's a very clever person.'

'I begin to see it!' cried the Baroness. Her brother, making no rejoinder, leaned back in his chair, and there was a long silence.

At last, with an altered accent, Madame Münster put another question, 'You expect, at any rate, to marry?'

'I shall be greatly disappointed if we don't.'

'A disappointment or two will do you good!' the Baroness declared. 'And afterwards, do you mean to turn American?'

'It seems to me I am a very good American already. But we shall go to Europe. Gertrude wants extremely to see the world.'

'Ah, like me, when I came here!' said the Baroness with a little laugh.

'No, not like you,' Felix rejoined, looking at his sister with a certain gentle seriousness. While he looked at her she rose from her chair, and he also got up. 'Gertrude is not at all like you,' he went on; 'but in her own way she is almost as clever.' He paused a moment; his soul was full of an agreeable feeling, and of a lively disposition to express it. His sister, to his spiritual vision, was always like the lunar disk when only a part of it is lighted. The shadow on this bright surface seemed to him to expand and to contract; but whatever its proportions, he always appreciated the moonlight. He looked at the Baroness, and then he kissed her. 'I am very much in love with Gertrude,' he said. Eugenia turned away and walked about the room, and Felix continued, 'She is very interesting, and very different from what she seems. She has never had a chance. She is very brilliant. We will go to Europe and amuse ourselves.'

The Baroness had gone to the window, where she stood looking out. The day was drearier than ever; the rain was doggedly falling. 'Yes, to amuse yourselves,' she said at last, 'you had decidedly better go to Europe!' Then she turned round, looking at her brother. A chair stood near her; she leaned her hands upon the back of it. 'Don't you think it is very good of me,' she asked, 'to come all this way with you simply to see you properly married – if properly it is?'

'Oh, it will be properly,' cried Felix, with light eagerness.

The Baroness gave a little laugh. 'You are thinking only of yourself, and you don't answer my question. While you are amusing yourself – with the brilliant Gertrude – what shall I be doing?'

'Vous serez de la partie!'[5] cried Felix.

'Thank you; I should spoil it.' The Baroness dropped her eyes for some moments. 'Do you propose, however, to leave me here?' she inquired.

Felix smiled at her. 'My dearest sister, where you are concerned I never propose. I execute your commands.'

'I believe,' said Eugenia slowly, 'that you are the most heartless person living. Don't you see that I am in trouble?'

'I saw that you were not cheerful, and I gave you some good news.'

'Well, let me give you some news,' said the Baroness. 'You probably will not have discovered it for yourself. Robert Acton wants to marry me.'

'No, I had not discovered that. But I quite understand it. Why does it make you unhappy?'

'Because I can't decide.'

'Accept him, accept him!' cried Felix joyously. 'He is the best fellow in the world.'

'He is immensely in love with me,' said the Baroness.

'And he has a large fortune. Permit me in turn to remind you of that.'

'Oh, I am perfectly aware of it,' said Eugenia. 'That's a great item in his favour. I am terribly candid.' And she left her place and came nearer her brother, looking at him hard. He was turning over several things; she was wondering in what manner he really understood her.

There were several ways of understanding her: there was what she said, and there was what she meant, and there was something, between the two, that was neither. It is probable that, in the last analysis, what she meant was that Felix should spare her the necessity of stating the case more exactly, and should hold himself commissioned to assist her by all honourable means to marry the best fellow in the world. But in all this it was never discovered what Felix understood.

'Once you have your liberty, what are your objections?' he asked.

'Well, I don't particularly like him.'

'Oh, try a little.'

'I am trying now,' said Eugenia. 'I should succeed better if he didn't live here. I could never live here.'

'Make him go to Europe,' Felix suggested.

'Ah, there you speak of happiness based upon violent effort,' the Baroness rejoined. 'That is not what I am looking for. He would never live in Europe.'

'He would live anywhere, with you!' said Felix gallantly.

His sister looked at him still, with a ray of penetration in her charming eyes; then she turned away again. 'You see, at all events,' she presently went on, 'that if it had been said of me that I had come over here to seek my fortune it would have to be added that I have found it!'

'Don't leave it lying!' urged Felix, with smiling solemnity.

'I am much obliged to you for your interest,' his sister declared, after a moment. 'But promise me one thing: *pas de zèle!*[6] If Mr Acton should ask you to plead his cause, excuse yourself.'

'I shall certainly have the excuse,' said Felix, 'that I have a cause of my own to plead.'

'If he should talk of me – favourably,' Eugenia continued, 'warn him against dangerous illusions. I detest importunities; I want to decide at my leisure, with my eyes open.'

'I shall be discreet,' said Felix, 'except to you. To you I will say, Accept him outright.'

She had advanced to the open doorway, and she stood looking at him. 'I will go and dress, and think of it,' she said; and he heard her moving slowly to her apartments.

Late in the afternoon the rain stopped, and just afterwards there was a great flaming, flickering, trickling sunset. Felix sat in his painting-room and did some work; but at last, as the light, which had not been brilliant, began to fade, he laid down his brushes and came out to the little piazza of the cottage. Here he walked up and down for some time, looking at the splendid blaze of the western sky, and saying, as he had often said before, that this was certainly the country of sunsets. There was something in these glorious deeps of fire that quickened his imagination; he always found images and promises in the western sky. He thought of a good many things – of roaming about the world with Gertrude Wentworth; he seemed to see their possible adventures, in a glowing frieze, between the cloud-bars; then of what Eugenia had just been telling him. He wished very much that Madame Münster would make a comfortable and honourable marriage. Presently, as the sunset expanded and deepened, the fancy took him of making a note of so magnificent a piece of colouring. He returned to his studio and fetched out a small panel, with his palette and brushes, and, placing the panel against a window-sill, he began to daub with great gusto. While he was so occupied he saw Mr Brand, in the distance, slowly come down from Mr Wentworth's house, nursing a large folded umbrella. He walked with a joyless, meditative tread, and his eyes were bent upon the ground. Felix poised his brush for a moment, watching him; then, by a sudden impulse, as he drew nearer, advanced to the garden gate and signalled to him – the palette and bunch of brushes contributing to this effect.

Mr Brand stopped and started; then he appeared to decide to accept Felix's invitation. He came out of Mr Wentworth's gate and passed along the road; after which he entered the little garden of the cottage. Felix had gone back to his sunset; but he made his visitor welcome while he rapidly brushed it in.

'I wanted so much to speak to you that I thought I would call you,' he said, in the friendliest tone. 'All the more that you have been to see me so little. You have come to see my sister; I know that. But you haven't come to see me – the celebrated artist. Artists are very sensitive, you know; they notice those things.' And Felix turned round, smiling, with a brush in his mouth.

Mr Brand stood there with a certain blank, candid majesty, pulling together the large flaps of his umbrella. 'Why should I come to see you?' he asked. 'I know nothing of Art.'

'It would sound very conceited, I suppose,' said Felix, 'if I were to say that it would be a good little chance for you to learn something. You would ask me why you should learn; and I should have no answer to that. I suppose a minister has no need for Art, eh?'

'He has need for good temper, sir,' said Mr Brand, with decision.

Felix jumped up, with his palette on his thumb and a movement of the liveliest deprecation. 'That's because I keep you standing there while I splash my red paint! I beg a thousand pardons! You see what bad manners Art gives a man; and how right you are to let it alone. I didn't mean you should stand either. The piazza, as you see, is ornamented with rustic chairs; though indeed I ought to warn you that they have nails in the wrong places. I was just making a note of that sunset. I never saw such a blaze of different reds. It looks as if the Celestial City[7] were in flames, eh? If that were really the case I suppose it would be the business of you theologians to put out the fire. Fancy me – an ungodly artist – quietly sitting down to paint it!'

Mr Brand had always credited Felix Young with a certain impudence, but it appeared to him that on this occasion his impudence was so great as to make a special explanation – or even an apology – necessary. And the impression, it must be added, was sufficiently natural. Felix had at all times a brilliant assurance of manner which was simply the vehicle of his good spirits and his good will; but at present he had a special design, and as he would have admitted that the design was audacious, so he was conscious of having summoned all the arts of conversation to his aid. But he was so far from desiring to offend his visitor that he was rapidly asking himself what personal compliment he could pay the young clergyman that would gratify him most. If he could think of it, he was prepared to pay it down. 'Have you been preaching one of your beautiful sermons today?' he suddenly asked, laying down his palette. This was not what Felix had been trying to think of, but it was a tolerable stop-gap.

Mr Brand frowned – as much as a man can frown who has very fair, soft eyebrows, and, beneath them, very gentle, tranquil eyes. 'No, I have not preached any sermon today. Did you bring me over here for the purpose of making that inquiry?'

Felix saw that he was irritated, and he regretted it immensely; but he had no fear of not being, in the end, agreeable to Mr Brand. He looked at him, smiling, and laying his hand on his arm. 'No, no, not for that – not for that. I wanted to ask you something; I wanted to tell you something. I am sure it will interest you very much. Only – as it is something rather private – we had better come into my little studio. I have a western window; we can still see the sunset. *Andiamo!*[8] And he gave a little pat to his companion's arm.

He led the way in; Mr Brand stiffly and softly followed. The twilight had thickened in the little studio; but the wall opposite the western window was covered with a deep pink flush. There were a great many sketches and half-finished canvases suspended in this rosy glow, and the corners of the room were vague and dusky. Felix begged Mr Brand to sit down; then glancing round him, 'By Jove, how pretty it looks!' he cried. But Mr Brand would not sit down; he went and leaned against the window; he wondered what Felix wanted of him. In the shadow, on the darker parts of the wall, he saw the gleam of three or four pictures that looked fantastic and surprising. They seemed to represent naked figures. Felix stood there with his head a little bent and his eyes fixed upon his visitor, smiling intensely, pulling his moustache. Mr Brand felt vaguely uneasy. 'It is very delicate – what I want to say,' Felix began. 'But I have been thinking of it for some time.'

'Please to say it as quickly as possible,' said Mr Brand.

'It's because you are a clergyman, you know,' Felix went on. 'I don't think I should venture to say it to a common man.'

Mr Brand was silent a moment. 'If it is a question of yielding to a weakness, of resenting an injury, I am afraid I am a very common man.'

'My dearest friend,' cried Felix, 'this is not an injury; it's a benefit – a great service! You will like it extremely. Only it's so delicate!' And, in the dim light, he continued to smile intensely. 'You know I take a great interest im my cousins – in Charlotte and Gertrude Wentworth. That's very evident from my having travelled some five thousand miles to see them.' Mr Brand said nothing, and Felix proceeded. 'Coming into their society as a perfect stranger I received of course a great many new impressions, and my impressions had a great freshness, a great keenness. Do you know what I mean?'

'I am not sure that I do; but I should like you to continue.'

'I think my impressions have always had a good deal of freshness,' said Mr Brand's entertainer; 'but on this occasion it was perhaps particularly natural that – coming in, as I say, from outside – I should be struck with things that passed unnoticed among yourselves. And then I had my sister to help me; and she is simply the most observant woman in the world.'

'I am not surprised,' said Mr Brand, 'that in our little circle two intelligent persons should have found food for observation. I am sure that, of late, I have found it myself!'

'Ah, but I shall surprise you yet!' cried Felix, laughing. 'Both my sister and I took a great fancy to my cousin Charlotte.'

'Your cousin Charlotte?' repeated Mr Brand.

'We fell in love with her from the first!'

'You fell in love with Charlotte?' Mr Brand murmured.

*'Dame!'*⁹ exclaimed Felix, 'she's a very charming person; and Eugenia was especially smitten.' Mr Brand stood staring, and he pursued, 'Affection, you know, opens one's eyes, and we noticed something. Charlotte is not happy! Charlotte is in love.' And Felix, drawing nearer, laid his hand again upon his companion's arm.

There was something akin to an acknowledgment of fascination in the way Mr Brand looked at him; but the young clergyman retained as yet quite enough self-possession to be able to say, with a good deal of solemnity, 'She is not in love with you.'

Felix gave a light laugh, and rejoined with the alacrity of a maritime adventurer who feels a puff of wind in his sail. 'Ah no; if she were in love with me I should know it! I am not so blind as you.'

'As I?'

'My dear sir, you are stone blind. Poor Charlotte is dead in love with *you*!'

Mr Brand said nothing for a moment; he breathed a little heavily. 'Is that what you wanted to say to me?' he asked.

'I have wanted to say it these three weeks. Because of late she has been worse. I told you,' added Felix, 'it was very delicate.'

'Well, sir' – Mr Brand began; 'well, sir –'

'I was sure you didn't know it,' Felix continued. 'But don't you see – as soon as I mention it – how everything is explained?' Mr Brand answered nothing; he looked for a chair and softly sat down. Felix could see that he was blushing; he had looked straight at his host hitherto, but now he looked away. The foremost effect of what he had heard had been a sort of irritation of his modesty. 'Of course,' said Felix, 'I suggest nothing; it would be very presumptuous in me to advise you. But I think there is no doubt about the fact.'

Mr Brand looked hard at the floor for some moments; he was oppressed with a mixture of sensations. Felix, standing there, was very sure that one of them was profound surprise. The innocent young man had been completely unsuspicious of poor Charlotte's hidden flame. This gave Felix great hope; he was sure that Mr

Brand would be flattered. Felix thought him very transparent, and indeed he was so; he could neither simulate nor dissimulate. 'I scarcely know what to make of this,' he said at last, without looking up; and Felix was struck with the fact that he offered no protest or contradiction. Evidently Felix had kindled a train of memories – a retrospective illumination. It was making, to Mr Brand's astonished eyes, a very pretty blaze; his second emotion had been a gratification of vanity.

'Thank me for telling you,' Felix rejoined. 'It's a good thing to know.'

'I am not sure of that,' said Mr Brand.

'Ah, don't let her languish!' Felix murmured, lightly and softly.

'You *do* advise me, then?' And Mr Brand looked up.

'I congratulate you!' said Felix, smiling. He had thought at first his visitor was simply appealing; but he saw he was a little ironical.

'It is in your interest; you have interfered with me,' the young clergyman went on.

Felix still stood and smiled. The little room had grown darker, and the crimson glow had faded; but Mr Brand could see the brilliant expression of his face. 'I won't pretend not to know what you mean,' said Felix at last. 'But I have not really interfered with you. Of what you had to lose – with another person – you have lost nothing. And think what you have gained!'

'It seems to me I am the proper judge, on each side,' Mr Brand declared. He got up, holding the brim of his hat against his mouth and staring at Felix through the dusk.

'You have lost an illusion!' said Felix.

'What do you call an illusion?'

'The belief that you really know – that you have ever really known – Gertrude Wentworth. Depend upon that,' pursued Felix. 'I don't know her yet; but I have no illusions; I don't pretend to.'

Mr Brand kept gazing, over his hat. 'She has always been a lucid, limpid nature,' he said solemnly.

'She has always been a dormant nature. She was waiting for a touchstone.[10] But now she is beginning to awaken.'

'Don't praise her to me!' said Mr Brand, with a little quaver in his voice. 'If you have the advantage of me that is not generous.'

'My dear sir, I am melting with generosity!' exclaimed Felix. 'And I am not praising my cousin. I am simply attempting a scientific definition of her. She doesn't care for abstractions. Now I think the contrary is what you have always fancied – is the basis on which you have been building. She is extremely preoccupied with the concrete. I care for the concrete too. But Gertrude is stronger than I; she whirls me along!'

Mr Brand looked for a moment into the crown of his hat. 'It's a most interesting nature.'

'So it is,' said Felix. 'But it pulls – it pulls – like a runaway horse. Now, I like the feeling of a runaway horse; and if I am thrown out of the vehicle it is no great matter. But if *you* should be thrown, Mr Brand,' – and Felix paused a moment – 'another person also would suffer from the accident.'

'What other person?'

'Charlotte Wentworth!'

Mr Brand looked at Felix for a moment sidewise, mistrustfully; then his eyes slowly wandered over the ceiling. Felix was sure he was secretly struck with the romance of the situation. 'I think this is none of our business,' the young minister murmured.

'None of mine, perhaps; but surely yours!'

Mr Brand lingered still, looking at the ceiling; there was evidently something he wanted to say. 'What do you mean by Miss Gertrude being strong?' he asked abruptly.

'Well,' said Felix meditatively, 'I mean that she has had a great deal of self-possession. She was waiting – for years; even when she seemed, perhaps, to be living in the present. She knew how to wait; she had a purpose. That's what I mean by her being strong.'

'What do you mean by her purpose?'

'Well – the purpose to see the world!'

Mr Brand eyed his strange informant askance again; but he said nothing. At last he turned away, as if to take leave. He seemed bewildered, however; for instead of going to the door he moved toward the opposite corner of the room. Felix stood and watched him for a moment – almost groping about in the dusk; then he led him to the door, with a tender, almost fraternal movement. 'Is that all you have to say?' asked Mr Brand.

'Yes, it's all – but it will bear a good deal of thinking of.'

Felix went with him to the garden gate, and watched him slowly walk away into the thickening twilight with a relaxed rigidity that tried to rectify itself. 'He is offended, excited, bewildered, perplexed – and enchanted!' Felix said to himself. 'That's a capital mixture.'

CHAPTER 11

SINCE that visit paid by the Baroness Münster to Mrs Acton, of which some account was given at an earlier stage of this narrative, the intercourse between these two ladies had been neither frequent nor intimate. It was not that Mrs Acton had failed to appreciate Madame Münster's charms; on the contrary, her perception of the graces of manner and conversation of her brilliant visitor had been only too acute. Mrs Acton was, as they said in Boston, very 'intense,' and her impressions were apt to be too many for her. The state of her health required the restriction of emotion; and this is why, receiving, as she sat in her eternal arm-chair, very few visitors, even of the soberest local type, she had been obliged to limit the number of her interviews with a lady whose costume and manner recalled to her imagination – Mrs Acton's imagination was a marvel – all that she had ever read of the most stirring historical periods. But she had sent the Baroness a great many quaintly-worded messages, and a great many nosegays from her garden, and baskets of beautiful fruit. Felix had eaten the fruit, and the Baroness had arranged the flowers and returned the baskets and the messages. On the day that followed that rainy Sunday of which mention has been made, Eugenia determined to go and pay the beneficent invalid a *'visite d'adieux'*;[1] so it was that, to herself, she qualified her enterprise. It may be noted that neither on the Sunday evening nor on the Monday morning had she received that expected visit from Robert Acton. To his own consciousness, evidently, he was 'keeping away'; and as the Baroness, on her side, was keeping away from her uncle's, whither, for several days, Felix had been the unembarrassed bearer of apologies and regrets for absence, chance had not taken the cards from the hands of design. Mr Wentworth and his daughters had respected Eugenia's seclusion; certain intervals of mysterious retirement appeared to them, vaguely, a natural part of the graceful, rhythmic movement of so remarkable a life. Gertrude especially held these periods in honour; she wondered what Madame Münster did at such times, but she would not have permitted herself to inquire too curiously.

The long rain had freshened the air, and twelve hours' brilliant sunshine had dried the roads; so that the Baroness, in the late afternoon, proposing to walk to Mrs Acton's, exposed herself to no great discomfort. As with her charming undulating step she moved along the clean, grassy margin of the road, beneath the thickly-hanging boughs of the orchards, through the quiet of the hour and place, and the rich maturity of the summer, she was even conscious of a sort of luxurious melancholy. The Baroness had the amiable weakness of attaching herself to places – even when she had begun with a little aversion; and now, with the prospect of departure, she felt tenderly toward this well-wooded corner of the Western world, where the sunsets were so beautiful and one's ambitions were so pure. Mrs Acton was able to receive her; but on entering this lady's large, freshly-scented room the Baroness saw that she was looking very ill. She was wonderfully white and transparent, and, in her flowered arm-chair, she made no attempt to move. But she flushed a little – like a young girl, the Baroness thought – and she rested her clear, smiling eyes upon those of her visitor. Her voice was low and monotonous, like a voice that had never expressed any human passions.

'I have come to bid you good-bye,' said Eugenia. 'I shall soon be going away.'

'When are you going away?'

'Very soon – any day.'

'I am very sorry,' said Mrs Acton. 'I hoped you would stay – always.'

'Always?' Eugenia demanded.

'Well, I mean a long time,' said Mrs Acton, in her sweet, feeble tone. 'They tell me you are so comfortable – that you have got such a beautiful little house.'

Eugenia stared – that is, she smiled; she thought of her poor little chalet, and she wondered whether her hostess were jesting.

'Yes, my house is exquisite,' she said; 'though not to be compared to yours.'

'And my son is so fond of going to see you,' Mrs Acton added. 'I am afraid my son will miss you.'

'Ah, dear madam,' said Eugenia, with a little laugh, 'I can't stay in America for your son!'

'Don't you like America?'

The Baroness looked at the front of her dress. 'If I liked it – that would not be staying for your son!'

Mrs Acton gazed at her with her grave tender eyes, as if she had not quite understood. The Baroness at last found something irritating in the sweet, soft stare of her hostess; and if one were not bound to be merciful to great invalids she would almost have taken the liberty of pronouncing her, mentally, a fool. 'I am afraid, then, I shall never see you again,' said Mrs Acton. 'You know I am dying.'

'Ah, dear madam,' murmured Eugenia.

'I want to leave my children cheerful and happy. My daughter will probably marry her cousin.'

'Two such interesting young people,' said the Baroness vaguely. She was not thinking of Clifford Wentworth.

'I feel so tranquil about my end,' Mrs Acton went on. 'It is coming so easily, so surely.' And she paused, with her mild gaze always on Eugenia's.

The Baroness hated to be reminded of death; but even in its imminence, so far as Mrs Acton was concerned, she preserved her good manners. 'Ah, madam, you are too charming an invalid,' she rejoined.

But the delicacy of this rejoinder was apparently lost upon her hostess, who went on in her low, reasonable voice. 'I want to leave my children bright and comfortable. You seem to me all so happy here – just as you are. So I wish you could stay. It would be so pleasant for Robert.'

Eugenia wondered what she meant by its being pleasant for Robert; but she felt that she would never know what such a woman as that meant. She got up; she was afraid Mrs Acton would tell her again that she was dying. 'Good-bye, dear madam,' she said. 'I must remember that your strength is precious.'

Mrs Acton took her hand and held it a moment. 'Well, you *have* been happy here, haven't you? And you like us all, don't you? I wish you would stay,' she added, 'in your beautiful little house.'

She had told Eugenia that her waiting-woman would be in the hall, to show her downstairs; but the large landing outside her door was empty, and Eugenia stood there looking about. She felt irritated; the dying lady had not *'la main heureuse'*.[2] She passed slowly downstairs, still looking about. The broad staircase made a great bend, and in the angle was a high window, looking westward, with a deep bench, covered with a row of flowering plants in curious old pots of blue China-ware. The yellow afternoon light came in through the flowers and flickered a little on the white wainscots. Eugenia paused a moment; the house was perfectly still, save for the ticking, somewhere, of a great clock. The lower hall stretched away at the foot of the stairs, half covered over with a large Oriental rug. Eugenia lingered a little, noticing a great many things. *'Comme c'est bien!'*[3] she said to herself; such a large, solid, irreproachable basis of existence the place seemed to her to indicate. And then she reflected that Mrs Acton was soon to withdraw from it. The reflexion accompanied her the rest of the way downstairs, where she paused again, making more observations. The hall was extremely broad, and on either side of the front door was a wide, deeply-set window, which threw the shadows of everything back into the house. There were high-backed chairs along the wall and big Eastern vases upon tables and, on either side, a large cabinet with a glass front and little curiosities within, dimly gleaming. The doors were open – into the darkened parlour, the library, the dining-room. All these rooms seemed empty. Eugenia passed along, and stopped a moment on the threshold of each. *'Comme c'est bien!'* she murmured again; she had thought of just such a house as this when she decided to come to America. She opened the front door for herself – her light tread had summoned none of the servants – and on the threshold she gave a last look. Outside, she was still in the humour for curious contemplation; so instead of going directly down the little drive, to the gate, she wandered away toward the garden, which lay to the right of the house. She had not gone many yards over the grass before she paused quickly; she perceived a gentleman stretched upon the level verdure, beneath a tree. He had not heard her coming, and he lay motionless, flat on his back, with his hands clasped under his head, staring up at the sky; so that the Baroness was able to reflect, at her leisure, upon the question of his identity. It was that of a person who had lately been much in her thoughts; but her first impulse, nevertheless, was to turn away; the last thing she desired was to have the air of coming in quest of Robert Acton. The gentleman on the grass, however, gave her no time to decide; he could not long remain unconscious of so agreeable a presence. He rolled back his eyes, stared, gave an exclamation, and then jumped up. He stood an instant, looking at her.

'Excuse my ridiculous position,' he said.

'I have just now no sense of the ridiculous. But, in case you have, don't imagine I came to see you.'

'Take care,' rejoined Acton, 'how you put it into my head! I was thinking of you.'

'The occupation of extreme leisure!' said the Baroness. 'To think of a woman when you are in that position is no compliment.'

'I didn't say I was thinking well!' Acton affirmed, smiling.

She looked at him, and then she turned away. 'Though I didn't come to see you,' she said, 'remember at least that I am within your gates.'

'I am delighted – I am honoured! Won't you come into the house?'

'I have just come out of it. I have been calling upon your mother. I have been bidding her farewell.'

'Farewell?' Acton demanded.

'I am going away,' said the Baroness. And she turned away again, as if to illustrate her meaning.

'When are you going?' asked Acton, standing a moment in his place. But the Baroness made no answer, and he followed her.

'I came this way to look at your garden,' she said, walking back to the gate, over the grass. 'But I must go.'

'Let me at least go with you.' He went with her, and they said nothing till they reached the gate. It was open, and they looked down the road, which was darkened over with long bosky shadows. 'Must you go straight home?' Acton asked.

But she made no answer. She said, after a moment, 'Why have you not been to see me?' He said nothing, and then she went on, 'Why don't you answer me?'

'I am trying to invent an answer,' Acton confessed.

'Have you none ready?'

'None that I can tell you,' he said. 'But let me walk with you now.'

'You may do as you like.'

She moved slowly along the road, and Acton went with her. Presently he said, 'If I had done as I liked I would have come to see you several times.'

'Is that invented?' asked Eugenia.

'No, that is natural. I stayed away because –'

'Ah, here comes the reason, then!'

'Because I wanted to think about you.'

'Because you wanted to lie down!' said the Baroness. 'I have seen you lie down – almost – in my drawing-room.'

Acton stopped in the road, with a movement which seemed to beg her to linger a little. She paused, and he looked at her a while; he thought her very charming. 'You are jesting,' he said; 'but if you are really going away it is very serious.'

'If I stay,' and she gave a little laugh, 'it is more serious still!'

'When shall you go?'

'As soon as possible.'

'And why?'

'Why should I stay?'

'Because we all admire you so.'

'That is not a reason. I am admired also in Europe.' And she began to walk homeward again.

'What could I say to keep you?' asked Acton. He wanted to keep her, and it was a fact that he had been thinking of her for a week. He was in love with her now; he was conscious of that, or he thought he was; and the only question with him was whether he could trust her.

'What can you say to keep me?' she repeated. 'As I want very much to go it is not in my interest to tell you. Besides, I can't imagine.'

He went on with her in silence; he was much more affected by

what she had told him than appeared. Ever since that evening of
his return from Newport her image had had a terrible power to
trouble him. What Clifford Wentworth had told him – that had
affected him, too, in an adverse sense; but it had not liberated
him from the discomfort of a charm of which his intelligence was
impatient. 'She is not honest, she is not honest,' he kept murmuring
to himself. That is what he had been saying to the summer sky,
ten minutes before. Unfortunately, he was unable to say it finally,
definitively; and now that he was near her it seemed to matter
wonderfully little. 'She is a woman who will lie,' he had said to
himself. Now, as he went along, he reminded himself of this
observation; but it failed to frighten him as it had done before.
He almost wished he could make her lie and then convict her of
it, so that he might see how he should like that. He kept thinking
of this as he walked by her side, while she moved forward with
her light, graceful dignity. He had sat with her before; he had driven
with her; but he had never walked with her.

'By Jove, how *comme il faut*[4] she is!' he said, as he observed
her sidewise. When they reached the cottage in the orchard she
passed into the gate without asking him to follow; but she turned
round, as he stood there, to bid him good-night.

'I asked you a question the other night which you never
answered,' he said. 'Have you sent off that document – liberating
yourself?'

She hesitated for a single moment – very naturally. Then, 'Yes,'
she said simply.

He turned away; he wondered whether that would do for his
lie. But he saw her again that evening, for the Baroness reappeared
at her uncle's. He had little talk with her, however; two gentlemen
had driven out from Boston, in a buggy, to call upon Mr Wentworth and his daughters, and Madame Münster was an object
of absorbing interest to both of the visitors. One of them, indeed,
said nothing to her; he only sat and watched with intense gravity,
and leaned forward solemnly, presenting his ear (a very large one),
as if he were deaf, whenever she dropped an observation. He had
evidently been impressed with the idea of her misfortunes and
reverses; he never smiled. His companion adopted a lighter, easier
style; sat as near as possible to Madame Münster; attempted to

draw her out, and proposed every few moments a new topic of conversation. Eugenia was less vividly responsive than usual, and had less to say than, from her brilliant reputation, her interlocutor expected, upon the relative merits of European and American institutions; but she was inaccessible to Robert Acton, who roamed about the piazza with his hands in his pockets, listening for the grating sound of the buggy from Boston as it should be brought round to the side door. But he listened in vain, and at last he lost patience. His sister came to him and begged him to take her home, and he presently went off with her. Eugenia observed him leaving the house with Lizzie; in her present mood the fact seemed a contribution to her irritated conviction that he had several precious qualities. 'Even that *mal-élevée*[5] little girl,' she reflected, 'makes him do what she wishes.'

She had been sitting just within one of the long windows that opened upon the piazza; but very soon after Acton had gone away she got up abruptly, just when the talkative gentleman from Boston was asking her what she thought of the 'moral tone' of that city. On the piazza she encountered Clifford Wentworth, coming round from the other side of the house. She stopped him; she told him she wished to speak to him.

'Why didn't you go home with your cousin?' she asked.

Clifford stared. 'Why, Robert has taken her,' he said.

'Exactly so. But you don't usually leave that to him.'

'Oh,' said Clifford, 'I want to see those fellows start off. They don't know how to drive.'

'It is not, then, that you have quarrelled with your cousin?'

Clifford reflected a moment, and then with a simplicity which had, for the Baroness, a singularly baffling quality, 'Oh no; we have made up!' he said.

She looked at him for some moments; but Clifford had begun to be afraid of the Baroness's looks, and he endeavoured, now, to shift himself out of their range. 'Why do you never come to see me any more?' she asked. 'Have I displeased you?'

'Displeased me? Well, I guess not!' said Clifford, with a laugh.

'Why haven't you come, then?'

'Well, because I am afraid of getting shut up in that back room.'

Eugenia kept looking at him. 'I should think you would like that.'

'Like it!' cried Clifford.

'I should, if I were a young man calling upon a charming woman.'

'A charming woman isn't much use to me when I am shut up in that back room!'

'I am afraid I am not of much use to you anywhere!' said Madame Münster. 'And yet you know how I have offered to be.'

'Well,' observed Clifford, by way of response, 'there comes the buggy.'

'Never mind the buggy. Do you know I am going away?'

'Do you mean now?'

'I mean in a few days. I leave this place.'

'You are going back to Europe?'

'To Europe, where you are to come and see me.'

'Oh yes, I'll come out there,' said Clifford.

'But before that,' Eugenia declared, 'you must come and see me here.'

'Well, I shall keep clear of that back room!' rejoined her simple young kinsman.

The Baroness was silent a moment. 'Yes, you must come frankly – boldly. That will be very much better. I see that now.'

'I see it!' said Clifford. And then, in an instant, 'What's the matter with that buggy?' His practised ear had apparently detected an unnatural creak in the wheels of the light vehicle which had been brought to the portico, and he hurried away to investigate so grave an anomaly.

The Baroness walked homeward, alone, in the starlight, asking herself a question. Was she to have gained nothing – was she to have gained nothing?

Gertrude Wentworth had held a silent place in the little circle gathered about the two gentlemen from Boston. She was not interested in the visitors; she was watching Madame Münster, as she constantly watched her. She knew that Eugenia also was not interested – that she was bored; and Gertrude was absorbed in study of the problem how, in spite of her indifference and her absent attention, she managed to have such a charming manner. That was the manner Gertrude would have liked to have; she determined to cultivate it, and she wished that – to give her the charm – she might in future very often be bored. While she was engaged in these researches, Felix Young was looking for Charlotte, to whom he had something to say. For some time now he had had something to say to Charlotte, and this evening his sense of the propriety of holding some special conversation with her had reached the motive point – resolved itself into acute and delightful desire. He wandered through the empty rooms on the large ground-floor of the house, and found her at last in a small apartment denominated, for reasons not immediately apparent, Mr Wentworth's 'office': an extremely neat and well-dusted room, with an array of law-books, in time-darkened sheepskin, on one of the walls; a large map of the United States on the other, flanked on either side by an old steel engraving[6] of one of Raphael's[7] Madonnas;[8] and on the third several glass cases containing specimens of butterflies and beetles.[9] Charlotte was sitting by a lamp, embroidering a slipper. Felix did not ask for whom the slipper was destined; he saw it was very large.

He moved a chair toward her and sat down, smiling as usual, but, at first, not speaking. She watched him, with her needle poised, and with a certain shy, fluttered look which she always wore when he approached her. There was something in Felix's manner that quickened her modesty, her self-consciousness; if absolute choice had been given her she would have preferred never to find herself alone with him; and, in fact, though she thought him a most brilliant, distinguished, and well-meaning person, she had exercised a much larger amount of tremulous tact than he had ever suspected to circumvent the accident of *tête-à-tête*. Poor Charlotte could have given no account of the matter that would not have seemed unjust both to herself and to her foreign kinsman; she could only have said – or rather, she would never have said it – that she did not like so much gentleman's society at once. She was not reassured, accordingly, when he began, emphasising his words with a kind of admiring radiance, 'My dear cousin, I am enchanted at finding you alone.'

'I am very often alone,' Charlotte observed. Then she quickly added, 'I don't mean I am lonely!'

'So clever a woman as you is never lonely,' said Felix. 'You have company in your beautiful work.' And he glanced at the big slipper.

'I like to work,' declared Charlotte simply.

'So do I!' said her companion. 'And I like to idle too. But it is not to idle that I have come in search of you. I want to tell you something very particular.'

'Well,' murmured Charlotte; 'of course, if you must –'

'My dear cousin,' said Felix, 'it's nothing that a young lady may not listen to. At least I suppose it isn't. But *voyons*; you shall judge. I am terribly in love.'

'Well, Felix,' began Miss Wentworth gravely. But her very gravity appeared to check the development of her phrase.

'I am in love with your sister; but in love, Charlotte – in love!' the young man pursued. Charlotte had laid her work in her lap; her hands were tightly folded on top of it; she was staring at the carpet. 'In short, I'm in love, dear lady,' said Felix. 'Now I want you to help me.'

'To help you?' asked Charlotte, with a tremor.

'I don't mean with Gertrude; she and I have a perfect understanding; and oh, how well she understands one! I mean with your father and with the world in general, including Mr Brand.'

'Poor Mr Brand!' said Charlotte slowly, but with a simplicity which made it evident to Felix that the young minister had not repeated to Miss Wentworth the talk that had lately occurred between them.

'Ah, now, don't say "poor" Mr Brand! I don't pity Mr Brand at all. But I pity your father a little, and I don't want to displease him. Therefore, you see, I want you to plead for me. You don't think me very shabby, eh?'

'Shabby?' exclaimed Charlotte softly, for whom Felix represented the most polished and iridescent qualities of mankind.

'I don't mean in my appearance,' rejoined Felix, laughing; for Charlotte was looking at his boots. 'I mean in my conduct. You don't think it's an abuse of hospitality?'

'To – to care for Gertrude?' asked Charlotte.

'To have really expressed one's self. Because I *have* expressed myself, Charlotte; I must tell you the whole truth – I have! Of course I want to marry her – and here is the difficulty. I held off as long as I could; but she is such a terribly fascinating person! She's a strange creature, Charlotte; I don't believe you really know her.' Charlotte took up her tapestry again, and again she laid it down. 'I know your father has had higher views,' Felix continued; 'and I think you have shared them. You have wanted to marry her to Mr Brand.'

'Oh no,' said Charlotte, very earnestly. 'Mr Brand has always admired her. But we did not want anything of that kind.'

Felix stared. 'Surely marriage was what you proposed?'

'Yes; but we didn't wish to force her.'

'*A la bonne heure!*[10] That's very unsafe, you know. With these arranged marriages there is often the deuce to pay.'

'Oh, Felix,' said Charlotte, 'we didn't want to "arrange."''

'I am delighted to hear that. Because in such cases – even when the woman is a thoroughly good creature – she can't help looking for a compensation. A charming fellow comes along – and *voilà!*'[11] Charlotte sat mutely staring at the floor, and Felix presently added, 'Do go on with your slipper. I like to see you work.'

Charlotte took up her variegated canvas, and began to draw vague blue stitches in a big round rose. 'If Gertrude is so – so strange,' she said, 'why do you want to marry her?'

'Ah, that's it, dear Charlotte! I like strange women; I always have liked them. Ask Eugenia! And Gertrude is wonderful; she says the most beautiful things!'

Charlotte looked at him, almost for the first time, as if her meaning required to be severely pointed. 'You have a great influence over her.'

'Yes – and no!' said Felix. 'I had at first, I think; but now it is six of one and half a dozen of the other; it is reciprocal. She affects me strongly – for she *is* so strong. I don't believe you know her; it's a beautiful nature.'

'Oh yes, Felix; I have always thought Gertrude's nature beautiful.'

'Well, if you think so now,' cried the young man, 'wait and see! She's a folded flower. Let me pluck her from the parent tree and you will see her expand. I'm sure you will enjoy it.'

'I don't understand you,' murmured Charlotte. 'I *can't*, Felix.'

'Well, you can understand this – that I beg you to say a good word for me to your father. He regards me, I naturally believe, as a very light fellow, a Bohemian, an irregular character. Tell him I am not all this; if I ever was, I have forgotten it. I am fond of pleasure – yes; but of innocent pleasure. Pain is all one; but in pleasure, you know, there are tremendous distinctions. Say to him that Gertrude is a folded flower and that I am a serious man!'

Charlotte got up from her chair, slowly rolling up her work. 'We know you are very kind to everyone, Felix,' she said. 'But we are extremely sorry for Mr Brand.'

'Of course you are – you especially! Because,' added Felix hastily, 'you are a woman. But I don't pity him. It ought to be enough for any man that you take an interest in him.'

'It is not enough for Mr Brand,' said Charlotte simply. And she stood there a moment, as if waiting conscientiously for anything more that Felix might have to say.

'Mr Brand is not so keen about his marriage as he was,' he presently said. 'He is afraid of your sister. He begins to think she is wicked.'

Charlotte looked at him now with beautiful appealing eyes – eyes into which he saw the tears rising. 'Oh, Felix, Felix!' she cried, 'what have you done to her?'

'I think she was asleep; I have waked her up!'

But Charlotte, apparently, was really crying; she walked straight out of the room. And Felix, standing there and meditating, had the apparent brutality to take satisfaction in her tears.

Late that night Gertrude, silent and serious, came to him in the garden; it was a kind of appointment. Gertrude seemed to like appointments. She plucked a handful of heliotrope and stuck it into the front of her dress, but she said nothing. They walked together along one of the paths, and Felix looked at the great, square, hospitable house, massing itself vaguely in the starlight, with all its windows darkened.

'I have a little of a bad conscience,' he said. 'I oughtn't to meet you this way till I have got your father's consent.'

Gertrude looked at him for some time. 'I don't understand you.'

'You very often say that,' he said. 'Considering how little we understand each other, it is a wonder how well we get on!'

'We have done nothing but meet since you came here – but meet alone. The first time I ever saw you we were alone,' Gertrude went on. 'What is the difference now? Is it because it is at night?'

'The difference, Gertrude,' said Felix, stopping in the path, 'the difference is that I love you more – more than before!' And then they stood there, talking, in the warm stillness and in front of the closed dark house. 'I have been talking to Charlotte – been trying to bespeak her interest with your father. She has a kind of sublime perversity; was ever a woman so bent upon cutting off her own head?'

'You are too careful,' said Gertrude; 'you are too diplomatic.'

'Well,' cried the young man, 'I didn't come here to make anyone unhappy!'

Gertrude looked round her a while in the odorous darkness. 'I will do anything you please,' she said.

'For instance?' asked Felix, smiling.

'I will go away. I will do anything you please.'

Felix looked at her in solemn admiration. 'Yes, we will go away,' he said. 'But we will make peace first.'

Gertrude looked about her again, and then she broke out passionately, 'Why do they try to make one feel guilty? Why do they make it so difficult? Why can't they understand?'

'I will make them understand!' said Felix. He drew her hand into his arm, and they wandered about in the garden, talking, for an hour.

CHAPTER 12

FELIX allowed Charlotte time to plead his cause; and then, on the third day, he sought an interview with his uncle. It was in the morning; Mr Wentworth was in his office; and, on going in, Felix found that Charlotte was at that moment in conference with her father. She had, in fact, been constantly near him since her interview with Felix; she had made up her mind that it was her duty to repeat very literally her cousin's passionate plea. She had accordingly followed Mr Wentworth about like a shadow, in order to find him at hand when she should have mustered sufficient composure to speak. For poor Charlotte, in this matter, naturally lacked composure; especially when she meditated upon some of Felix's intimations. It was not cheerful work, at the best, to keep giving small hammer-taps to the coffin in which one had laid away, for burial, the poor little unacknowledged offspring of one's own misbehaving heart; and the occupation was not rendered more agreeable by the fact that the ghost of one's stifled dream had been summoned from the shades by the strange, bold words of a talkative young foreigner. What had Felix meant by saying that Mr Brand was not so keen? To herself her sister's justly-depressed suitor had shown no sign of faltering. Charlotte trembled all over when she allowed herself to believe for an instant now and then that, privately, Mr Brand might have faltered; and as it seemed to give more force to Felix's words to repeat them to her father, she was waiting until she should have taught herself to be very calm. But she had now begun to tell Mr Wentworth that she was extremely anxious. She was proceeding to develop this idea, to enumerate the objects of her anxiety, when Felix came in.

Mr Wentworth sat there, with his legs crossed, lifting his dry, pure countenance from the Boston *Advertiser*.[1] Felix entered smiling, as if he had something particular to say, and his uncle looked at him as if he both expected and deprecated this event. Felix vividly expressing himself had come to be a formidable figure to his uncle, who had not yet arrived at definite views as to a proper tone. For the first time in his life, as I have said, Mr Wentworth shirked a responsibility; he earnestly desired that it might not be laid upon him to determine how his nephew's lighter propositions should be treated. He lived under an apprehension that Felix might yet beguile him into assent to doubtful inductions, and his conscience instructed him that the best form of vigilance was the avoidance of discussion. He hoped that the pleasant episode of his nephew's visit would pass away without a further lapse of consistency.

Felix looked at Charlotte with an air of understanding, and then at Mr Wentworth, and then at Charlotte again. Mr Wentworth bent his refined eyebrows upon his nephew and stroked down the first page of the *Advertiser*. 'I ought to have brought a bouquet,' said Felix, laughing. 'In France they always do.'

'We are not in France,' observed Mr Wentworth gravely, while Charlotte earnestly gazed at him.

'No, luckily, we are not in France, where I am afraid I should have a harder time of it. My dear Charlotte, have you rendered me that delightful service?' And Felix bent toward her as if someone had been presenting him.

Charlotte looked at him with almost frightened eyes; and Mr Wentworth thought this might be the beginning of a discussion. 'What is the bouquet for?' he inquired, by way of turning it off.

Felix gazed at him, smiling. *'Pour la demande!'*[2] And then, drawing up a chair, he seated himself, hat in hand, with a kind of conscious solemnity.

Presently he turned to Charlotte again. 'My good Charlotte, my admirable Charlotte,' he murmured, 'you have not played me false – you have not sided against me?'

Charlotte got up, trembling extremely, though imperceptibly. 'You must speak to my father yourself,' she said. 'I think you are clever enough.'

But Felix, rising too, begged her to remain. 'I can speak better to an audience!' he declared.

'I hope it is nothing disagreeable,' said Mr Wentworth.

'It's something delightful, for me!' And Felix, laying down his hat, clasped his hands a little between his knees. 'My dear uncle,' he said, 'I desire, very earnestly, to marry your daughter Gertrude.' Charlotte sank slowly into her chair again, and Mr Wentworth sat staring, with a light in his face that might have been flashed back from an iceberg. He stared and stared; he said nothing. Felix fell back, with his hands still clasped. 'Ah – you don't like it. I was afraid!' He blushed deeply, and Charlotte noticed it – remarking to herself that it was the first time she had ever seen him blush. She began to blush herself, and to reflect that he might be much in love.

'This is very abrupt,' said Mr Wentworth at last.

'Have you never suspected it, dear uncle?' Felix inquired. 'Well, that proves how discreet I have been. Yes, I thought you wouldn't like it.'

'It is very serious, Felix,' said Mr Wentworth.

'You think it's an abuse of hospitality!' exclaimed Felix, smiling again.

'Of hospitality? – an abuse?' his uncle repeated very slowly.

'That is what Felix said to me,' said Charlotte conscientiously.

'Of course you think so; don't defend yourself!' Felix pursued. 'It *is* an abuse, obviously; the most I can claim is that it is perhaps a pardonable one. I simply fell head over heels in love; one can hardly help that. Though you are Gertrude's progenitor I don't believe you know how attractive she is. Dear uncle, she contains the elements of a singularly – I may say a strangely – charming woman!'

'She has always been to me an object of extreme concern,' said Mr Wentworth. 'We have always desired her happiness.'

'Well, here it is!' Felix declared. 'I will make her happy. She believes it, too. Now, hadn't you noticed that?'

'I had noticed that she was much changed,' Mr Wentworth declared, in a tone whose unexpressive, unimpassioned quality appeared to Felix to reveal a profundity of opposition. 'It may be that she is only becoming what you call a charming woman.'

'Gertrude, at heart, is so earnest, so true,' said Charlotte very softly, fastening her eyes upon her father.

'I delight to hear you praise her!' cried Felix.

'She has a very peculiar temperament,' said Mr Wentworth.

'Eh, even that is praise!' Felix rejoined. 'I know I am not the man you might have looked for. I have no position and no fortune; I can give Gertrude no place in the world. A place in the world – that's what she ought to have; that would bring her out.'

'A place to do her duty!' remarked Mr Wentworth.

'Ah, how charmingly she does it – her duty!' Felix exclaimed, with a radiant face. 'What an exquisite conception she has of it! But she comes honestly by that, dear uncle.' Mr Wentworth and Charlotte both looked at him as if they were watching a greyhound doubling. 'Of course with me she will hide her light under a bushel,' he continued; 'I being the bushel! Now I know you like me – you have certainly proved it. But you think I am frivolous and penniless and shabby! Granted – granted – a thousand times granted. I have been a loose fish – a fiddler, a painter, an actor. But there is this to be said: In the first place, I fancy you exaggerate; you lend me qualities I haven't had. I have been a Bohemian – yes; but in Bohemia I always passed for a gentleman. I wish you could see some of my old *camarades*³ – they would tell you! It was the liberty I liked, but not the opportunities! My sins were all peccadilloes; I always respected my neighbour's property – my neighbour's wife. Do you see, dear uncle?' Mr Wentworth ought to have seen; his cold blue eyes were intently fixed. 'And then, *c'est fini!* It's all over. *Je me range.*⁴ I have settled down to a jog-trot. I find I can earn my living – a very fair one – by going about the world and painting bad portraits. It's not a glorious profession, but it is a perfectly respectable one. You won't deny that, eh? Going about the world, I say? I must not deny that, for that I am afraid I shall always do – in quest of agreeable sitters. When I say agreeable, I mean susceptible of delicate flattery and prompt of payment. Gertrude declares she is willing to share my wanderings and help to pose my models. She even thinks it will be charming; and that brings me to my third point. Gertrude likes me. Encourage her a little and she will tell you so.'

Felix's tongue obviously moved much faster than the imagination of his auditors; his eloquence, like the rocking of a boat in a deep, smooth lake, made long eddies of silence. And he seemed to be pleading and chattering still, with his brightly eager smile, his uplifted eyebrows, his expressive mouth, after he had ceased speaking, and while, with his glance quickly turning from the father to the daughter, he sat waiting for the effect of his appeal. 'It is not your want of means,' said Mr Wentworth, after a period of severe reticence.

'Now it's delightful of you to say that! Only don't say it's my want of character. Because I have a character – I assure you I have; a small one, a little slip of a thing, but still something tangible.'

'Ought you not to tell Felix that it is Mr Brand, father?' Charlotte asked, with infinite mildness.

'It is not only Mr Brand,' Mr Wentworth solemnly declared. And he looked at his knee for a long time. 'It is difficult to explain,' he said. He wished, evidently, to be very just. 'It rests on moral grounds, as Mr Brand says. It is the question whether it is the best thing for Gertrude.'

'What is better – what is better, dear uncle?' Felix rejoined urgently, rising in his urgency and standing before Mr Wentworth. His uncle had been looking at his knee; but when Felix moved he transferred his gaze to the handle of the door which faced him. 'It is usually a fairly good thing for a girl to marry the man she loves!' cried Felix.

While he spoke Mr Wentworth saw the handle of the door begin to turn; the door opened and remained slightly ajar until Felix had delivered himself of the cheerful axiom just quoted. Then it opened altogether, and Gertrude stood there. She looked excited; there was a spark in her sweet dull eyes. She came in slowly, but with an air of resolution, and closing the door softly, looked round at the three persons present. Felix went to her with tender gallantry, holding out his hand, and Charlotte made a place for her on the sofa. But Gertrude put her hands behind her and made no motion to sit down.

'We are talking of you!' said Felix.

'I know it,' she answered. 'That's why I came.' And she fastened her eyes on her father, who returned her gaze very fixedly. In his own cold blue eyes there was a kind of pleading, reasoning light.

'It is better you should be present,' said Mr Wentworth. 'We are discussing your future.'

'Why discuss it?' asked Gertrude. 'Leave it to me.'

'That is, to me!' cried Felix.

'I leave it, in the last resort, to a greater wisdom than ours,' said the old man.

Felix rubbed his forehead gently. 'But *en attendant*⁵ the last resort, your father lacks confidence,' he said to Gertrude.

'Haven't you confidence in Felix?' Gertrude was frowning; there was something about her that her father and Charlotte had never seen. Charlotte got up and came to her, as if to put her arm round her; but suddenly, she seemed afraid to touch her.

Mr Wentworth, however, was not afraid 'I have had more confidence in Felix than in you,' he said.

'Yes, you have never had confidence in me – never, never! I don't know why.'

'Oh, sister, sister!' murmured Charlotte.

'You have always needed advice,' Mr Wentworth declared. 'You have had a difficult temperament.'

'Why do you call it difficult? It might have been easy, if you had allowed it. You wouldn't let me be natural. I don't know what you wanted to make of me. Mr Brand was the worst.'

Charlotte at last took hold of her sister. She laid her two hands upon Gertrude's arm. 'He cares so much for you,' she almost whispered.

Gertrude looked at her intently an instant; then kissed her. 'No, he does not,' she said.

'I have never seen you so passionate,' observed Mr Wentworth, with an air of indignation mitigated by high principles.

'I am sorry if I offend you,' said Gertrude.

'You offend me, but I don't think you are sorry.'

'Yes, father, she is sorry,' said Charlotte.

'I would even go further, dear uncle,' Felix interposed. 'I would question whether she really offends you. How can she offend you?'

To this Mr Wentworth made no immediate answer. Then, in a moment, 'She has not profited as we hoped.'

'Profited? *Ah voilà!*' Felix exclaimed.

Gertrude was very pale; she stood looking down. 'I have told Felix I would go away with him,' she presently said.

'Ah, you have said some admirable things!' cried the young man.

'Go away, sister?' asked Charlotte.

'Away – away; to some strange country.'

'That is to frighten you,' said Felix, smiling at Charlotte.

'To – what do you call it?' asked Gertrude, turning an instant to Felix. 'To Bohemia.'

'Do you propose to dispense with preliminaries?' asked Mr Wentworth, getting up.

'Dear uncle, *vous plaisantez!*'[6] cried Felix. 'It seems to me that these are preliminaries.'

Gertrude turned to her father. 'I *have* profited,' she said. 'You wanted to form my character. Well, my character is formed – for my age. I know what I want; I have chosen. I am determined to marry this gentleman.'

'You had better consent, sir,' said Felix, very gently.

'Yes, sir, you had better consent,' added a very different voice.

Charlotte gave a little jump, and the others turned to the direction from which it had come. It was the voice of Mr Brand, who had stepped through the long window which stood open to the piazza. He stood patting his forehead with his pocket-handkerchief; he was very much flushed; his face wore a singular expression.

'Yes, sir, you had better consent,' Mr Brand repeated, coming forward. 'I know what Miss Gertrude means.'

'My dear friend!' murmured Felix, laying his hand caressingly on the young minister's arm.

Mr Brand looked at him; then at Mr Wentworth; lastly at Gertrude. He did not look at Charlotte. But Charlotte's earnest eyes were fastened to his own countenance; they were asking an immense question of it. The answer to this question could not come all at once; but some of the elements of it were there. It was one of the elements of it that Mr Brand was very red, that he held his head very high, that he had a bright excited eye and an air of embarrassed boldness – the air of a man who has taken a resolve in the execution of which he apprehends the failure, not of his moral, but of his personal, resources. Charlotte thought he looked very grand; and it is incontestable that Mr Brand felt very grand. This, in fact, was the grandest moment of his life; and it was natural that such a moment should contain opportunities of awkwardness for a large, stout, modest young man.

'Come in, sir,' said Mr Wentworth, with an angular wave of his hand. 'It is very proper that you should be present.'

'I know what you are talking about,' Mr Brand rejoined. 'I heard what your nephew said.'

'And he heard what you said!' exclaimed Felix, patting him again on the arm.

'I am not sure that I understood,' said Mr Wentworth, who had angularity in his voice as well as in his gestures.

Gertrude had been looking hard at her former suitor. She had been puzzled, like her sister; but her imagination moved more quickly than Charlotte's. 'Mr Brand asked you to let Felix take me away,' she said to her father.

The young minister gave her a strange look. 'It is not because I don't want to see you any more,' he declared, in a tone intended as it were for publicity.

'I shouldn't think you would want to see me any more,' Gertrude answered gently.

Mr Wentworth stood staring. 'Isn't this rather a change, sir?' he inquired.

'Yes, sir.' And Mr Brand looked everywhere; only still not at Charlotte. 'Yes, sir,' he repeated. And he held his handkerchief a few moments to his lips.

'Where are our moral grounds?' demanded Mr Wentworth, who had always thought Mr Brand would be just the thing for a younger daughter with a peculiar temperament.

'It is sometimes very moral to change, you know,' suggested Felix.

Charlotte had softly left her sister's side. She had edged gently toward her father, and now her hand found its way into his arm. Mr Wentworth had folded up the *Advertiser* into a surprisingly small compass, and, holding the roll with one hand, he earnestly clasped it with the other. Mr Brand was looking at him; and yet, though Charlotte was so near, his eyes failed to meet her own. Gertrude watched her sister.

'It is better not to speak of change,' said Mr Brand. 'In one sense there is no change. There was something I desired – something I asked of you; I desire something still – I ask it of you.' And he paused a moment; Mr Wentworth looked bewildered.

'I should like, in my ministerial capacity, to unite this young couple.'

Gertrude, watching her sister, saw Charlotte flushing intensely, and Mr Wentworth felt her pressing upon his arm. 'Heavenly Powers!' murmured Mr Wentworth. And it was the nearest approach to profanity he had ever made.

'That is very nice; that is very handsome!' Felix exclaimed.

'I don't understand,' said Mr Wentworth; though it was plain that everyone else did.

'That is very beautiful, Mr Brand,' said Gertrude, emulating Felix.

'I should like to marry you. It will give me great pleasure.'

'As Gertrude says, it's a beautiful idea,' said Felix.

Felix was smiling, but Mr Brand was not even trying to. He himself treated his proposition very seriously. 'I have thought of it, and I should like to do it,' he affirmed.

Charlotte, meanwhile, was staring with expanded eyes. Her imagination, as I have said, was not so rapid as her sister's, but now it had taken several little jumps. 'Father,' she murmured, 'consent!'

Mr Brand heard her; he looked away. Mr Wentworth, evidently, had no imagination at all. 'I have always thought,' he began slowly, 'that Gertrude's character required a special line of development.'

'Father,' repeated Charlotte, 'consent.'

Then at last Mr Brand looked at her. Her father felt her leaning more heavily upon his folded arm than she had ever done before; and this, with a certain sweet faintness in her voice, made him wonder what was the matter. He looked down at her and saw the encounter of her gaze with the young theologian's; but even this told him nothing, and he continued to be bewildered. Nevertheless, 'I consent,' he said at last, 'since Mr Brand recommends it.'

'I should like to perform the ceremony very soon,' observed Mr Brand, with a sort of solemn simplicity.

'Come, come, that's charming!' cried Felix profanely.

Mr Wentworth sank into his chair. 'Doubtless, when you understand it,' he said, with a certain judicial asperity.

Gertrude went to her sister and led her away, and Felix having passed his arm into Mr Brand's and stepped out of the long window with him, the old man was left sitting there in unillumined perplexity.

Felix did no work that day. In the afternoon, with Gertrude, he got into one of the boats, and floated about with idly-dipping oars. They talked a good deal of Mr Brand – though not exclusively.

'That was a fine stroke,' said Felix. 'It was really heroic.'

Gertrude sat musing, with her eyes upon the ripples. 'That was what he wanted to be; he wanted to do something fine.'

'He won't be comfortable till he has married us,' said Felix. 'So much the better.'

'He wanted to be magnanimous; he wanted to have a fine moral pleasure. I know him so well,' Gertrude went on. Felix looked at her; she spoke slowly, gazing at the clear water. 'He thought of it a great deal, night and day. He thought it would be beautiful. At last he made up his mind that it was his duty, his duty to do just that – nothing less than that. He felt exalted; he felt sublime. That's how he likes to feel. It is better for him than if I had listened to him.'

'It's better for me,' smiled Felix. 'But do you know, as regards the sacrifice, that I don't believe he admired you when this decision was taken quite so much as he had done a fortnight before?'

'He never admired me. He admires Charlotte; he pitied me. I know him so well.'

'Well, then, he didn't pity you so much.'

Gertrude looked at Felix a little, smiling. 'You shouldn't permit yourself,' she said, 'to diminish the splendour of his action. He admires Charlotte,' she repeated.

'That's capital!' said Felix laughingly, and dipping his oars. I cannot say exactly to which member of Gertrude's phrase he alluded; but he dipped his oars again, and they kept floating about.

Neither Felix nor his sister, on that day, was present at Mr Wentworth's at the evening repast. The two occupants of the chalet dined together, and the young man informed his companion that his marriage was now an assured fact. Eugenia congratulated him, and replied that if he were as reasonable a husband as he had been, on the whole, a brother, his wife would have nothing to complain of.

Felix looked at her a moment, smiling. 'I hope,' he said, 'not to be thrown back on my reason.'

'It is very true,' Eugenia rejoined, 'that one's reason is dismally flat. It's a bed with the mattress removed.'

But the brother and sister, later in the evening, crossed over to the larger house, the Baroness desiring to compliment her prospective sister-in-law. They found the usual circle upon the piazza, with the exception of Clifford Wentworth and Lizzie Acton; and as everyone stood up as usual to welcome the Baroness, Eugenia had an admiring audience for her compliment to Gertrude.

Robert Acton stood on the edge of the piazza, leaning against one of the white columns, so that he found himself next to Eugenia while she acquitted herself of a neat little discourse of congratulation.

'I shall be so glad to know you better,' she said; 'I have seen so much less of you than I should have liked. Naturally; now I see the reason why! You will love me a little, won't you? I think I may say I gain on being known.' And terminating these observations with the softest cadence of her voice, the Baroness imprinted a sort of grand official kiss upon Gertrude's forehead.

Increased familiarity had not, to Gertrude's imagination, diminished the mysterious impressiveness of Eugenia's personality, and she felt flattered and transported by this little ceremony. Robert Acton also seemed to admire it, as he admired so many of the gracious manifestations of Madame Münster's wit.

They had the privilege of making him restless, and on this occasion he walked away, suddenly, with his hands in his pockets, and then came back and leaned against his column. Eugenia was now complimenting her uncle upon his daughter's engagement, and Mr Wentworth was listening with his usual plain yet refined politeness. It is to be supposed that by this time his perception of the mutual relations of the young people who surrounded him had become more acute; but he still took the matter very seriously, and he was not at all exhilarated.

'Felix will make her a good husband,' said Eugenia. 'He will be a charming companion; he has a great quality – indestructible gaiety.'

'You think that's a great quality?' asked the old man.

Eugenia meditated, with her eyes upon his. 'You think one gets tired of it, eh?'

'I don't know that I am prepared to say that,' said Mr Wentworth.

'Well, we will say, then, that it is tiresome for others but delightful for one's self. A woman's husband, you know, is supposed to be her second self; so that, for Felix and Gertrude, gaiety will be a common property.'

'Gertrude was always very gay,' said Mr Wentworth. He was trying to follow this argument.

Robert Acton took his hands out of his pockets and came a little nearer to the Baroness. 'You say you gain by being known,' he said. 'One certainly gains by knowing you.'

'What have *you* gained?' asked Eugenia.

'An immense amount of wisdom.'

'That's a questionable advantage for a man who was already so wise!'

Acton shook his head. 'No, I was a great fool before I knew you!'

'And being a fool you made my acquaintance! You are very complimentary.'

'Let me keep it up,' said Acton, laughing. 'I hope, for our pleasure, that your brother's marriage will detain you.'

'Why should I stop for my brother's marriage when I would not stop for my own?' asked the Baroness.

'Why shouldn't you stop in either case, now that, as you say, you have dissolved that mechanical tie that bound you to Europe?'

The Baroness looked at him a moment. 'As I say? You look as if you doubted it.'

'Ah,' said Acton, returning her glance, 'that is a remnant of my old folly! We have other attractions,' he added. 'We are to have another marriage.'

But she seemed not to hear him; she was looking at him still. 'My word was never doubted before,' she said.

'We are to have another marriage,' Acton repeated, smiling.

Then she appeared to understand. 'Another marriage?' And she looked at the others. Felix was chattering to Gertrude; Charlotte, at a distance, was watching them; and Mr Brand, in quite another quarter, was turning his back to them and, with his hands under his coat-tails and his large head on one side, was looking at the small, tender crescent of a young moon. 'It ought to be Mr Brand and Charlotte,' said Eugenia, 'but it doesn't look like it.'

'There,' Acton answered, 'you must judge just now by contraries. There is more than there looks to be. I expect that combination one of these days; but that is not what I meant.'

'Well,' said the Baroness, 'I never guess my own lovers; so I can't guess other people's.'

Acton gave a loud laugh, and he was about to add a rejoinder when Mr Wentworth approached his niece. 'You will be interested to hear,' the old man said, with a momentary aspiration toward jocosity, 'of another matrimonial venture in our little circle.'

'I was just telling the Baroness,' Acton observed.

'Mr Acton was apparently about to announce his own engagement,' said Eugenia.

Mr Wentworth's jocosity increased. 'It is not exactly that; but it is in the family. Clifford, hearing this morning that Mr Brand had expressed a desire to tie the nuptial knot for his sister, took it into his head to arrange that, while his hand was in, our good friend should perform a like ceremony for himself and Lizzie Acton.'

The Baroness threw back her head and smiled at her uncle; then turning, with an intenser radiance, to Robert Acton, 'I am certainly very stupid not to have thought of that,' she said. Acton looked down at his boots, as if he thought he had perhaps reached the limits of legitimate experimentation, and for a moment Eugenia said nothing more. It had been, in fact, a sharp knock, and she needed to recover herself. This was done, however, promptly enough. 'Where are the young people?' she asked.

'They are spending the evening with my mother.'

'Is not the thing very sudden?'

Acton looked up. 'Extremely sudden. There had been a tacit understanding; but within a day or two Clifford appears to have received some mysterious impulse to precipitate the affair.'

'The impulse,' said the Baroness, 'was the charms of your very pretty sister.'

'But my sister's charms were an old story; he had always known her.' Acton had begun to experiment again.

Here, however, it was evident the Baroness would not help him. 'Ah, one can't say! Clifford is very young; but he is a nice boy.'

'He's a likeable sort of boy, and he will be a rich man.' This was Acton's last experiment; Madame Münster turned away.

She made but a short visit, and Felix took her home. In her little drawing-room she went almost straight to the mirror over the chimney-piece, and, with a candle uplifted, stood looking into it. 'I shall not wait for your marriage,' she said to her brother. 'Tomorrow my maid shall pack up.'

'My dear sister,' Felix exclaimed, 'we are to be married immediately! Mr Brand is too uncomfortable.'

But Eugenia, turning and still holding her candle aloft, only looked about the little sitting-room at her gimcracks and curtains and cushions. 'My maid shall pack up,' she repeated. '*Bonté divine*, what rubbish! I feel like a strolling actress; these are my "properties."'

'Is the play over, Eugenia?' asked Felix.

She gave him a sharp glance. 'I have spoken my part.'

'With great applause!' said her brother.

'Oh, applause – applause!' she murmured. And she gathered up two or three of her dispersed draperies. She glanced at the beautiful brocade, and then, 'I don't see how I can have endured it!' she said.

'Endure it a little longer. Come to my wedding.'

'Thank you; that's your affair. My affairs are elsewhere.'

'Where are you going?'

'To Germany – by the first ship.'

'You have decided not to marry Mr Acton?'

'I have refused him,' said Eugenia.

Her brother looked at her in silence. 'I am sorry,' he rejoined at last. 'But I was very discreet, as you asked me to be. I said nothing.'

'Please continue, then, not to allude to the matter,' said Eugenia.

Felix inclined himself gravely. 'You shall be obeyed. But your position in Germany?' he pursued.

'Please to make no observations upon it.'

'I was only going to say that I supposed it was altered.'

'You are mistaken.'

'But I thought you had signed –'

'I have not signed!' said the Baroness.

Felix urged her no further, and it was arranged that he should immediately assist her to embark.

Mr Brand was indeed, it appeared, very impatient to consummate his sacrifice and deliver the nuptial benediction which would set it off so handsomely; but Eugenia's impatience to withdraw from a country in which she had not found the fortune she had come to seek was even less to be mistaken. It is true she had not made any very various exertion; but she appeared to feel justified in generalising – in deciding that the conditions of action on this provincial continent were not favourable to really superior women. The elder world was, after all, their natural field. The unembarrassed directness with which she proceeded to apply these intelligent conclusions appeared to the little circle of spectators who have figured in our narrative but the supreme exhibition of a character to which the experience of life had imparted an inimitable pliancy. It had a distinct effect upon Robert Acton, who, for the two days preceding her departure, was a very restless and irritated mortal. She passed her last evening at her uncle's, where she had never been more charming; and in parting with Clifford Wentworth's affianced bride she drew from her own finger a curious old ring and presented it to her with the prettiest speech and kiss. Gertrude, who as an affianced bride was also indebted to her gracious bounty, admired this little incident extremely, and Robert Acton almost wondered whether it did not give him the right, as Lizzie's brother and guardian, to offer in return a handsome present to the Baroness. It would have made him extremely happy to be able to offer a handsome present to the Baroness; but he abstained from this expression of his sentiments, and they were in consequence, at the very last, by so much the less comfortable. It was almost at the very last that he saw her – late the night before she went to Boston to embark.

'For myself, I wish you might have stayed,' he said. 'But not for your own sake.'

'I don't make so many differences,' said the Baroness. 'I am simply sorry to be going.'

'That's a much deeper difference than mine,' Acton declared; 'for you mean you are simply glad!'

Felix parted with her on the deck of the ship. 'We shall often meet over there,' he said.

'I don't know,' she answered. 'Europe seems to me much larger than America.'

Mr Brand, of course, in the days that immediately followed, was not the only impatient spirit; but it may be said that of all the young spirits interested in the event none rose more eagerly to the level of the occasion. Gertrude left her father's house with Felix Young; they were imperturbably happy, and they went far away. Clifford and his young wife sought their felicity in a narrower circle, and the latter's influence upon her husband was such as to justify, strikingly, that theory of the elevating effect of easy intercourse with clever women which Felix had propounded to Mr Wentworth. Gertrude was for a good while a distant figure, but she came back when Charlotte married Mr Brand. She was present at the wedding feast, where Felix's gaiety confessed to no change. Then she disappeared, and the echo of a gaiety of her own, mingled with that of her husband, often came back to the home of her earlier years. Mr Wentworth at last found himself listening for it; and Robert Acton, after his mother's death, married a particularly nice young girl.

NOTES

In compiling these notes I have avoided annotation for its own sake, and have tried instead to concentrate on those points which will, perhaps, enhance the reader's understanding and appreciation of the novel.

There are, for example, several notes on period and topographical details, since Thomas Wentworth Higginson's strictures (see Introduction) seem to me to be not only irrelevant but also, in the main, unfair.

Some of the themes explored in the Introduction have also been singled out for comment: for example, the significance of the characters' names; the fairy-tale element; the importance of clothes. There are also occasions where a note is designed to bring out the difference between the European and the New England cultures.

As for the potted biographies of the Empress Josephine and other women: my concern here was to stress the parallels with Eugenia's situation, or to bring out more clearly the misconceptions of the other characters concerning her.

Finally, I have offered translations of all the foreign words and phrases; if competent linguists find these superfluous, they need not, of course, refer to them.

PATRICIA CRICK

CHAPTER 1

1. (p. 33) *a gloomy-looking inn*. Subsequent topographical details indicate the Tremont Hotel.

2. (p. 33) *upwards of thirty years since*. The novel was published in 1878.

3. (p. 33) *her much-trimmed skirts were voluminous*. As well as being more elaborately flounced and trimmed, skirts were becoming progressively fuller throughout this period, until they culminated in the crinolined skirts of the late forties onwards.

4. (p. 34) *a huge, low omnibus*. These horsecars did not appear in Boston before the fifties (see Introduction), although they were already established in New York by 1832.

5. (p. 34) *the pavement*. i.e. the roadway.

6. (p. 34) *a tall wooden church spire, painted white*. This would be Park

Street Church, built in 1809 for the orthodox Congregationalists whose original churches had gone over to the Unitarians. Because gunpowder was stored there during the 1812 war with the British, the site became known as 'Brimstone Corner'; the name persisted, however, because it was linked in the popular imagination with the hellfire sermons preached in the church.

7. (p. 35) *Hebe*. The cup-bearer of the gods in Greek mythology.

8. (p. 35) *affreux*. Dreadful.

9. (p. 36) *an alchemist's laboratory*. The alchemists of the Middle Ages were in many respects the forerunners of modern science; sometimes, however (as in their search for the Philosopher's Stone, which they believed would transmute base metals into gold), they more closely resembled wizards.

10. (p. 36) *Ce sera clair, au moins*. At least it will be obvious.

11. (p. 37) *Voyons*. Let's see.

12. (p. 38) *Bonté divine*. Good heavens.

13. (p. 38) *Mid-May's Eldest Child*. Felix is proposing this title ironically. The reference is to Keats's 'Ode to a Nightingale':

> Fast fading violets cover'd up in leaves;
> And mid-May's eldest child,
> The coming musk-rose, full of dewy wine,
> The murmurous haunt of flies on summer eves.

14. (p. 38) *Qu'en savez-vous?* What do you know about it? Note that whereas Felix uses *tu* to his sister, she addresses him, with aristocratic formality, as *vous*.

15. (p. 38) *a steamer*. Regular crossings of the Atlantic by steamship only began in 1838. But it was still rather a haphazard affair, and for several decades steamships were also equipped with a complete set of masts and rigging, in case the boilers broke down or the supply of coal ran out.

16. (p. 39) *Felix*. The name means 'happy'.

17. (p. 39) *Bohemian*. This use of the word (which arose from the erroneous belief that the gipsies originally came from Bohemia) was common in the nineteenth century to denote a person of free-and-easy habits, and was particularly applied to artists and writers.

18. (p. 40) *Tu vas voir*. You'll see.

19. (p. 41) *Comme c'est bariolé*. How gaily-coloured it is.

20. (p. 41) *'The young women are not Mohametan'*. The reference is to the Islamic custom of women veiling their faces.

21. (p. 42) *désagréments*. Annoyances.

22. (p. 42) *a large public garden*. This may be Boston Common, or it may be the Public Garden proper, although in the 1840s this was smaller than it is now.

23. (p. 43) *Puritan*. The Puritans were the early colonizers of New England. As a political entity, Puritanism had largely disappeared by the eighteenth century, but the Puritan ethic continued to exert an influence on American society.

24. (p. 44) *some letters*. It was normal practice, when one went to a new place, to take letters of introduction from friends or acquaintances which would ensure ready acceptance into an unfamiliar society.

25. (p. 44) *voix du sang*. Ties of blood.

26. (p. 45) *mise en scène*. Setting.

CHAPTER 2

1. (p. 46) *waist*. Bodice or blouse.

2. (p. 46) *piazza*. Verandah.

3. (p. 49) *thread gloves*. i.e. gloves of woven or knitted material. A more elegant young man would have worn gloves of fine leather (though his 'high hat' is fashionable enough).

4. (p. 51) *the golden age*. In Greek and Roman myth, this was the first age of the world, in which men were virtuous, and everything was perfect.

5. (p. 51) *silvery prime*. The silver age, or second age of the world, was inferior to the first, and produced a race of men who were dependent on their mothers for an inordinate time ('a hundred years', says Hesiod).

6. (p. 51) *None of them were forbidden books*. It was not unusual at this period for young unmarried women's reading to be censored by their parents.

7. (p. 52) *the Arabian Nights*. A collection of (mainly) fairy stories and fabulous romances written in Arabic, which first became popular in the Western world during the eighteenth century. Although all the early translations of these stories were expurgated, they still retain a strongly erotic flavour.

8. (p. 52) *Prince Camaralzaman and the Princess Badoura*. Camaralzaman, a young man of extraordinary beauty, is the son of the King of Khalidan (adjacent to Persia). Badoura, who is no less beautiful, is the daughter of the King of the Interior Islands, in the region of China.

9. (p. 54) *comme vous devez avoir raison*. How right you are.

10. (p. 55) *dinner ... At two o'clock*. At the beginning of the nineteenth

century this was the normal dinnertime throughout the English-speaking world; as the century wore on, fashionable people (following the example of the French) took to dining later and later in the day. As we saw in Chapter 1, Felix and Eugenia dine in the evening.

11. (p. 56) *The Queen of Sheba came to Solomon*. This Biblical episode is described in 1 Kings X. However, it should be noted that Sheba and Solomon were mutually impressed.

12. (p. 56) *Silberstadt-Schreckenstein*. Silberstadt (silver-town) is perfectly acceptable as a German place-name; Schreckenstein (horror-stone), with its sibilants and guttural, is ludicrous.

13. (p. 57) *en l'air*. Unsettled.

CHAPTER 3

1. (p. 59) *they killed the fatted calf*. A reference to the Parable of the Prodigal son (Luke XV), who wastes his inheritance in riotous living, but is nevertheless well received by his father when he eventually returns home.

2. (p. 59) *C'est bien vague*. That's very vague.

3. (p. 59) *lionised*. i.e. treated as a celebrity.

4. (p. 59) *nous n'avons qu'à nous tenir*. We only have to do the right thing.

5. (p. 59) *swells*. Socially distinguished people.

6. (p. 60) *bon*. Good.

7. (p. 60) *ton*. Tone, in the sense of prevailing mood.

8. (p. 60) *aisance*. Affluence.

9. (p. 60) *portioning*. Giving a dowry to.

10. (p. 61) *epicurean*. Devoted to pleasure.

11. (p. 62) *barouche*. A four-wheeled horse-drawn carriage with seating for four passengers.

12. (p. 62) *plans reculés*. The background. This is the vocabulary of drawing or painting.

13. (p. 63) *Mrs Morgan*. The reader may also be reminded of Morgan le Fay, the witch woman who seduces and destroys the white-wizard Merlin, in Malory's *Morte d'Arthur*.

14. (p. 64) *cachette*. Hiding-place.

15. (p. 65) *General Washington*. George Washington (1732–99), American general who led the War of Independence against England and became first President of the United States.

16. (p. 65) *I have heard of Washington*. The general was particularly popular

in France, partly because he fought the British (La Fayette, the French general, raised a force and went to fight on the American side), and partly because the revolutionary ideals of America were seen as marking the way for the French Revolution. The Baroness *should* surely have been aware of this.

17. (p. 66) *Empress Josephine*. The wife of Napoleon I, noted for her charm, her scheming, and her sexual promiscuity. After thirteen years of childless marriage, Napoleon obtained an annulment, and then married Marie Louise, daughter of the Austrian emperor Francis I.

18. (p. 67) *par exemple!* Really!

19. (p. 67) *beau cousin*. Handsome cousin.

20. (p. 69) *salon*. Literally, drawing-room, but also refers to the social circle which meets there. In Paris the *salons*, from the mid-seventeenth to the early nineteenth century, were not merely social gatherings, but the main centres of intellectual and artistic discussion.

21. (p. 69) *habitués*. Frequent visitors.

22. (p. 69) *A Protestant*. Eugenia is, presumably, a Roman Catholic, and in those pre-ecumenical days, convent-bred girls were not encouraged to understand the distinctions between the various branches of Protestantism.

23. (p. 69) *Unitarian*. The movement seems to have originated in the Socinianism of sixteenth-century Transylvania. In the late eighteenth century, it became prevalent in the Congregational churches of New England, and was established as a separate denomination by about 1815. As the name implies, its followers reject the doctrine of the Trinity, claiming that God exists in only one person. As a young man, Emerson was a Unitarian pastor for a time, and it was partly under his influence that it developed in the nineteenth century as a religion of reason.

CHAPTER 4

1. (p. 75) *boudoir*. A lady's small private dressing-cum-sitting room.

2. (p. 76) *court-plaster*. Sticking plaster.

3. (p. 76) *soubrette*. Actress taking the part of a maid or similar minor character in a comedy.

4. (p. 76) *penetralia*. The innermost shrine.

5. (p. 77) *intime*. Intimate.

6. (p. 77) *en famille*. With the family.

7. (p. 77) *porte à porte*. Cheek by jowl.

8. (p. 77) *bombazine apron*. An apron of twilled material, usually black,

which was part of the uniform of convent-educated girls in the nineteenth century.

9. (p. 77) *Quakerism*. Quakers did settle in New England, but the Baroness has no real justification for supposing the Wentworths to be such.

10. (p. 78) *eleemosynary*. Granted as a form of charity.

11. (p. 78) *dans cette galère*. In this odd situation. A reference to Molière's *Scapin*, whose young hero has (allegedly) been carried off in a pirate galley.

12. (p. 79) *Il faudra . . . lui faire un peu de toilette*. We shall have to dress it up a bit.

13. (p. 79) *portières*. Door-hangings.

14. (p. 79) *wax candles*. These were for drawing-rooms and elegant occasions; lamps or tallow candles were for common, everyday use.

15. (p. 79) *India shawls*. These, and the other details given, are typical accessories of a French drawing-room of the 1840s.

16. (p. 80) *quatrième*. Lodgings on the fourth floor (Amer. fifth floor) – not a sought-after situation.

17. (p. 80) *cornucopias*. Horns of plenty.

18. (p. 80) *contact so unrestricted with young unmarried ladies*. In Europe, such young ladies were heavily chaperoned at this period.

19. (p. 81) *buggy*. A four-wheeled vehicle.

20. (p. 82) *ennui*. Boredom (a common Romantic ailment).

21. (p. 84) *local colour*. Exotic touches, much favoured by authors of the Romantic era.

22. (p. 84) *Madame de Staël*. (1766–1817), noted French authoress and hostess of a *salon*. She was interested in defining national types, and worked to promote the cross-fertilization of cultures. Having yearned after romantic love all her life, she finally found happiness with a younger man.

23. (p. 84) *Madame Récamier*. (1777–1849), hostess of a brilliant *salon* during the French Restoration period, whose semi-reclining portrait by David is well known. She had many male admirers with whom her relationships were almost certainly platonic, though public opinion thought otherwise.

CHAPTER 5

1. (p. 85) *tea*. In households where dinner was in the early afternoon, tea-time would be in the early evening.

2. (p. 89) *beau vieillard*. A handsome old man.

3. (p. 89) *daguerrotype*. An early type of photograph, invented in 1838.

4. (p. 90) *do paint me while I am asleep*. Prince Camaralzaman sees Princess Badoura for the first time, and falls in love with her, while she is asleep.

5. (p. 94) *Nicholas Nickleby*. The novel by Dickens, published in 1839, whose picaresque hero, like Felix, is 'a momentary ornament of a group of strolling actors'. The Wentworths are quite up-to-date in their reading.

CHAPTER 6

1. (p. 100) *vous vous y prenez mal*. You are setting about it in the wrong way.

2. (p. 102) *corsage*. Bodice.

3. (p. 103) *nous n'en sommes pas là*. We are not at that stage.

4. (p. 104) *Schloss*. Castle.

5. (p. 105) *Que voulez-vous!* What do you expect!

6. (p. 106) *putting your trust in princes*. A reference to the Prayer Book. 'O put not your trust in princes, nor in any child of man: for there is no help in them.'

7. (p. 107) *tête-à-tête*. A private conversation between two persons.

8. (p. 107) *chinoiseries*. Ornaments and furniture from China.

9. (p. 107) *Celestial Empire*. The native name for China.

10. (p. 108) *bric-à-brac*. Ornaments.

11. (p. 109) *Emerson*. (1803–82), the American philosophic writer, whose First Series of *Essays* was published in 1841. (See Introduction). In his Phi Beta Kappa oration, entitled 'The American Scholar', in 1837, Emerson had advocated independence from the European cultural tradition.

CHAPTER 7

1. (p. 113) *Philistine*. The original Philistines are portrayed in the Bible as the enemies of the Israelites. In the nineteenth century, however, the word came to mean an uncultured person.

2. (p. 114) *Sicurissimo!* Most certainly.

3. (p. 115) *C'est de son âge*. It's appropriate to his years.

4. (p. 119) *Leghorn hats*. Simple, wide-brimmed straw hats from Italy.

5. (p. 121) *making la cour*. Paying court to.

6. (p. 122) *Je n'y comprends rien.* I don't understand it at all.

7. (p. 125) *an epithalamium.* A bridal poem or song.

CHAPTER 8

1. (p. 131) *chaussures.* Shoes.

2. (p. 131) *the Common.* Boston Common, in the fashionable centre of the city.

3. (p. 132) *doctrine of wild oats.* The belief that a young man should be allowed to 'sow his wild oats', i.e. commit youthful follies, before settling down.

4. (p. 133) *make the tour.* The Grand Tour of Europe was considered an important part of the education of the young eighteenth-century English gentleman; something of the same idea persisted in nineteenth-century America.

5. (p. 133) *relations.* i.e. social contacts.

6. (p. 134) *married by the left hand.* In a morganatic marriage ceremony the bride and bridegroom take each other by the left instead of the right hand.

7. (p. 134) *vrai monde.* i.e. orthodox society, as opposed to the *demi-monde* of the courtesan.

CHAPTER 9

1. (p. 139) *Newport.* The fashionable resort in Rhode Island, situated about fifty miles from Boston, where Henry James spent part of his boyhood.

2. (p. 140) *the North American Review.* This periodical was started in 1815 as a bi-monthly, but by the 1840s it had become a quarterly. It published articles on literary, cultural and scientific topics.

3. (p. 141) *He was not quoting.* No, indeed, though his words here have a distinct flavour of the Pauline *Epistles* about them.

4. (p. 142) *Mais entrez donc!* But do come in!

5. (p. 144) *a galant homme.* A gentleman.

CHAPTER 10

1. (p. 152) *je n'en suis pas là.* I'm not in such a state.

2. (p. 153) *Les beaux jours sont passés.* The good days are over.

3. (p. 153) *making les yeux doux.* Gazing lovingly.

4. (p. 154) *Je ne la crains pas*. I'm not afraid of it/her.

5. (p. 155) *Vous serez de la partie*. You'll be one of us. Note that Felix is now calling his sister 'vous'.

6. (p. 157) *pas de zèle*. Don't be too enthusiastic.

7. (p. 159) *the Celestial City*. Heaven.

8. (p. 159) *Andiamo!* Let's go!

9. (p. 161) *Dame!* Indeed!

10. (p. 162) *a touchstone*. A piece of basanite used for testing the fineness of gold and silver alloys according to the colour of the streak produced by rubbing them on it. Felix seems to be using the word with a slightly different meaning, as if there were something magic about it.

CHAPTER 11

1. (p. 165) *visite d'adieux*. Farewell visit.

2. (p. 168) *la main heureuse*. A tactful manner.

3. (p. 168) *Comme c'est bien!* How nice it is!

4. (p. 171) *comme il faut*. Correct.

5. (p. 172) *mal-élevée*. Badly brought up.

6. (p.174) *steel engraving*. Before the advent of photogravure, the normal method of reproducing paintings was by monochrome engravings from copper plates. Pure copper is too soft to stand up to multiple impressions, so where a large number of reproductions was required, the original copper plate would be coated with a thin layer of steel.

7. (p. 174) *Raphael*. (1483–1520), the great painter of the Italian Renaissance.

8. (p. 174) *Madonnas*. Representations of the Virgin Mary. It is interesting that the only portraits in this house of which we have any details are these, and that of the Empress Josephine mentioned on page 66, representing, perhaps, the age-old stereotyping of woman as either saint or whore.

9. (p. 174) *butterflies and beetles*. Collecting such specimens was a favourite nineteenth-century hobby.

10. (p. 176) *A la bonne heure!* That's all very well!

11. (p. 176) *voilà*. That's it.

CHAPTER 12

1. (p. 179) *the Boston Advertiser*. This daily paper was published from 1813 to 1859.

NOTES

2. (p. 180) *Pour la demande.* For the proposal.

3. (p. 182) *camarades.* Comrades.

4. (p. 182) *C'est fini . . . Je me range.* It's over . . . I'm settling down.

5. (p. 184) *en attendant.* While waiting for.

6. (p. 185) *vous plaisantez.* You are joking.

FOR THE BEST IN PAPERBACKS, LOOK FOR THE

In every corner of the world, on every subject under the sun, Penguin represents quality and variety – the very best in publishing today.

For complete information about books available from Penguin – including Pelicans, Puffins, Peregrines and Penguin Classics – and how to order them, write to us at the appropriate address below. Please note that for copyright reasons the selection of books varies from country to country.

In the United Kingdom: For a complete list of books available from Penguin in the U.K., please write to *Dept E.P., Penguin Books Ltd, Harmondsworth, Middlesex, UB7 0DA*

In the United States: For a complete list of books available from Penguin in the U.S., please write to *Dept BA, Penguin, 299 Murray Hill Parkway, East Rutherford, New Jersey 07073*

In Canada: For a complete list of books available from Penguin in Canada, please write to *Penguin Books Canada Ltd, 2801 John Street, Markham, Ontario L3R 1B4*

In Australia: For a complete list of books available from Penguin in Australia, please write to the *Marketing Department, Penguin Books Australia Ltd, P.O. Box 257, Ringwood, Victoria 3134*

In New Zealand: For a complete list of books available from Penguin in New Zealand, please write to the *Marketing Department, Penguin Books (NZ) Ltd, Private Bag, Takapuna, Auckland 9*

In India: For a complete list of books available from Penguin, please write to *Penguin Overseas Ltd, 706 Eros Apartments, 56 Nehru Place, New Delhi, 110019*

In Holland: For a complete list of books available from Penguin in Holland, please write to *Penguin Books Nederland B.V., Postbus 195, NL–1380 AD Weesp, Netherlands*

In Germany: For a complete list of books available from Penguin, please write to *Penguin Books Ltd, Friedrichstrasse 10 – 12, D–6000 Frankfurt Main 1, Federal Republic of Germany*

In Spain: For a complete list of books available from Penguin in Spain, please write to *Longman Penguin España, Calle San Nicolas 15, E–28013 Madrid, Spain*

The Aspern Papers and
The Turn of the Screw
Edited by Anthony Curtis

The two tales in this edition, *The Aspern Papers* and *The Turn of the Screw*, reveal at its finest James's genius for creating a world out of a single incident and charging it with unforgettable dramatic tension.

A story of 'spoils and stratagems', *The Aspern Papers* is set in a crumbling Venetian palazzo where an old woman treasures up some letters sent to her by the great American poet, Aspern. When a zealous literary historian arrives, and attempts to prise the letters from her, he finds his charm, ingenuity and morals stretched to breaking-point.

'It is a most wonderful, lurid, poisonous little tale,' wrote Oscar Wilde of *The Turn of the Screw*, James's most puzzling and controversial work. In the story of a governess newly in charge of two small children, haunted by ghosts, our imagination is miraculously set free to conjure up terrors never precisely named, or explained.

The Wings of the Dove

'She couldn't dream it away, nor walk it away, nor read it away, nor think it away . . . She couldn't have lost it if she had tried – that was what it was to be really rich . . .'

Milly Theale is as fabulously rich, young and alone in the world as a fairytale princess. Suffering (we gradually realize) from a grave illness, she arrives in Europe with her companion, Mrs Stringham, willing to be captivated and eager for happiness. In a corner of London drawing-room society she meets the vibrantly dazzling Kate Croy, and is introduced to Merton Densher, an attractive journalist who, for expediency's sake, would fall in love with her if he could . . .

Human greed and human tragedy are the themes of this beautifully worked novel which, with *The Ambassadors* and *The Golden Bowl*, represents (in Walter Allen's words) 'the final flowering of James's genius'.

'He is as solitary in the history of the novel as Shakespeare in the history of poetry' – Graham Greene.

BY THE SAME AUTHOR

The Bostonians
Edited by Charles Anderson

'. . . I asked myself what was the most salient and peculiar point in our social life. The answer was: the situation of women, the decline of the sentiment of sex, the agitation on their behalf.'

Such was Henry James's theme, brilliantly realized in *The Bostonians*. The story of Basil Ransome, a Mississippi lawyer, Olive Chancellor, a radical feminist, and their struggle for exclusive possession of the beautiful Verena Tarrant, has attracted virtually as much controversy as it has readers.

Is it simply a Victorian novel of love and marriage? If it is a novel of ideas, does it embody the triumph of chauvinism, or mourn the tragic collapse of *avant garde* feminism? Certainly, in the glitter and moral illumination of its comedy, *The Bostonians* ranks with James's greatest novels in its portrayal of what it means to be fully human, for both men and women.

Washington Square
Edited by Brian Lee

At the age of twenty-two, Catherine Sloper is regarded as a rather mature blossom, such as could be plucked from the stem only with a vigorous jerk.

Yet although she is neither clever nor beautiful (her taste in dress verges on the vulgar), Morris Townsend finds Catherine exceedingly charming. Less, it must be admitted, because of her evident goodness and truth than because she is due to inherit a substantial fortune. Meanwhile, the curious spectacle of his daughter's being courted by a handsome, athletic fortune-hunter is, for Doctor Sloper, at once an entertainment and a challenge . . .

Washington Square (1880), set in New York, belongs with Henry James's early novels. It is a spare and intensely moving story of divided loyalties and innocence betrayed, and it is also, as Graham Greene has said, 'perhaps the only novel in which a man has successfully invaded the feminine field and produced a work comparable to Jane Austen's'.